ALSO BY KATHRYN DAWN O'BRIEN

MURDER HAS A MEMORY

MURDER
HOLDS A
SEANCE

A ROBERTA LAW MYSTERY

KATHRYN DAWN O'BRIEN

KING PELLEY PUBLISHING

MURDER HOLDS A SEANCE

Library of Congress Control Number: 2016909347

ISBN 978-0-9839713-2-0

Published by:

King Pelley Publishing
Sherman Oaks, CA 91413
www.robertalawmysteries.com

Book design by Kimberly Martin

First Edition

For Lil & Jack O'Brien,
thanks for all the love and laughter

ACKNOWLEDGEMENTS

The author wishes to offer her sincerest thanks to the following individuals and organizations, as well as to acknowledge certain books and works that were particularly helpful in the course of her research. Ms. Lee Jones and The Spiritualist Center™; The Beatles; Unbound Productions and Wicked Lit; Mountain View Cemetery; Holy Family Church; Temple Emanuel; California Institute of Abnormalarts; United States Forest Service; the Cobb Estate; Devil's Gate Dam; Sage Vegan Bistro; Real Food Daily; The Pie Hole; Coast to Coast AM; the Los Angeles Times; the Los Angeles Public Library; Robert W. Chambers' "In the Court of the Dragon;" Stephen King's "You Know They Got a Hell of a Band;" Lewis Carroll's *Through the Looking-Glass, and What Alice Found There*; Aleister Crowley's *The Book of the Law* and *The Book of Lies*; Lord Alfred Tennyson's "In Memoriam A.H.H.;" William Wordsworth's "The Tables Turned;" Greg Bishop, Joe Oesterle, and Mike Marinaccci's *Weird California*; Gary Lachman's *Aleister Crowley: Magick, Rock and Roll, and the Weirdest Man in the World*; my ever diligent editor, Geraldine Farrell; and last, but not least, the loving, loyal and supportive staff at King Pelley Publishing, Lucky, Laci, and Jimmy.

CONTENTS

CHAPTER ONE

Sunday In Echo Park With Louie

I LOOKED OUT THE CAR window at the dappled early morning light, a rare sight for a night owl like me. October is one of my favorite months in Southern California. Goldilocks time, as Louie likes to call it. Not too hot, not too cold, not too wet, not too dry—just right.

"Remind me why I let you drag me out of bed at such an ungodly hour on a Sunday morning."

"To have brunch with my dear Aunt Lupe, sweet Roberta." Louie shot me one of his I-need-something-from-you smiles.

"I agreed to go to one of her gigs with you. How did that turn into brunch?"

"Well, this is a gig—sort of." Louie pulled off the Hollywood Freeway and headed toward Echo Park Avenue. "She's singing before brunch."

For those of you who don't already know me from my previous adventure, "Murder Has a Memory" (shameless plug, but a girl's gotta make a living), my name is Roberta Law. And here are my Vital Stats:

OCCUPATION: Hypnotherapist.
PREVIOUS OCCUPATION: Actress.
HEIGHT: Five-Foot-Eight.
EYES: Green.
HAIR: Auburn.
AGE: Old enough to be on my second career.
WEIGHT: That's on a need-to-know basis only.

Louie, you ask? Swarthy Latin Lover looks, but unfortunately, plays for the other team. An actor turned talent manager, and my best pal.

As for his aunt? Lupe Lopez is not your typical octogenarian. She fancies herself a chic cabaret chanteuse. But she's more Charo meets Delores Delago, a feisty Latina blend of retrofitted tack.

"Since when does your aunt get up before three in the afternoon?" I yawned.

"She's on a new kick."

We made our way into the quaint enclave of Angelino Heights, the second oldest district in Los Angeles. An area filled with Craftsman, Mission Revival, Art Deco and classic Victorian homes in various states of repair and disrepair.

"This is your aunt's neighborhood. Are we picking her up, too? Has that 1970 Corvette convertible of hers finally given up the ghost?"

"Ghost? Who said anything about ghosts?" Louie sounded agitated. As a matter of fact, he didn't seem at all like his usual self. No quips, no smart-ass comebacks.

"It's just an expression. Calm down. What's the matter with you today?"

"You'll see in a minute." Louie brought his black SUV to a sudden stop in front of Lupe's formidable Queen Anne style Victorian. "Almost missed it. Keep forgetting about the new paint job."

The once sedately colored home was being reimagined in the most garish shade of lavender I had ever seen.

Louie opened his car door, "Okay, let's do this."

"I'll just wait here while you get her. It looks like that paint might still be wet."

"Oh, I'm not getting her. The show's going on inside."

I stepped out of the car and saw two guys in painter overalls standing on a scaffold. They hoisted a large wooden sign onto the second story of the house. Painted in bright rainbow colors, it read: "A. B. C. D. E."

"Is she turning her place into a daycare center or something?"

"I only wish." We hiked up the front steps leading to the porch. "The sign stands for Abundant Beings Church of Divine Energy."

"Don't do cults. Gotta go!" I turned around and headed back down the stairs.

"Hey, wait a minute. You promised," Louie shouted.

"Oh no, I didn't. I never signed up for this."

Louie ran after me. "You won't have to sign up for anything. I need you to check someone out and give me your professional opinion."

"I'm a hypnotherapist, not a psychiatrist or a deprogramming expert. You should be dragging Danny to this." Danny is my brother and Louie's ex-partner—romance, not business. A groundbreaking psychiatrist turned card-carrying schizophrenic, in-between lucid moments he dabbles in religion. The last time I saw him he was a Zen Buddhist.

"I can't. He's the one who got Aunt Lupe hooked on this group. And now look," he pointed to the fresh paint job and the newly hung sign, "they're taking over."

That stopped me dead in my tracks. "Louie, when will you ever learn? Danny's a ticking time bomb. He never stays on his meds. I thought you two were finally through."

"Love is a fickle mistress, my friend."

"What do you want me to do?"

"These people are part of some sort of renegade Spiritualist Church. I need you to check out their founder and main channeler, Madame Mestral."

"In what way?"

"Let me know if you think she's legit."

I rolled my eyes. "I can do that from here. Uh—no."

"Come on, Roberta, I'm serious." I knew he was. Louie had never gone this long without making some sort of joke, usually tied to a song title. "Take a look at this woman and see if she really is going into some sort of trance and communing with the spirits of the dearly departed. Please... Aunt Lupe is my only living relative in LA."

Guilt ropes me in every time. "All right."

* * *

Upon entering Lupe's foyer we were greeted by a portly matron bestowing exuberant unsolicited hugs on everyone. She locked her sights on Louie and me. "Welcome, my angels! I feel the spirits are with us today."

I ducked out of the trajectory of the impending embrace, leaving a dazed Louie in her clutches, and glommed onto an elderly gentleman handing out programs. "Please take a seat," he said, ushering me into the cathedral-ceilinged living room on his right.

Except for the baby grand piano, all of Lupe's furniture had been replaced by rows of stackable white chairs. A raised platform sat between the fireplace and the stained glass bay windows. The place was abuzz with activity. At least fifty seats were packed in to the space and they were filling up fast. The congregants were mostly Latino, predominantly women—middle-aged or older— with a smattering of artsy-looking millennial hipsters thrown into the mix.

Louie caught up with me. "Thanks for leaving me in the lurch."

"Hola, Luis!" Lupe called out from beside the piano. "Is that Roberta with you?" She looked at us through a pair of bejeweled, gold opera glasses.

Too vain to wear eyeglasses, she reluctantly wore contacts when driving. Though no stranger to the cosmetic scalpel, LASIK eye surgery was out of the question. As a Latina, she considered her sapphire blue eyes to be priceless, and proved it by insuring them with Lloyd's of London years ago.

Lupe pointed to the first row of chairs, "I saved a place up front for you."

We found two seats, dead center, with place cards on them. One read: "UNCLE LUIS LOPEZ." The other: "FUTURE MRS. LUIS LOPEZ."

I picked my card up and sat down. "How many times have you come out to your aunt?"

"Every time I see her."

"Something tells me it's not sticking."

Louie stared at his card. "Maybe she's in the early stages of Alzheimer's. My Uncle Luis has been dead for years."

Lupe pushed through the milling people, rushing at us with a sheet of music clutched in her hand. She wore a skin-tight, indigo sequined, micro-mini cocktail dress with a plunging neckline on her birdlike hundred pound frame. The whole ensemble was topped off with a matching turban, concealing god knows what color of hair. Her size D boob implants had held up much better than her now sagging facelift. Though only five-foot-two, she made up for this by wearing a pair of five-inch high, glittering red, hooker heels.

"Please excuse my shoes," Lupe swooped in to hug me. "I'm having a hard time letting go of red. It's my signature color." Shaking her head, "There I go again. It *was* my signature color."

"What do you mean *was*?" Louie asked.

"Madame Mestral says I need to raise my vibrational level. Red is the color of the base chakra. Which is all well and fine for regular entertaining, but I am attempting to do so much more with my act now." She tapped a long crimson fingernail on the center of Louie's forehead. "Indigo is the color of the third eye chakra."

"Come on, you can't be serious, Cousin Lupe."

It was a long established Lopez family tradition that Lupe's true age was never to be revealed. She felt it would be detrimental to her timeless music career. So whenever they were around other people Louie was instructed to refer to her as his cousin, never his aunt. How this made any sense was beyond me, but it seemed to make Lupe happy.

Lupe put her hand over Louie's mouth. "Shhh, Luis! I think we're going to have to drop this business of you being my cousin," she said in a hushed tone. "You're getting a little old looking." Wow, that took a lot of nerve. Louie had just turned forty, he was two years younger than me for god's sake! "But we'll discuss this matter later in private."

Louie and I looked down at the discarded "UNCLE LUIS LOPEZ" sign by our feet. Then we looked at each other knowing the inevitable conclusion to this mystery. The Cousin Lupe Era had drawn to a close and a new epoch in Lopez Family History had begun.

"Thanks to the guidance of Madame Mestral," Lupe continued, "I am channeling the greats—Josephine Baker, Marlene Dietrich! Last week, 'The Little Sparrow' came through."

"You're channeling birds, too?" Louie quipped.

"Don't be ridiculous! I'm speaking of the legendary Piaf!" Lupe took in a series of deep breaths while waving her arms up and down her body in a crisscross motion. "I must not allow myself to get so worked up. This passionate energy of mine will disturb the spirits." She paused and stood perfectly still. "It's these damn red shoes! They must go!" She kicked off her heels like they had erupted in flames, then let out a sigh. "That's better." Lupe turned to me. "So when are you two going to set a date?"

"Never," I replied. "He's gay, remember?"

Lupe broke out into a hysterical laugh. "That's just a phase. His Tío Ramón went through the same thing."

"He's gay, too," Louie said.

She continued laughing. "Tell that to his wife!"

"He lives with a drag queen," Louie replied.

"Enough with this frivolity. The service will be starting any minute now. I must finish preparing my song." Brandishing the sheet music in her hand, she headed back over to the piano.

"Did you get a look at the music she was holding?" I asked Louie, who was down on the floor looking for Lupe's discarded shoes. "A Piaf number, 'No Regrets.' If she is channeling her, why does she need to study a chart?"

"See what I mean? This Mestral woman has got her all twisted up. She's always been a little nuts, but never totally crazy." Louie sat back down in his chair.

I stared at the rescued ruby footwear sitting in his lap.

"Don't give me that look, Missy. The West Hollywood Halloween Carnaval is coming up. I'm not letting pumps this fabulous go to waste."

An angelic sounding voice came over the loudspeaker, "Everyone please take your seats and turn off all electronic devices, the service is about to begin."

A series of chimes rang. A young man shut the door connecting the living room to the foyer. A couple of women drew the heavy purple velvet curtains across the windows. Then all the lights in the room dimmed to black. We sat in silence.

I felt a hot moist breath on my neck. "I'm scared," Louie whispered.

A pinhole baby pink spotlight focused on the makeshift stage. The light slowly opened to reveal Madame Mestral, in all of her glory, seated on a purple and gold throne. The piano played a short, familiar intro followed by Lupe singing, "You Light Up My Life." Yes, the Debby Boone song.

"Now I'm scared," I whispered.

Clothed in a flowing white robe, Madame Mestral's jet-black hair spilled over her shoulders and down her back. She looked to be somewhere in her late fifties. The song came to a close. Mestral sat motionless, her piercing gaze fixed on the congregation. "Sing, make it wild and loud," she commanded in a lisping Spanish accent. "The vibrational level of the room must soar."

The house lights rose slightly, everyone jumped to their feet and launched into a rousing rendition of "Sing A Song." First Debby

Boone, now the Carpenters. For some reason the spirit world was locked in a Seventies pop time warp.

Madame Mestral—eyes closed—placed her hands in front of her, in what appeared to be some sort of yogic posture. Middle fingers straight, pointing forward, touching at the top; other fingers bent, touching at the knuckles; thumbs pointed toward her and touching at the top.

As the song progressed, the congregation grew louder and wilder. People were singing at the top of their lungs, stomping their feet, clapping their hands, and banging their chairs up and down on the antique redwood floors.

Lupe, a cordless mic in hand, wove through the room interjecting her singing with shouts of, "That's it!" and "Let's raise the roof!"

Madame Mestral's head bobbed up and down, faster and faster, until it finally dropped to her chest. She appeared to be going into a trance, but I wasn't close enough to detect any significant rapid eye movement. Then out of nowhere, Madame Mestral let out an ear-piercing shriek. The music and singing came to an abrupt halt. Mestral's head bolted upright.

What an opener!

No one moved. All eyes were fixed on the mystic diva atop her throne.

"Samir is at the door. Do you wish to let him in?" she bellowed in a deep Middle Eastern accent.

"If somebody starts singing the Wings' tune 'Let 'Em In,' I'm outta here," I whispered to Louie.

"Welcome, Samir!" someone cried from the back of the room.

"Please come in, Samir!" the woman next to me spoke.

"We've missed you, Samir!" a young man standing near the foyer door called out.

9

"Ahlan, Samir!" Lupe said.

Madame Mestral let out a robust belly laugh. "Ahhh, that is the word I have been waiting to hear. Ahlan wa Sahlan, my little songbird. Your companion in evening talk doesn't usually like to come out and play in the day. But it must be evening somewhere on this big blue marble, right? Drinks, anyone?" This was followed by another boisterous laugh.

Louie looked over at me. "I don't get it. Is she supposed to be Samir, Allan, Allan Samir or Allan Washalan? And what's all the laughing about?"

"The entity's name is Samir," a familiar voice answered from behind us. "The word 'Ahlan' is an Arabic greeting of welcome. 'Ahlan wa Sahlan' is a traditional reply. He's laughing because he made a little joke. His name, Samir, loosely translates in to 'companion in evening talk' in English."

Louie looked puzzled. "Huh? She's a he?"

"Samir is a man. He lived in ancient Egypt and was involved with the building of the great pyramid at Giza."

I turned to face my older brother, Danny. "But, of course."

"Still a cynic I see, Roberta," Danny said. He looked good. The graying black curls on his head and emerging crow's feet around his dark blue eyes suited him.

Samir thundered, "I have an important message for someone in the room." All unnecessary chatter ground to a halt. "It's from a spirit named Tommy. Does anyone in the room know a Tommy?"

A number of hopeful hands shot up in the air. Not the most unusual name.

"I'm having difficulty getting a clear impression of the last name. Something beginning with an 'F' perhaps?"

The old cold reading scam, typical phony psychic ploy. Throw out a vague tidbit of info and see who bites.

"He is a young man, in his twenties, wearing some sort of battle uniform. I believe he died in the nineteen hundred and sixties, anno Domini, as you call it."

Deceased war veteran with a common first name, pretty safe bet.

"But the death did not come in battle. He was on leave. Hiking in a forest." Madame Mestral fidgeted in her seat. "A last name is coming through. It is like the Riddle of the Sphinx. He is a forest in a forest."

Oh, brother, what a ham.

"Forrester! The name is Forrester!" Lupe ran to the platform crying. "It's my Tommy! Tommy Forrester, the love of my life. He died hiking in the Angeles National Forest. It was an accident, he tripped and fell from a cliff."

"Correct," Samir pronounced. A look of consternation came over Madame Mestral's face. "Wait. Not all correct. Tommy is writing something he does not have the strength to speak. M—U—R ... MURDER!"

Lupe screamed, then fell in a heap at the foot of the channeler's throne.

CHAPTER TWO

Whatever Lupe Wants

L OUIE RUSHED TO Lupe's side. "Somebody get some water," he shouted, fanning her with his program.

No one else made a move. So I jumped up, dashed into the kitchen, and grabbed a bottle of water from the fridge. By the time I returned Lupe was sitting up, cradled in Madame Mestral's arms.

"There, there, my dear," Madame Mestral stroked Lupe's forehead. "I've warned you about your blood sugar." She no longer sounded like Samir, but there was no trace of her Spanish accent either. "You cannot exist on air and water alone, you must eat more." Her intonation was unmistakably British.

Lupe batted her eyes. "I know, Dr. Greystoke. But If I don't watch my figure, no one else will."

Oh, good grief, not another entity.

Louie took out his cell. "I'm calling 9-1-1."

"Whatever for?" Lupe reached up and took the water from me. "My doctor is here."

"Where?" Louie looked around the room.

Lupe pointed at Madame Mestral. "Right here."

"Dr. Neville Greystoke, at your service." Madame Mestral held her right hand out to Louie.

"Are you kidding me?" Louie said, ignoring the outstretched hand.

"Not at all old chap, graduated with honors from King's College London. Class of '90. Studied under the renowned surgeon, Sir Joseph Lister. Perhaps you've heard of him?"

"The Listerine guy? He wasn't around in 1990." Louie seemed proud to know this little historical tidbit.

"Well, you're correct about that," Greystoke answered. "It was, in fact, 1890. However, as the father of modern surgery, I doubt Sir Lister considered being the inspiration for a popular American mouthwash his greatest achievement." Mestral helped Lupe up off the floor and onto her stool beside the piano. "Now will someone please get this precious lady some saltines with honey on them, so we may continue with the service."

"Is Tommy with you, Dr. Greystoke?"

"Regretfully, I have not had the pleasure of making the acquaintance of your long lost beau."

"Neither have I," Lupe replied.

Louie turned to Danny, "Will you please take a look at her? She's not making any sense."

"If you will excuse me then, I will take my leave and let my noble colleague take over." Madame Mestral patted my brother on the back and returned to the platform.

Danny stood in front of Lupe, scanning her face. "What do you mean, you haven't met him?"

"Here's your snack." A young man, with a series of multicolor gauges running up his left ear, handed Lupe a plate.

"Thank you, Gunnar." Lupe took a bite from a cracker. "Would you be a darling? Run back into the kitchen and bring me the newspaper clipping I have pinned on the icebox." She looked to Danny. "This will explain everything."

Gunnar returned with the clipping and handed it to Lupe. "Could you please read this to everyone for me, Roberta? My eyes are tired."

I took the clipping from Lupe. It was from the obituary section of the *Los Angeles Times* dated last October. There was a black and white photograph of a handsome young man wearing a Marine Corps dress blues uniform. Above his picture were the words, "In Memoriam." I read aloud what was written underneath, "In loving memory of Private First Class Thomas (Tommy) Forrester, a devoted son, brother, fiancé, and friend. Taken from us suddenly on October 16, 1966 at the tender age of nineteen. Gone, but never forgotten." I put the paper down. "How very sad."

"Don't forget the beautiful Tennyson poem at the end," Lupe said. "I know it by heart:

> 'A hand that can be clasp'd no more -
> Behold me, for I cannot sleep,
> And like a guilty thing I creep
> At earliest morning to the door.' "

Louie grimaced. "It's kinda creepy."

I nodded my head. "It is an unusual quote to choose."

"No, I meant the date he died. Today is the sixteenth of October."

"No wonder my Tommy came through today."

"How is he your Tommy, if you've never even met him?" Louie asked his aunt. "And how does this clipping explain anything?"

"As you know, Luis, I have never married. Though there have been many suitors and numerous proposals over the years, I have always kept my heart out of reach. When I ran across this notice in the paper last year, I finally understood why. The moment I laid eyes on him everything fell into place. Here was my soul mate. Star-crossed lovers, fated to never meet in this lifetime." Lupe was prone to fantastic notions, but this was a doozy even for her. "Let us continue with the service, this is much too upsetting to talk about any longer. Does anyone have a tissue?"

Louie handed her one. "You still look pale to me."

"Nothing a little blush won't fix." She pulled out a tiny compact from behind the music on her stand. "Please go back and join the others."

"I think she's going to be okay." Danny pulled Louie and me aside on the way back to our seats. "But, to be on the safe side, I recommend scheduling a check-up with her corporeal world physician." It was good to see my brother back on terra firma, perhaps he could help us put an end to this mess he started.

Madame Mestral, or Samir, or Dr. Greystoke, I really had no idea by this point, had resumed their seat on the throne. The pianist played an ethereal instrumental piece while five chairs and a small lectern were set up on the platform. If you ignored the throne with the sleeping seer in it, and that we were sitting in Lupe's living room, the addition of these new items lent a more conventional feel to the proceedings.

The hugging matron from the front door took the stage, positioning herself behind the lectern. "I have some announcements to make, please see me after the service if you require any further information." She rifled through some notes. "Dolores Gonzales is back in the hospital. She's having her gall bladder removed this time. Dr. Greystoke will be assisting."

I'd love to be a fly on the wall for that one.

"Please remember Dolores in your prayers. The Christmas Bake Sale sign-up sheet is located on the activities table in the foyer. Don't forget to add your name to the list. There's still time to join our Seers Symposium. We meet here every Monday night at seven. Once again, look for the sheet on the table out front."

If you changed Seers Symposium to Ladies Auxiliary and made the imaginary doctor real, these announcements sounded like something you could have heard at Aunt Bee's church in Mayberry. Of course, from a visual standpoint, there was still the problem of the catnapping clairvoyant.

Next up was the old guy with the programs. He cleared his throat and tapped on the mic clipped to his lapel several times. "Please turn to page sixty-five in your hymn books."

Hymn books? This should be interesting.

The woman on my right reached under her seat and nodded at me to follow suit. Based on the day's earlier tunes, I was half expecting to find a three ring binder covered with Rickie Tickie Stickies and filled with popular song lyric sheets ripped out of vintage *16* and *Tiger Beat* magazines. Instead I found an unassuming black leather book with the word "HYMNAL" embossed in gold on front. I turned to the requested page. "In the Sweet By-and-By," lyrics by S. Fillmore Bennett, music by Joseph P. Webster, published in 1868. A quote from the Bible was written before the beginning of the song, "In my Father's house are many mansions: if it were not so, I would not have told you. I go to prepare a place for you." - John 14:2.

After the singing of the hymn, the floor was thrown open to members of the Seers Symposium. Five of Madame Mestral's students—a Goth girl in her twenties; a middle-aged Latina woman; another elderly gentleman; my brother, Danny; and Lupe—took the stage. They sat up there meditating, for what seemed like hours, while the rest of us watched and waited. Obviously, they were not as adept at this technique as their fearless leader, still snoozing on her purple perch. Every now and then one of the members of the group let out a grunt or a moan and someone in the audience coughed or opened a candy wrapper.

I nudged Louie, "Can we go and wait in the kitchen? I'm starving."

"Soon," he said. "I want to catch this next part. This is the first time I've seen Aunt Lupe get up there."

"I have a message for Maria," the Latina woman sitting far stage right spoke. "It's from Juan. Please let his wife know he's sorry he left the way he did that night, but he is very happy now in his new life."

"Can you name that tune? I can," Louie said. " 'Take a Letter, Maria.' "

I stifled a laugh. "Maybe she's channeling an oldies radio station."

"I'm sorry, that's all I can get today." The Latina woman stepped down off the stage.

"Her antenna must be loose," Louie said.

"Stop it!" I gave him a playful slap.

"Bash a ram, she lala vaneer," Danny yelled out. "Cor aveno par silaman. Repto kali neesho."

I sighed. "This is not good, he's speaking in tongues again."

"Flo ena cara pavorum. Solinga kai noba—"

The heavenly ramblings were cut short by the song stylings of the late, yet just in the nick of time today, Edith Piaf. The adoring crowd was treated to three of her legendary tunes, plus an encore, all in French. Lupe really knew how to work a room. She closed her impromptu act to thunderous applause.

"Do you think Madame Mestral's okay, Louie? How can she possibly sleep through all this noise?"

"Maybe she's consulting with Samir or some other ancient spook? Don't worry, I'm sure Dr. Greystoke will look after her if she's not feeling well."

Ushers passing collection baskets made their way through the room.

"Anything you can spare to continue this great work will be most appreciated," a lispy Spanish voice spoke.

"She's baaaack," Louie joked.

I nodded, "Must be the revitalizing smell of money."

Madame Mestral turned to the members of the Seers Symposium still on stage. "Thank you, my darlings, you may return to your seats now." Her voice was stronger. "Anyone wanting a special healing today please move to a chair up front, immediately following the service. Dr. Greystoke and his students will attend to your needs."

"I wonder how much that's going to cost?"

"Nothing, Roberta." Danny stepped down off the platform. "Not everything in the world is about money."

"Maybe not." The woman next to me passed a collection basket. "But everything in *this world* seems to be."

* * *

Louie and I joined Danny and Lupe in the dining room for brunch. While we ate, Dr. Greystoke and students attended to the needs of the volunteer guinea pigs in the other room.

"Is there any more coffee left?" Louie drained the last drops from the carafe on the oak table.

"I'll go in the kitchen and make some more," Lupe stood up.

"Let me do it," Danny said, taking the empty pot from Louie. "Continue your conversation." He walked through the swinging door into the adjoining kitchen.

"What's going on with you and these people?" Louie asked. "They've taken over. This is your home, not a church."

"I like the company. What harm is there in it?" Lupe picked up a pink Depression glass serving platter. "More eggs, anyone?"

"Don't go trying to change the topic. I know you're tricks." Louie scooped some more scrambled eggs onto his plate. "Is there any bacon left?"

Lupe stood up, "I'll make some."

I grasped Lupe's wrist. "He's devoured more than his fill of bacon."

"How dare you call me fat!" Louie pushed away his half-eaten third helping.

"You're the one who said you felt like a beluga whale at the Palm Springs White Party this year."

"Oh, what an adorable couple you two make. I can't wait for the day I sing at your wedding."

Louie rolled his eyes. "Let's not get back on that merry-go-round. Why did you let them paint the outside of this place lavender?"

"It made them happy. And it worked."

"What worked?" I asked.

"They raised the vibrational level."

"How can you tell?" Louie scoffed. "What proof is there?"

"My Tommy came back to me, that is all the proof I need."

"How could he come back when he wasn't with you in the first place? You've never even met him." Louie looked to me for help. "Can you please talk some sense into this woman?"

"How long have you had the clipping pinned to the fridge?" I asked.

"Ever since I first saw it."

"So about a year?" I prodded.

Lupe nodded.

"Don't you think it's possible Madame Mestral saw it hanging there?" I continued.

"Of course. But what difference does it make?"

Louie threw up his hands. "Don't you see she's conning you?"

"If she's conning me, why would she say Tommy was murdered?" Lupe's voice rose in pitch, "She wouldn't know such a thing, only Tommy would."

I took Lupe's hand, hoping to calm her. "The clipping said he died suddenly, it didn't specify how."

"Madame Mestral probably made the whole thing up or assumed it was murder," Louie added.

"Even more proof she was in contact with my Tommy. Why not make up or assume he died in Vietnam? He had his uniform on in the picture."

She did make a good point. Why murder? Why go there?

"Even the police didn't think it was murder," Lupe continued. "They ruled the death an accident."

Danny returned with a fresh pot of coffee and topped off Louie's mug. "Anyone else for a refill?"

I passed him my cup. "How do you know this, Lupe? It's not mentioned in the paper."

"I did a little research in the archives at the library. I wanted to read Tommy's original obituary."

Louie extended his palm to Lupe, "Hand it over."

Lupe went over to the antique wooden cabinet on the opposite side of the dining room. She opened the top drawer and took out a small silver box. "It's in here," she said, handing the box to Louie.

"I knew you'd have it," he said.

"Have what?" Danny took a sip of coffee.

Louie opened the box. "This," he took out a folded piece of paper. "A copy of the guy's obituary." He scanned the sheet. "It says he died in a hiking accident."

"It wasn't an accident," Lupe said. "He was pushed off a cliff."

"It doesn't mention a thing in here about pushing or a cliff." Louie handed me the paper.

"There were other articles about the investigation in to his death," Lupe was defensive, "they mentioned the cliff."

Louie put out his hand again, "Let me have them."

"I didn't make copies of those. They were too depressing."

And an obituary isn't?

"Besides they didn't tell me anything about my sweet Tommy."

No fuel for her imaginary lover fantasy.

"She's acting like one of those women who fall for death row prisoners." Louie turned to Danny, "You're a psychiatrist, isn't there a name for this type of thing?"

"You're talking about hybristophilia, a very complex psychological phenomena." Danny rubbed his chin, "This situation is entirely different."

"See Daniel understands. Those men are murderers. Tommy is a victim. And I'm going to seek justice for him, if it takes every last cent I have."

Madame Mestral entered the dining room carrying a large empty tray.

"Right on cue," I said.

She nodded her head at me. "Good day. You must be Master Lopez's friend, the mesmerist." Madame Mestral picked up my dirty plate.

Master Lopez? Awfully formal of her. I hope Louie doesn't get too attached to his new title. "Yes, Roberta Law. I'm a hypnotherapist. We haven't called ourselves mesmerists for a few centuries now."

She blushed.

"And you are Madame Mestral, no doubt."

"Oh my, no," she sounded flustered. "I'm just a friend of hers. My name's Sheila O'Hara."

I thought I detected an Irish brogue.

She continued clearing the table. "I'm Lady Lopez's parlor maid."

Will the real Madame Mestral please stand up?

"I don't know why people keeping mixing me and The Madame up?"

Perhaps it's because you share the same body.

"If you need anything else your Ladyship," she finished loading the tray, "I'll be in the scullery."

"Why don't you take the rest of the day off, Sheila?" Lupe said. "You need to be at your best for tonight."

"Thank you, m'Lady. That is very kind of you." She exited through the swinging door.

Louie was the first to speak, "Now that's just downright weird."

"You certainly ate enough of her food though," Lupe chastised him.

"She made brunch for us?" I was astonished. "When did she have time?"

"The poor woman was up at the crack of dawn," Danny answered. "She woke me up with all of those banging pots and pans."

"You slept here?" I said.

"Yes, Lupe was gracious enough to offer me a room while I'm on leave from the Zen Center."

"They kicked you out, didn't they?" I was well aware of my brother's checkered history of living arrangements.

"There was the matter of a small fire."

"You're starting fires now?"

"Calm down," Louie said. "It wasn't his fault. I gave him an oil lantern to use in his cabin up at Mt. Baldy. He fell asleep and his cat knocked it over."

"What!"

"Don't worry the gato is okay," Lupe added. "Here puss, puss." A sleek black cat jumped onto her lap. "His name is Hector."

At this point I had to wonder if I was the only sane one in the house.

"Look I really have to go," I rose from my seat. "I would have loved to meet the real Madame Mestral, but she appears to be a very elusive character."

"We can't leave yet!" Louie grabbed onto my arm and dragged me over to the far corner of the room—out of earshot of Danny and Lupe. "You promised me a professional assessment of this woman. Is she legit or not?"

While every part of my rational mind screamed, "NO WAY." I couldn't ignore the nagging feeling at the back of my subconscious mind, preventing me from coming to a definitive conclusion. "Can't say for sure. I need to get closer and see her in action some more."

"Will you come back with me next Sunday? I'm really worried Lupe is going to give everything she has to this woman, especially now that Mestral's working this Tommy Forrester angle with her."

I took a moment before answering. "One last time. Maybe I can figure how to get Danny out of her clutches by next week, too."

"Thanks, you're the best." Louie gave me a peck on the cheek. He turned to Lupe, "Thanks for everything. We had a great time. If it's all right with you we'd like to come again next week."

"I knew you two lovebirds would be impressed by Madame Mestral," Lupe beamed. "We'll see you tomorrow night at seven sharp."

"Tomorrow?" Louie and I said in unison.

"I signed you up for the last two slots in the Seers Symposium."

CHAPTER THREE

Little Yellow Corvette

M Y CLIENT LOAD was light that Monday. Only three appointments scheduled, all in the afternoon. I was up at nine to feed my son, Lex. Okay, he's actually a beagle. But don't hold that against him. He's the smartest, most loving, loyal male I have ever had the pleasure to know and adore.

"Here you go, boy." I put a fresh bowl of kibble down on his official USDA Beagle Brigade placemat. "I picked up a new brand for you to try."

Lex sidled up to the stainless steel dish, took a brief whiff, and looked up at me with those big amber eyes.

"I know. New brand, but same old diet. Come on, give it a taste."

He waddled from the kitchen into the living room and hopped onto his favorite easy chair.

"Well, you can jump again. You've got to at least thank me for that."

Lex was thirty pounds overweight when I found him at Beagle Rescue and, though he had slimmed down considerably, it was a constant Battle of the Beagle Bulge.

Coffee brewing, I grabbed a plain, fat-free, Greek yogurt and half a grapefruit from the fridge before sitting down in the dining room to resume my own lifelong campaign against the creeping pounds.

My half-read Sunday edition of the *LA Times* was scattered on the table. I liked getting my news the old fashioned way, blocks of story rather than bites of sound. Searching for the crossword, I ran across the obits. There was another "In Memoriam" notice for Tommy Forrester. This year's version had some lines from a Wordsworth poem:

> "One impulse from a vernal wood
> May teach you more of man,
> Of moral evil and of good,
> Then all the sages can."

Someone was placing the weirdest epitaphs I had ever seen for this guy.

I picked up my cordless handset and put a call in to Louie. "Hey, it's me. Did you happen to see the obituary section of yesterday's *Times*? There's a new Tommy Forrester memorial in there, with another cryptic poetry excerpt."

"Let's hope my Aunt Lupe didn't see it. We've got to get her off this Tommy obsession or I'll never get those kooks out of her house."

"We?"

"Come on, I need your help on this."

"I am helping you. After I make my assessment of Madame Mestral tonight, you're on your own, buddy."

"What about your brother? Danny was the first one to get mixed up in this mess."

"He's a big boy. Besides I can't do much if he's not on his meds."

"I saw him take them this morning after breakfast."

"Spent the night, did he?"

"No, he dropped by to tell me what we needed to bring with us tonight."

"Dropped by? Why didn't he just call?"

Louie hesitated, "He thinks his phone's being tapped again."

"Back on his meds, huh? Must've been a Tic Tac you saw him swallow. So who's spying on him this time? CIA? The Vatican?" I heard a stuttered beep. "Another call's coming in, or maybe my phone's being tapped, too."

"Very funny. Before you go," Louie raced through the next part, "you have to bring a large mason jar filled with natural spring water and one fertilized free-range chicken egg with you tonight."

"What the he—"

"No plastic!" He was gone.

The beep tone pulsed again in my ear. I looked at the Caller ID. It was Ben Cohen, my erstwhile lover. Well, not exactly lover. More my would've been, could've been, should've been lover. Impossibly handsome—dark brown hair, slight graying at the temples, steel blue eyes—all wrapped up in a six-foot-one, forty-five year old, irresistible package.

"Good morning, Mr. Cohen."

"Good morning, Ms. Law. I see we are on formal terms today. May I ask why?"

"Just keeping things on a business level, as we agreed."

Ben is the Founding Director of the California Center for Parapsychology and Paranormal Research. When my hypnotherapy practice veers off the straight and narrow, he helps me navigate the less familiar unearthly realms I sometimes wind up in.

Ben chuckled. "I thought we agreed to let things cool off a bit."

"That's what I'm doing." Though I wish I wasn't.

"Brrr, mind if we turn the heat up a notch or two?"

Mind? I'm ready for a four-alarm fire. "You're not doing that annoying mental telepathy thing right now, are you?"

Ben and I have this strange Vulcan mind meld thing going on between us—he's much better at it though. He believes we share this ability because we are "Twin Flames," one eternal soul split in two, sort of an amped up soul mate. They don't incarnate together often, but when they do—look out! Crazy, I know, but there you have it. Oh, one last important note, he thinks we—and by "we" I mean "he"—need to remain celibate until we're ready to take on our inevitable sacred sexual reunion. As a Retired Catholic, I don't do celibate. So, needless to say, we have reached an impasse in our personal relationship.

"I've kept my promise," Ben said. "No more cerebral voyeurism."

God, that sounds sexy the way he says it.

"You left me a message yesterday, I'm returning your call."

"I might need your assistance with a situation."

"What kind of situation?"

"Do mediums come under your purview?"

"As in channeler?"

"As in con artist."

"Let's not jump to any conclusions. Yes, many of them are fakes and frauds, but not all. Edgar Cayce comes to mind."

"Great. Could you get in touch with him and see if he knows a Madame Mestral?"

"Sure, but I'll require the services of a necromancer."

"Let me run that by Louie. How much will it cost?"

Ben laughed. "Nothing. I was being a smart ass. Cayce died in 1945. He was the most documented psychic of the twentieth century, they called him the 'sleeping prophet.' But I could get in touch with my contacts at the Association for Research and Enlightenment, the non-profit he founded to continue his work."

"Would you, please?"

"What's Louie got to do with this? Is he adding a new line-up to his talent roster?"

"It's his loopy Aunt Lupe. She's hooked up with a bunch of crazies, courtesy of my med-free brother, and they've turned her house into some sort of way station for the dead."

"It could be a 'thin place.' Maybe I should drop by there with you one day and take some energy readings with my EMF meter."

Thin place? EMF meter? "You've lost me."

"Tell you what, meet me for lunch tomorrow afternoon and I'll explain. One o'clock, my office?"

It had been awhile since we'd last seen each other and I missed him. "I can do that."

"Till tomorrow, angel. I mean, Ms. Law."

* * *

I lolled around in my PJs till quarter past eleven, put the finishing touches on my Halloween decorations, and was sitting behind the desk in my office by half past twelve. One of the many benefits of having a home based practice.

Lex was relaxing on the Persian style area rug that lay between my desk and the black leather recliner reserved for clients.

"Stop eyeing the chair, buddy. It's off limits."

Lex let out a deep sigh.

I continued prepping the new client intake forms for my first
appointment of the day. It was an interesting case, a referral from
one of Danny's former colleagues, Carl Jenkins, a psychologist.
He was treating the woman for panic disorder, but the problem
had worsened. Talk therapy was not working for her and she was
phobic about taking any kind of medication. Feeling hypnosis
might be the best route to follow at this point and not a trained
hypnotist himself, he asked if I would assist in her treatment.

My phone rang. "Roberta Law, speaking."

"Hi, Roberta. It's Carl. Has my patient, Angela Fowler,
shown up yet?"

"She's scheduled to come in at one. Do you need to speak
with her?"

"No, I'm doing some follow-up. She missed her appointment
with me last week and hasn't returned any of my calls. I want to
make sure she's all right, plus give you a heads-up. She now has
full blown thanatophobia, an abnormal fear of death. The next
couple of weeks will be rough. With Halloween coming up and
all the spooky, ghoulish decorating people like to do these days,
she may get a whole lot worse before she starts to get any better.
It may be the reason she never showed up for our last session."

I flashed to an image of my front yard, decked out in full
ghastly horror.

"Will you call me after your session with her today and let me
know how she's doing?"

"No problem, Carl. And thanks for the referral."

I quickly hung up the phone and looked at my watch, it was ten
minutes to one. "You can do this, Roberta."

Dashing outside—I raced round my property, yanking down
every cobweb, pulling up every tombstone, trashing any noticeable

sign of my Fright Fest decor. Caught up in my harrowed purge, I didn't pay much attention to the blonde-haired woman in dark sunglasses, sitting in the canary yellow Corvette parked across the street.

After dumping my horror decorations by the side of the house, it dawned on me the woman sitting in the car had been staring at me, taking in my frenzied panic, for the past ten minutes.

Looking to the heavens, I muttered under my breath, "Please don't let this be my new client."

I approached the vehicle. She didn't look familiar, but her car sure did.

"Can I help you?" I called out.

The car's engine started.

"Are you looking for Roberta Law's office?"

The mysterious stranger peeled away from the curb—in Lupe Lopez's Corvette.

CHAPTER FOUR

Have An Egg Roll, Ms. Law

O
N THE DRIVE TO Angelino Heights that evening, I thought about my no-show new client and the blonde in the Corvette. They had to be the same person, it was too much of a coincidence. But what was she doing in Lupe's car? When I called Carl Jenkins back to explain what happened, he was very understanding. He confirmed his client was a blonde, but had no idea what make of vehicle she drove.

I pulled up in front of the Abundant Beings Church of Divine Energy, aka Lupe's house, at quarter to seven. Before going in, I made a quick scan for the yellow Corvette. It was nowhere in sight.

Louie greeted me at the front door. "You made it."

"Where's Lupe's car? I didn't notice it parked out front."

"She mentioned something about having to take her car into the shop. Why?"

"Thought I saw it on my street today."

"Did you get the license number?"

All I could remember was that woman staring me down. "I wasn't paying attention to the plates."

"A lot of people drive classic cars in this town."

"Yeah, you're right."

Louie clapped his hands. "So did you bring the stuff?"

"What stuff?"

"The water and the egg?"

"I thought you were joking."

Louie pulled me into the kitchen. "Aunt Lupe must have extra in here somewhere." He rifled through the fridge. "Open one of those cupboards and look for a large mason jar."

"Really?"

"Yes, really. Madame Mestral takes this business very seriously. She won't let you in there without it." Louie pulled out an egg. "One down."

"Where is everybody?"

"It's a small group. They meet upstairs in the library." He slammed the fridge door. "Damn! She doesn't have any natural spring water in there."

"This'll do." I took a mason jar and filled it with tap water. "They'll never know the difference."

"Don't bet on it. The Madame gives me the creeps. Do you think she might be a mind reader?"

"You've been spending too much time around Danny and Lupe."

"What about the way you and Ben can read minds?"

He had me there. "That's different." I screwed the lid on the jar. "We can only read each other's minds."

"Yeah, but Ben's assistant, Nancy, can read anybody's mind."

This was true. I hated it when Louie was logical. "Fine, to be on the safe side, let's watch what we think when we're in her presence." How we would accomplish this feat was beyond me. "I'm all set, let's go."

Louie grabbed me by the shoulders and looked in to my eyes. "Are you ready for this mission to seek out and destroy fakes, frauds and phonies wherever you may find them?" It was nice to see he was getting his sense of humor back.

Putting on my best British accent, "How can your lowly squire not be, Sir? What with me trusty egg and jar of water by me side."

"Alrighty then," he thrust an imaginary sword in the air, "to the library!"

We exited the kitchen through the servants' entrance and climbed the creaking wooden steps to the third story turret, where Lupe's library was located. I loved this room with its built-in wrap-around bookshelves filled with worn, musty tomes.

Louie knocked before turning the cut crystal doorknob. Slowly, he opened the heavy door to reveal a circled gathering of eight chairs—two of which were vacant. Lupe, Danny, plus the other three members of the Seers Symposium, who I recognized from Sunday's service—the Goth girl, the Latina, and the old man—all sat quietly while Madame Mestral spoke.

"Please take a seat," she called from her purple and gold throne.

I wonder what poor sucker had to drag that thing up here?

"Remove the lids from your jars," she continued, "and place the water under your seat. Deposit your eggs in the nest on the mantle above the fireplace."

It was a cool evening. An inviting fire crackled in the filigreed cast iron fireplace, with polished mahogany surround. The lights were dimmed in the tulip shaped glass sconces, flanking either side of the mantelpiece. We carefully slipped our eggs into the large nest and returned to our chairs.

Madame Mestral, once again adorned in flowing white robes (I hope she has more than one of these outfits), rose from her perch and glided over to the nest. She passed her hands over the contents three times, mumbling something under her breath. Cradling the aerie in her arms, she moved into the center of the circle of chairs.

"Consuelo!" Mestral's lisping voice boomed with an undertone of Samir thrown into the mix.

The Latina woman, who channeled the message for Maria at the previous day's service, darted to her augur's side. "Sí, su santidad."

"English," Mestral barked.

I wonder if The Madame even speaks Spanish?

Consuelo bowed. "Forgive me, Mad—" She hesitated, probably not sure whether the directive to speak only in English applied to all words.

"Hold this," Mestral thrust the nest into her confused devotee's chest. "Please rise." She pointed at Louie and me; we clasped hands as we stood. "The initiation will begin."

Initiation? Wait a minute. I stepped forward to voice my protest and felt the sweat break out on Louie's palm.

Mestral ignored my movement. "Who will vouch for these two?"

Danny stood and grabbed my free hand. Lupe took Louie's. "We do," they said in unison.

Mestral reached into the bird's nest. Taking an egg in each hand, she passed them to Lupe and Danny. "Let the cleansing begin!"

Counselo shouted, "Limpia, vamos!"

Mestral glared at her.

Believe me, I was ready to *vamos* right about then. But Danny pulled me back and whispered in my ear, "Be patient. It's a traditional shamanic ritual."

Letting go of our respective hands, Lupe positioned herself in front of Louie and Danny hovered behind me.

I felt the egg perched on top of my head, poised between my cranium and my brother's palm. It brought back memories of a game I played as a kid, the one where you would crack an imaginary egg on a friend's scalp and feign it oozing down their skull. "If he cracks that egg now, I'm going to kill him," I thought.

The fragile oval moved to my forehead, then over my eyes and down the rest of my face. Louie received the exact same ministrations from his aunt. They maneuvered those uncooked eggs all over our bodies in a series of swift downward sweeping motions.

The egg rolling competition came to a conclusion and Counselo moved forward holding two small glass bowls. One was presented to Louie, the other to me.

Danny and Lupe placed our eggs in the bowls before escorting us to Mestral's throne.

Louie looked a little shaky as he stood before The Madame. I do hope he's granted courage and I get to return home. Where are Lupe's ruby slippers when you need them most?

Madame Mestral cracked Louie's egg open into his bowl. She surveyed the contents for a brief moment. "You are clear. Resume sitting."

I was next.

Mestral picked up my egg—sniffed it—shook it—and tapped it on the side of the bowl. The shell fractured through the center, the horrible scent of sulfur filled the air as black goop oozed out into the bowl.

I pinched my nose. "Eww."

Mestral handed the bowl to Consuelo. "This is not good."

No shit, Sherlock. Let's say we skip breakfast.

Mestral snapped her fingers. "Another egg."

"Sorry, I'm all out." I backed away from her. "But don't worry about me, I'm good."

"No, you are not! The evil eye has been cast, its gaze falls upon you!"

CHAPTER FIVE

I Could Have Channeled All Night

MADAME MESTRAL shook her head. "The black egg is a very bad omen. We must consult the oracle." Her eyes closed. "Samir are you near?"

Not Samir again, spare me the community theater dramatics. Mestral or one of her cohorts probably planted the egg. It was from Lupe's fridge, after all, and most likely intended for her.

The Madame's head wobbled back and forth, sluggish at the outset, but steadily picking up pace.

I had never seen anyone go into trance in quite this manner, if that was in fact what she was doing. This time I was at a close enough range to evaluate some of the observable physical signs of hypnosis, such as fluttering of the eyelids and subtle body twitching. But the quickening movement of her head and the dim lighting in the room made it very difficult to verify.

Consuelo rushed back into the room. "I have another one."

"Give me that thing." I snatched the new egg from her hands and examined the shell for any cracks or possible tampering.

Madame Mestral let out a deafening screech. "You can look for all eternity, but you cannot alter your destiny," the voice of Samir bellowed from the medium's body.

And they're off! Mestral falls back, Samir takes the lead.

"Go ahead, crack open the egg you hold." Mestral, eyes now wide open, looked directly at me. "The results will be the same."

I turned to Consuelo. "Where did this come from?"

She looked to Madame Mestral for direction.

Samir spoke, "Tell her."

"Un pollo."

A deep, boisterous, Samir laugh emitted from Mestral. "A chicken! Of course, what else but a chicken!" The Madame stood up, placed her hands under her armpits, and strutted round the room flapping her arms up and down. "Bwok, bwok, bwok."

The old cluck like a chicken bit.

Everyone in the room, including Louie, started laughing. Everyone, but me.

"Is this from Lupe's fridge?" I asked.

"Sí, señorita."

This was the second time in a row Consuelo had spoken in Spanish without an adverse reaction from Mestral, who was still busy pecking. She certainly knew how to stay in character.

"Samir," I called. "Doesn't it bother you when Consuelo speaks Spanish?"

The clucking subsided and Mestral returned to the throne. "Why should it?" Samir responded. "The sweet woman is teaching me the language and I am most grateful for her kindness." She pointed at the egg still in my hand. "Time to get cracking, as they say in your idiom."

"I didn't bring these eggs with me. They're both from Lupe's refrigerator."

"This does not matter. They are picking up on your energy." Mestral turned to Consuelo, "Are there any more in there?"

She nodded. "Cinco."

"Bring them all." Samir spoke to me, "The ones you have not touched will be unaffected." Mestral pointed at Louie. "You, there!"

"Y–y–yes, your Highness." Louie cautiously rose from his chair.

"Give her your vessel."

"My v–v–vess—"

"Give me your bowl," I said.

Louie picked it up from beside his chair and quickly handed it off to me.

Knowing full well this had to be a set-up, I cracked the egg into the bowl. The pungent stench of the rotted contents burned my nostrils. "Can we get rid of this now? I think I'm going to be sick."

The Goth girl came to my rescue and whisked the offensive material out of the library.

"Tch—tch—tch, the Limpia con Huevo did not remove the entire curse," Samir said. "We must repeat the ritual."

Think I'll take a pass. "Look, I'm sure I'll be fine after a couple of aspirins and a good night's sleep."

Consuelo returned with the carton of remaining eggs. The Goth girl trailed behind her with a fresh glass bowl.

"The remaining students will each select an egg." The Madame smiled at Consuelo. "Distribute the huevos." Mestral stood up and walked over to a two-foot high, brass hourglass resting atop a small marble table. "Electra."

The Goth girl moved forward

"Place the vessel underneath this table."

She deposited the bowl and returned to her seat.

"Are all the eggs distributed?"

Consuelo approached the table with a sheepish look on her face and one egg remaining in the carton. "Felix is asleep."

"Wake up, you old fool!" Lupe shouted at the man sitting next to her.

Felix didn't budge.

"I think he's dead," Louie said.

"Nonsense!" Samir boomed. "It is not his time yet."

By the looks of him, Felix had long overstayed his welcome on this planet.

"He's turned his hearing aids off again." Electra gently nudged Felix.

"Are we starting?" he asked, shaking off his slumber.

Consuelo offered him the egg.

"No, thank you," he said. "Doctor Greystoke says I need to watch my cholesterol."

"It's not for eating." An exasperated Lupe took the egg from Consuelo and shoved it into Felix's hands.

"You will hold the eggs between the palms of your hands," Mestral flipped the hourglass over, "until these sands run out."

Cue the flying monkeys.

Mestral turned her attention back to me. "If all the eggs are black when they enter the bowl, I will take your tampering theory under advisement."

Gee, thanks.

She returned to her throne. "In the meantime, think back. See if you remember being watched, spied on, or eyed suspiciously by anyone."

I flashed on the mystery blonde in the yellow Corvette. Sitting there, staring at me.

* * *

The rest of the evening proceeded in as humdrum a way as possible for a gathering of would-be spirit communicators. Samir took a siesta and Madame Mestral rejoined us as moderator. Lupe regaled the gathering with more selections from the Piaf catalogue, while Danny thought he had got a line on Brigham Young—but that one didn't pan out. The other members of the Symposium vacillated between long bouts of meditative silence and short bursts of meaningless monologues. Louie and I observed the whole thing with a grain of salt and a pound of apprehension.

"Before we bring tonight's session to a close," Madame Mestral watched the last of the sand drain from the top of the hourglass, "Samir has requested I have you crack the eggs you have been holding into this glass bowl. After doing so, you are dismissed."

Each of the students filed past the throne, depositing their perfectly normal looking whites and yolks into the clear receptacle. Consuelo, Electra and Felix left immediately after getting the all clear from Mestral. Danny returned to his seat and waited with Louie and me.

Lupe was the last to go up.

I anxiously awaited the result. If Lupe *was* the main target of an elaborate scam, someone would have managed to slip her a bum egg.

The shell clinked against the rim of the bowl and a putrid aroma flooded the room.

Just as I suspected, although Lupe's reaction took me by surprise.

"Not again," she sighed. "How does this keep happening to me, Madame Mestral?"

"You are a very talented and sensual woman, Lupe. Someone you know must be very jealous."

What a load of horse—

Lupe grabbed my arm. "I bet I know who it is…"

I cut her off before she revealed any more. "Can you not tell her who this person is Madame Mestral?"

"Regretfully, I do not possess the gift of second sight, my dear. I am but a humble medium."

Just hanging out on your "humble" throne.

"Drink your Ascended Lightworker water before going to sleep tonight, Lupe, and be sure to pay another visit to the botanica tomorrow. I advise you to do the same, Miss Law. " Madame Mestral rose from her throne. "I must retire for the evening."

I intercepted her at the door. "Could I chat with you for a moment before you leave?"

Mestral held her right hand to her forehead. "Perhaps some other time."

"I'll be brief," I said.

A pained look came across her face. "You really must excuse me." She rushed out of the room

"I'll check in on you later," Lupe called to Mestral. "Poor woman is constantly plagued by those spells of hers."

"Is she still living here?" Louie asked his aunt. "You told me it was only for a night or two."

"Her other accommodations fell through."

"Kind of convenient the way that spell of hers left us behind to do the cleanup." Louie held his nose and picked up the bowl of eggs.

Lupe retrieved the mason jar from underneath her chair and tightly screwed the lid back on. "Don't forget your Ascended Lightworker water everyone."

Danny held up an empty jar. "I already drank mine."

"That's the stuff she was telling me to drink? Ordinary ta—," Louie nudged me before I spilled the beans about the verboten liquid I had opted to use, "—sty, natural spring water."

"It's not ordinary anymore." Lupe took a sip. "It has been filled with divine healing energy."

"You don't say." I picked up my jar and examined it.

"She does say, and so do I." Danny sounded a little steamed.

I didn't back down. "And how does this miraculous transformation come about?"

Lupe was oblivious to my facetious tone. "Madame Mestral has assembled a team of the finest spirit doctors. Every week, while we are gathered here, they channel the group's elevated vibrational frequencies into the water. Before going to bed, we drink this magical elixir and our frequencies raise even higher."

Louie glanced my way. " 'Circle of Life,' Simba." He raised his jar in a toast.

Danny intercepted it mid-air. "Enough, you two."

"So you are endorsing this water?" I waited for my brother's response.

"Let's say I'm choosing to remain open to all possibilities."

"It doesn't cost much at all, Roberta." Lupe added. "You can pick some up when we visit Don Pardo tomorrow."

The announcer from *Saturday Night Live*?

"Are you planning a spirit communication?" Louie asked. "He's dead."

Lupe shook her head. "Impossible! Not my Don Juan Pardo!"

"You're confusing me." Louie finished stacking the folding chairs. "Which one are you talking about, the iconic TV announcer or fictional womanizer?"

Danny waded into the fray. "Neither. He's more like Castaneda's Don Juan—a brujo."

"A witch doctor," Louie said.

"Shaman," Danny countered.

"He owns a jewelry store in Beverly Hills." Lupe jiggled the gold charm bracelet on her right wrist. "Don Juan Pardo sold this to me earlier today."

I examined the intricate links and talismans on Lupe's wrist. "You said you bought water from him, too?"

"Yes, at his other business. The botanica—Pardo's Potions—in East Hollywood. It is so much better than the regular spring water you find in the grocery store."

Quite the entrepreneur.

Louie raised an eyebrow. "How much is he charging for this water of his and what's so special about it?"

"All this talk of water is making thirsty." Lupe steered the conversation in another direction. "Please join me downstairs for some coffee and tres leches cake."

* * *

We reconvened in Lupe's kitchen.

While Danny made the coffee and Lupe sliced the cake, Louie pulled me through the swinging door into the dining room. "This is worse than I thought. You've got to go with her tomorrow and meet this Don Pardo guy."

"Why me? Why don't you go?"

"I'm flying to Vegas to see a new client. It's her first night performing with Cirque du Soleil."

"I have sessions scheduled tomorrow and I'm meeting Ben for lunch."

"Bring him with you. He may be able to help us."

I knew Ben wouldn't mind, he'd already agreed to come to Lupe's house to take some kind of reading with that meter of his. "All right, I'll shift a couple of appointments around and see if Ben has enough time available to tag along."

Lupe entered the room with a tray full of cake and coffee. "Poor Daniel is so tired he went up to bed. He said to say goodnight to you."

"Do you know if he's taking his medication, Lupe?"

"Don't worry. He took another jar of Ascended Lightworker water upstairs with him." She put the tray down on the table. "May I ask a small favor of you, Roberta?"

"Sure."

"Would you mind driving me to Don Pardo's tomorrow? I don't think my car will be ready till late in the day." Lupe passed me a piece of cake. "Madame Mestral got waylaid on her way to my mechanic's this afternoon. They were closing the shop by the time she got there. Coffee?"

"No coffee for me, thanks." I turned my cup over. "Madame Mestral was driving your car?"

"Yes, I let her borrow it whenever I'm not using it. She's been so good to me, it's the least I can do. And wasn't it sweet of her to offer to run it into the shop for me?"

"Was she the only person you let use your car today?"

"Oh, yes. I'm very particular about who I let drive my car." Lupe patted Louie on the cheek. "Right, chiquito?"

"That accident wasn't my fault." Louie took a bite of his cake. "And it happened thirty years ago."

"You were driving a car at the age of ten?"

"I was the unfortunate passenger when Lupe was driving through Boyle Heights and thought she spotted Julio Iglesias hanging out in Mariachi Plaza. She let go of the wheel to reapply her makeup, I grabbed onto it for dear life and steered us away from the musicians. We hit a lamppost instead."

"Always so melodramatic this one. I've been touching up my war paint that way for as long as I can remember." Lupe took a sip of coffee. "Never one accident."

"You know what she did after we crashed? She flung open her door and ran out to look for Julio Iglesias."

Lupe sighed. "It was too late, we scared him away."

"Why would someone who was in the Top Five of the Billboard Hot 100 that year be hanging out in front of a donut shop in East LA trying to pick up a gig?"

"The heart wants what the heart wants. Anyone for another piece of cake?"

"None for me, thanks." I put my fork down on my plate. "It's time for me to call it a night. I'm meeting a colleague for lunch tomorrow. Do you mind if I bring him by with me? He's a parapsychologist and would like to take some energy readings on your house."

Lupe gave me a curious look. "Energy readings?"

"I know as much about it as you do. He'll explain everything tomorrow. I think you'll like him."

"Is he single?"

"As a matter of fact, he is."

Lupe smiled. "I like him already."

"We'll see you around two-thirty." I got up from the table. "Before I leave, may I ask you a question about the Piaf channeling you do?"

"Of course, Roberta."

"I noticed you holding a chart of one of her songs yesterday. If you are channeling her, why do you need to study sheet music?"

"I receive her in her mother tongue of French. Since I don't speak the language, I wanted to know exactly what I was singing."

Fair enough.

"But you've had French language Piaf numbers in your act for years," Louie added.

Lupe threw back her head. "So it's a crime to channel an artist I'm familiar with?"

"No, I'd say it's more of a curiosity than a crime."

"Don't forget, Luis." Lupe shook her finger. "La curiosidad mató al gato."

Louie didn't miss a beat. "Can you have Edith Piaf say that in French?"

"I can't find Madame Mestral!" Danny burst into the room. "She's disappeared!"

CHAPTER SIX

Ding-Dong! The Madame's Gone

A PANICKED LOOKING Lupe rose from her seat. "Maybe Madame Mestral forgot something in the library."

Danny shook his head. "That's the first place I looked when she wasn't in her room."

"Let's fan out and search the entire house, even the rooms you've already checked." Lupe joined Danny at the door to the kitchen. "Come on you two," she looked backed at Louie and me, "this is a big house. We need your help."

Louie glanced at his watch. "It's only ten o'clock. What are you so worried about? She probably couldn't sleep and went out for a stroll."

"God, I hope she hasn't gone outside," Danny said. "That could be terribly dangerous."

Sounds like my brother's paranoia is making a comeback. "Relax, Danny. This neighborhood's not so bad."

"Madame Mestral is a somnambulist," Danny said.

"You've hypnotized her?" In hypnotherapy parlance, a "somnambulist" is a subject with a high degree of suggestibility and prone to readily slip into trance.

"No, not that kind of somnambulist. She has noctambulism—Madame Mestral's a sleepwalker."

"She showed up in my room one night looking for a dwarf," Lupe added.

Louie laughed. "Maybe she was channeling Snow White."

"Don't be ridiculous, Luis. Snow White isn't a real person."

Louie and I followed Danny and Lupe into the kitchen.

"The dwarf happens to be the third dream symbol in Carl Jung's trip to the self," Danny continued, "and a very serious warning. They represent that which is hidden in one's quest for self-knowledge, the neglected or repressed parts of the psyche. Don't even get me started on the whole Snow White thing."

"Luis, please check the third floor. Roberta, if you could take the second floor? I'll do the ground floor while Daniel checks the basement."

We split up and headed to our assigned areas. I took the old service staircase up to the second story. Opening the doors to the three bedrooms, I quickly checked each suite until I came upon Mestral's lair. I knocked before entering, but like the others there was no one inside. This would be a good opportunity to snoop around.

The brass four-poster bed was unkempt and showed signs of being recently occupied. A half finished jar of Ascended Lightworker water sat on the nightstand. Next to it were a number of bottles of prescription meds—Thorazine, Prozac, Valium, and Dexedrine. Each label had a different patient name, not one of them was Mestral. I turned to leave the room.

"Nooo, mommy, nooo," a child's sobs came from the closet. "Please don't leave me in here. I'm scared of the dark."

I opened the door and turned on the interior light. The top shelf of the closet was lined with styrofoam head forms wearing wigs of all styles and colors. Underneath the tightly packed rack of clothes, I discovered Madame Mestral curled up in a ball weeping.

"Are you all right?" I asked.

She continued crying without acknowledging my presence.

"I'll be right back." Running out of the room, I called to the others, "She's up here!" I hurried to the third floor to look for Louie.

He was in the library, sitting on Mestral's throne, reading a copy of *Vogue*. "This chair is really comfortable."

"Come with me," I said. "I've located Madame Mestral, I think she's strung out on drugs."

By the time we hit the second landing, I heard Danny and Lupe making their way up from the main floor.

"Did you call for us, Roberta?" Lupe stepped off the staircase.

"Yes, I found Madame Mestral. But I think she needs medical attention."

Danny joined us. "What's wrong?"

"See for yourself." I led them into the guest room, opened the closet and pushed the clothes aside. No one was there. "She was in here a minute ago."

"Perhaps you saw a ghost." Danny said.

"No, it was Madame Mestral. She was crying like a baby. I think she might be having some sort of drug reaction."

"Drugs?" Lupe seemed shocked. "She's been a teetotaler her entire life. I doubt she would be messing around with dope."

"They were prescription drugs." I headed for the nightstand. All the pill bottles were gone. "I don't understand."

"Don't understand what, my dear?" Madame Mestral walked into the room.

Lupe rushed to the disappearing mystic's side and gave her a hug. "Daniel and I were so worried. Where have you been?"

"Outside, communing with the stars."

"I figured you went for a walk," Louie said.

"Forgive me, Madame Mestral," Danny said. "I sounded the alarm when I stopped by your room and couldn't locate you anywhere."

"You precious man," Mestral patted Danny on the cheek, "worried I was sleepwalking again?"

"I was concerned for your well being, too," Lupe added.

Mestral wrapped her arms around Danny and Lupe. "My darlings, no need to be troubled by such thoughts anymore. I believe I have the problem under tight control."

I looked The Madame straight in the eye. "What happened to all the meds I saw in here a moment ago?"

She didn't flinch. "Meds? No idea what you're talking about, I've never believed in such remedies. They are a hindrance to my gift."

I scanned the room, hoping to spot a stray pill bottle. Nada. Her transformation from teary-eyed child to phlegmatic sensitive was not only fast, it was thorough.

"All kudos for deliverance from my affliction are due to our beloved Don Pardo. The man is truly a miracle worker."

Or a very sly drug dealer.

* * *

On my drive home I called Louie. "I'm telling you I found her curled up in a fetal position. Which doesn't surprise me considering the extensive pharmacopoeia she had on hand."

"What kind of drugs?"

"Uppers, downers, antipsychotics—you name it."

"You think she's an addict?"

"Not one of those bottles had her name on it. Either she stole all those pills or she's prescription shopping under assumed names."

"Well, I'm glad you're going with Aunt Lupe tomorrow to see this Don Pardo guy."

"Yeah, it will be interesting to see if he peddles more than just jewelry and magic water."

"I'll call you when I get back from Vegas. Keep an eye on The Madame for me. I don't want her leading my aunt on any more Tommy Forrester afterlife excursions. Love ya!" Louie hung up.

My puzzling encounter with Madame Mestral kept looping in my mind. Was she taking those drugs I found? Had they created the shattered person hiding in the closet? Or was the calm and collected woman who joined us in the guest room their final product? I needed to discuss this with a competent mental health professional, but was afraid to trust my brother. He was too closely involved and prone to his own brand of erratic behavior. I decided to contact Carl Jenkins in the morning.

At half past eleven, I pulled into my driveway. Lex was waiting at the front door, leash in mouth.

"Sorry I'm late, buddy. It's been an unusual night. Will you forgive me if we make tonight's walk a short one?"

Lex dropped his lead at my feet and ran past me into the night.

"Okay, I get the message."

I scrambled for a flashlight. It's dark in LA at night, streetlights are few and far between. The city's fabled marriage to eternal sunshine was undermined by its clandestine affair with unfathomable darkness.

"Lex, where are you?" My voice was hushed, I lived in a quiet area. No need to wake the neighbors.

I ran to the southeast corner of my block and checked out the intersecting street. "Come on, Lex. It's too late for games."

About a block west of me, I caught sight of a waddling beagle butt rounding the corner, headed north. By the time I got there, Lex was halfway up the street poised to let it all hang out on someone's pristine lawn.

"Don't you dare! I forgot to bring a bag."

Leash in hand, I rushed the squatting hound, snapped the tether onto his collar and hauled his popping posterior to the curb. I looked around for a stray plastic bag to pick up after him.

"Looks like you're going to get a nice long walk after all."

We continued up the block and then circled back to our house. I ran inside, retrieved a poop bag, and then retraced our steps to the scene of the crime. After scooping up Exhibit A, we headed home for the night.

Turning back onto my street, about a half block away, I detected a yellow Corvette parked in front of my house. Picking up my already brisk pace, as I got closer to home, I spotted someone standing outside my office door. "May I help you?"

The figure darted for the vehicle.

"It's all right. Please wait, I'm Roberta Law."

Stopping short, outside the car door, the stranger turned and looked at me. It was the blonde-haired woman from earlier in the day.

Lex and I hurtled toward her. "Don't go!"

When we got within a few feet, she jumped into the driver's seat. The Corvette's engine revved.

I shined my flashlight on the rear plate—C A N T O R A.

The car sped away.

My high school Spanish was rusty. But I knew I could rely on my dear pal, Siri, to help me out. After several tries, I finally gave up and just googled it myself—CANTORA: Female Singer, Songbird.

All that was missing was a picture of Lupe Lopez.

CHAPTER SEVEN

A Cup Of Champurrado, Some Churros, And You

I WAS UP EARLY on Tuesday. Juggling client appointments to free some time for my afternoon excursion with Lupe. Luckily, Ben was able to do the same with his schedule and agreed to accompany me to Lupe's after lunch with his ghost-detecting machine in tow. I was hoping to run into Madame Mestral while we were there and get Ben's take on her, plus find out more about the exact whereabouts of Lupe's Corvette. Louie texted to confirm it was his aunt's vanity plate I had seen. How her car got into the hands of the enigmatic blonde was still an unknown. With one more call left to place, my day was off to an invigorating start.

"Good morning, Dr. Carl Jenkins office," a cheery voice came over my receiver. "How may I assist you?"

"Yes, good morning. It's Roberta Law calling. I was wondering if I could speak with Dr. Jenkins?"

"I'm sorry, he's in session at the moment. May I take a message?"

"Please let him know I called. He has the number."

I hung up the phone and finished prepping notes for my nine o'clock. It was the fourth and, most likely, last session for a screenwriter suffering from severe writer's block. The client was highly responsive to hypnosis, as most creative types are, and had made rapid progress. After I finished jotting down my final notations, I still had about a half hour to spare. To kill some time I googled the name Tommy Forrester. Over four thousand results popped up.

"Guess I need to be a tad more specific."

I walked to the dining room and fetched the Sunday *Times*.

"Let's try this again." I expanded my search field—Private First Class Thomas Forrester + deceased.

The top hit was one of those legacy memorial websites. I clicked on the link and landed on a page for the exact guy I was looking for—Lupe's Tommy. There was a photo gallery with images of her fantasy suitor at various ages. His original obituary had been added, along with a guest book for visitors to leave comments. Someone named Cissy sponsored the site.

I heard a knock on the outside door to my office. My writer was early.

"Just a minute!" I logged off the computer, made sure Lex wasn't hiding anywhere, shut the door connecting my office to the rest of the house, and went to let my client in.

No one was there. A small brown package sat on my stoop. "ROBERTA" was scribbled on top. There was no indication of who had sent the parcel or who had delivered it. I picked it up and went back inside.

I debated opening the unusual package. Was this a Homeland Security matter? Should I alert the police or something? My curiosity outweighing my suspicion, I ripped the paper off the package and discovered an old Keds shoebox underneath. Inside, a dog-eared copy of *The Book of Lies* by Aleister Crowley with a bookmark sticking out of it. Opening the book to the indicated page, I came across a highlighted quote:

"Dreams are imperfections of sleep; even so is consciousness the imperfection of waking. Dreams are impurities in the circulation of the blood; even so it's consciousness a disorder of life. Dreams are without proportion, without good sense, without truth; so also is consciousness. Awake from dream, the truth is known: awake from waking. The truth is: The Unknown."

Cryptic, to say the least. Who it was from and why it was delivered to me, I had absolutely no idea.

* * *

Since we were both heading over to Lupe's place after lunch, Ben suggested we grab a bite in Echo Park. My '68 VW Bug (Lupe wasn't the only one who had a thing for vintage yellow vehicles) circled Sunset Boulevard a couple of times before landing a prime parking spot on Logan Street. We were meeting at Sage Vegan Bistro. Ben recommended the restaurant—he liked to eat healthy. I just liked to eat.

"I know what a big burger fan you are, Roberta." Ben passed me a menu. "May I suggest the Classic Tempeh Burger?"

The words "tempeh" and "burger" had no business being together in my Jughead vision of "classic" American fare. "No cheeseburgers, I suppose?"

"They have some delicious cashew based cheeses."

"Anything cow based?"

"Sorry, this place is vegan not vegetarian."

I took a quick look at the menu. "Think I'll stick with a soup and salad."

We placed our orders with the server.

"Thanks for clearing your schedule this afternoon. This Madame Mestral business has Louie in a tizzy."

Ben looked incredulous. "More of a tizzy than usual?"

I laughed. "Hard to believe, I know. Any luck with your contacts at the Cayce center?"

"No one at the A.R.E. is familiar with a medium by the name of Madame Mestral."

"I knew there was something fishy about this woman." I looked at the munching veganistas sitting at the table beside us. "Sorry, poor choice of words."

"Wait a minute, Roberta. Don't go jumping to any conclusions."

Ben was always so levelheaded. I secretly wished he was more excitable, especially in the bedroom department. This celibacy fixation of his wasn't doing it for me.

"Just because they haven't heard of her doesn't necessarily make her a fake," Ben continued.

"See for yourself. She'll probably be lounging on her throne when we drop by Lupe's."

"You didn't mention we'd be meeting royalty today," Ben teased. "If I'd known, I would have worn a tie."

The less you have on, the better. As soon as that thought left my mind, a distinct twinkle danced in Ben's steel-blue eyes. I wasn't fully convinced his mind reading days were a thing of the past.

"Are you all right, Roberta?"

"Yes, why?"

"Your face got very red all of a sudden."

Do I detect a coy smirk with that line? "Ben Cohen are you snooping around in my head?"

The waiter arrived with our plates. "Hot Wing Salad and Jamaican Jerk Burger?"

"Hot one here." I looked at Ben—*the Jerk's over there.*

Ben smiled and took a big bite out of his burger.

* * *

We rang Lupe's bell at twenty past two. There was still no sign of her yellow Corvette on the street.

Lupe answered the door. "Welcome to my home, please come in." She escorted us into the foyer.

"Lupe, this is Ben Cohen—the man I told you about."

She batted her eyes and offered her hand. "Delighted to meet you, Mr. Cohen."

Having already given him a heads up about the amatory octogenarian, Ben played along with her harmless Blanche DuBois-esque fantasies. "Charmed to make your acquaintance, señorita." He gently kissed her liver-spotted hand. "And, please, call me by my first name."

"Can I interest anyone in some coffee or hot chocolate?"

"Nothing for me, thanks," I said.

"I could go for a hot chocolate, if it's Mexican hot chocolate," Ben said.

"It's champurrado," Lupe beamed. "I wouldn't think of serving anything else with Dia de los Muertos right around the corner. Please join me in the dining room."

"Will you ladies excuse me for a moment? I left my EMF meter in the car." Ben headed back outside.

I followed Lupe into the dining room. "Will Sheila O'Hara be serving us today?" The random appearance of Madame Mestral's channeled entities both amused and perturbed me.

"No, but she made the most delicious churros this morning." Lupe pointed to a platter in the center of the dining room table. "You must try one."

They did look tasty. I picked one up and took a bite. "Mmmm, these are good. For a deceased Irish woman, she makes a mighty wicked churro."

"She got the recipe from Pancho Villa's mother."

"Let me get this straight. The entities channel entities, too?"

"Not really. Some of them are aware of each other and can communicate, though I'm not quite sure how they do this. You'd have to ask Madame Mestral to explain it."

"Where is The Madame?

"She isn't in at the moment."

"Is she out making house calls with Dr. Greystoke?"

"Oh, Roberta." Lupe flicked my shoulder with her hand. "You're as bad as Luis sometimes. I can just imagine the niños you two are going to make."

That's quite the imagination you have.

Lupe held a teacup under the spout of her sterling silver samovar. "I think Ben fancies me, don't you?"

Earth to Lupe. Earth to Lupe. "Well, he's a very nice man—"

"And handsome, too."

I nodded my head. Oh, god. What mischief have I wrought? I shouldn't have told Ben to be so attentive.

Lupe set two cups and saucers down on the dining room table. "But, he's not my type."

Phew! Dodged a bullet this time. What do you mean *not your type*? What's the matter with him?

"Cohen is a Jewish name, is it not? I promised Papi I would marry in the Church. My Tommy was a good Catholic boy."

That's right, the online obituary mentioned his funeral was held at Holy Family Church in Pasadena.

"Tommy wants me to find his murderer, Roberta. So he can finally rest in eternal peace." Lupe took a napkin and dabbed a tear from her eye. "This morning at breakfast, Madame Mestral promised to do everything in her power to help me right the wrong done to my Tommy. I've contracted with her to do a series of private sittings for me." Her voice rose. "If it takes my very last penny, I vow to see my Tommy's death avenged!"

"Sorry I took so long," Ben called from the front door.

"We're back here," I shouted

"I almost got run over by a car," Ben said.

Lupe gasped. "Madame Mestral was right last night. The Evil Eye is upon us both, Roberta. No one in our lives will be safe from harm until we pay a visit to Don Pardo."

Ben joined us in the dining room.

"Are you all right?" I asked him.

"Far as I can tell." Ben looked down at himself. "I managed to jump out of the way of her yellow Corvette in the nick of time. That crazy blonde came barreling down the street out of nowhere."

CHAPTER EIGHT

You Could Drive A Hypnotist Crazy

I COULDN'T BELIEVE what I was hearing. A speeding blonde behind the wheel of a yellow Corvette had almost run down Ben. Was I being stalked? Why? I wasn't buying into any of the "evil eye" malarkey Mestral had sold Lupe on. "Did you manage to get a look at the license plate?"

"Not really. It all happened so fast. I think it had a specialty plate."

"Lupe, are you positive your car is still in the shop?"

"Yes, Madame Mestral has gone to pick it up for me."

"Would you mind if I give your mechanic a quick call?" I asked.

"Let me look for my purse, the phone number's in there." Lupe exited the dining room.

"What's this all about, Roberta?" Ben sounded concerned.

"I think someone has got a hold of Lupe's car and they're following me."

Lupe re-entered the room. "Here it is." She handed me a crumpled business card.

I reached into my handbag and fished around for my cell. "My phone's in here somewhere."

"I'll go to the living room and get you the cordless." Lupe turned to leave.

I dumped my bag out on the dining room table. "Found it!"

Lupe sat down and took a sip from her cup. "Drink your Champurrado, Benjamin. It's getting cold."

"Hello, I'm calling to check on Lupe Lopez's car…Yes, I can hold." I put the phone on speaker and returned the scattered contents of my life—lipstick, hairbrush, doggie treats, wallet, keys, condoms—to their rightful home.

Ben picked up the copy of Crowley's *Book of Lies* I had stuffed in there before heading out from my office. "Interested in the works of Thelema?"

"Thelma? I think some guy wrote the book."

"Some guy, indeed. Aleister Crowley was a renown English ceremonial magician."

"Don't think I ever caught his act." I handed the auto mechanic's card back to Lupe. "His book's kinda weird."

"Not that kind of magician. He was an occultist. *Thelema* is the name of the religion he founded. It's based on the philosophical law of Thelema—'Do what thou wilt shall be the whole of the Law. Love is the law, love under will.' "

"Guess he wasn't too creative in the naming things department. I'm surprised he didn't call his book Thelema, too."

"He did pen *The Holy Books of Thelema*. The Law of Thelema is found in the religion's central sacred text, *The Book of the Law*. He claimed it was transmitted to him over a three day period in Cairo, by an entity known as Aiwass."

Lupe's ears pricked up. "I wonder if he knows Samir?"

"Are you still there?" a gruff male voice came back on the line.

"Yes," I answered.

"The car's not here."

I dropped what I was doing and retrieved the phone. "Oh, it is… She has… No, that won't be necessary. Thank you." I threw my cell back in my purse and continued collecting my remaining possessions from the table.

Ben spoke first. "Care to share with the rest of the class, Roberta?"

"Madame Mestral was there picking up the car."

"Wonderful!" Lupe clapped her hands together. "I missed my little Chiquita Banana. But I still don't understand why you called about my car, Roberta. Do you not want to drive me to Don Pardo's?"

I felt completely ridiculous and paranoid. Still, I knew what I'd seen—a blonde driving around in Lupe Lopez's car. "No, Lupe, it's not that."

"What is it then?" Ben pressed.

"I thought someone might have stolen your car. I've seen a blonde-haired woman driving around in a yellow Corvette, with what I could have sworn was your license plate."

"Was she weeping?" Lupe asked.

"Not that I could tell."

"Rule out La Llorona. Was she wearing a nurse's uniform?"

"No."

"Not La Planchada either." Lupe shook her head. "Let's run it by Don Pardo when we see him."

I didn't have the foggiest notion what she was going on about.

Ben picked up on my confusion. "La Llorona and La Planchada are two well known ghosts in Mexican culture." He opened a small black leather pouch and took out a gray hand-held device. "Time to take some readings with my EMF meter."

"Is that the ghost machine?" Lupe held out her hand. "May I hold it?"

Ben nodded.

She cradled the gadget in her hands. "May I kiss it?"

"I don't see why not," Ben said.

"Tommy are you in there?" Lupe placed a soft kiss on the apparatus. "Benjamin has come to get you out."

"I'm afraid that's not quite how it works." Ben reached for the instrument and turned it on. A series of red, green, and yellow lights flashed at the top.

"Kind of Star Trek-ish," I said.

"First, I need to take some preliminary readings to establish a base level for the house." Ben got up from the table. "In a nutshell, this machine is reading electromagnetic fields. Every place has a number of areas of naturally occurring activity—usually from existing power lines, appliances, televisions, etcetera. Roberta, as we walk through the house will you please make note of the numbers I give you?"

I took out my iPhone.

"No," Ben said. "Do it the old-fashioned way—with pen and paper."

"I will get it for you, Roberta." Lupe walked over to the wooden cabinet across the room.

"Mobile phones work off of radio frequency energy, which is a form of electromagnetic radiation. I want to get as pristine a baseline as possible. Let's turn off all personal electronics."

Ben and I powered down our cells.

Lupe handed me a pen and paper. "I don't have such a phone."

Ben looked at Lupe. "I need you to go ahead of us and unplug anything not needed at the moment."

"Sí, I'll start in the kitchen." Lupe exited through the swinging door.

"We're looking for readings anywhere between .1 and 1.0 milligauss on the EMF scale, which is about standard for the average house." Ben moved slowly through the room." Any anomalous spikes above that range indicate the presence of something paranormal."

Following closely behind Ben, I peeked over his shoulder at the bouncing needle on the meter. Near the kitchen door, the indicator made a precipitous jump. "There's something! Did you see it?"

"I thought you didn't believe in ghosts, Roberta. Please note a sudden spike from .9 to 5." Ben looked back at me. "Also jot down, we were standing next to a light switch at the time of the occurrence."

"Is that significant?"

"Yes, we're picking up a reading for the electrical current running through the wall. This room is clear, nothing seems to be out of the ordinary."

Ben and I ploddingly made our way through the entire house in this manner; Lupe joined us on the second floor.

"Did you check the basement?" Lupe inquired.

"Yes," Ben said. "Everything checked out."

"I bet you find that rascal, Tommy, hiding in my bedroom."

Lupe led the way into her chamber. Obviously, she was still having trouble grasping the nature of what we were doing.

"It's not a person we're looking for per se, it's more like a portal." Ben surveyed the area. "The ancient Celts referred to them as 'thin places' because they believed the veil between the eternal and physical worlds was attenuated in these spots."

On second thought, Lupe wasn't the only one having trouble with the concept behind our mission. "Are we looking for some sort of vortex?"

"Pretty much."

"I'm not so sure I like this phantom scavenger hunt," I said.

"Another all clear," Ben said.

"Oh, pooh!" Lupe stamped her foot.

"That's the last room on this landing." Ben headed up the staircase to the third and final floor.

The library was checked first. Then we moved on to a small, dusty antechamber, which opened onto an attic stuffed with a lifetime's worth of memorabilia.

"I'm turning these two rooms into a recording studio," Lupe said. "Do they pass inspection?"

Ben paced the rooms, head down, tracking the output of the EMF meter. "Everything looks good."

"Nothing special about this house," I said, writing down the last note.

Lupe looked offended by my remark.

"Let me rephrase that, nothing *unusual* about this house."

"I'm not picking up any spectral activity," Ben said.

"So The Madame is making it all up?"

"Roberta! Bite your tongue," Lupe chastised.

"Not necessarily," Ben added. "A medium has a psychic gift. They don't have to be in a 'thin place' for it to work."

"So what was the point of this exercise?" I asked.

"All possibilities must be checked thoroughly before we can come up with any probable conclusions." Ben took the paper from my hand. "Thanks for taking notes, Roberta. I'll add them to my ongoing research in this field."

Lupe looked at her wristwatch. "It's almost four o'clock. We should be on our way to Don Pardo's. Are you coming with us, Benjamin?"

We left the attic and headed for the staircase.

"Sorry, have to take a rain check. First thing tomorrow morning I'm conducting a teleseminar on psychokinesis for the Institute of Noetic Sciences. I need to get back to the office and put the final polish on my presentation."

We reached the second landing.

Ben was putting the EMF meter back in its case. "Wow, this thing's going crazy."

"What do you mean?" I said.

"Look, see for yourself." Ben showed me the machine. Its needle was bouncing up and down erratically. The lights flashed over and over in rapid-fire sequence—green—yellow—red—green—yellow—red.

Lupe's voice was hushed. "Is Tommy here?"

"Something's here." Ben walked past each of the rooms on the floor. He stopped outside Mestral's door. "It's coming from in there."

"How can that be?" I asked. "The room had no noticeable activity when we were in there earlier."

"Maybe we should check it again." Lupe reached for the door-knob and screamed. "It's turning all by itself!"

I would have given anything to have a rosary in my hands right then.

The door creaked open.

Ben's eyes were glued to the EMF meter. "I've never seen such a high reading."

"Do you mind keeping it down out here?" Madame Mestral stood in the open doorway. "Who are you?" She moved toward Ben. "And what are you doing?"

"This needle's off the charts." He held the meter over The Madame's head. "It's coming from her!"

CHAPTER NINE

Don Pardo's Hideaway

"THIS MAN AND HIS apparatus are annoying me." Mestral turned to go back in her room.

"Don't be upset with him," Lupe pleaded. "He's trying to help me find my Tommy."

The Madame balked at the idea. "Utter nonsense. Only I can help you contact him."

Guess The Madame isn't too fond of competition.

"Any reputable medium should be able to assist her," Ben said. "I've never heard of spirits signing exclusivity contracts."

You go, boy. Put this ghost grifter in her place.

"That being said, I didn't come here to replace you. Ben Cohen's the name," he put out his hand, "I'm a parapsychologist. And with your permission, I would like to study you."

No! Now we'll never get rid of her. Louie's going to be livid.

Mestral gave Ben the once-over before cautiously extending her hand. "What would this involve? And how much remuneration would I receive?"

Funny how it always comes down to money.

"Most of my subjects are volunteers, but a small stipend can be arranged."

Mestral took a moment to ponder the offer on the table. "It's a deal." She shook Ben's hand. "Now you really must excuse me. My head has been bothering me again. I need to take a nap." She went inside her room and shut the door.

"Does she have a lot of problems with her head?" Ben turned off his EMF meter.

"Look what she does for a living," I said. "What do you think?"

We left the second floor landing and continued downstairs.

"The poor woman is plagued by these spells of hers," Lupe said. "I don't know how she stands it."

"Has she seen a physician?" Ben asked.

"She isn't fond of doctors. Roberta's brother, Daniel, is the only one she trusts."

"I don't think he'll be much help," I said. "He's on an indefinite hiatus."

"I was thinking more along the lines of an environmental health practitioner. She may have EHS, electromagnetic hypersensitivity. Her EMF readings are abnormally high, well beyond anything I've ever seen."

"That's a real thing?" I asked, stepping onto the main floor.

"Some say yes, and some say no. The main challenge will be how to reduce her exposure to EMF emissions."

"Why is that, Benjamin?" Lupe opened the front door.

"The disturbances don't appear to be coming from the external environment. They're coming from inside her."

* * *

From the street, Pardo's Potions was an unassuming shop tucked in-between a taquería and a medical marijuana dispensary. A serendipitous alignment that was a stoner's dream come true. Get high courtesy of Dr. Feelgood, pop next door to have your paranoia-induced curse removed, and top it off with a plate of enchiladas con mole.

The window of Pardo's mystical apothecary was chock-full of religious iconery representing every saint and deity known to man. Once inside, the pungent smell of incense took my breath away. Afro-Cuban jazz rhythms pulsated in the background.

At the front of the store an array of rosary beads hung near the cash register, and an eclectic assortment of mojo tchotchkes were neatly laid out beneath an enclosed glass counter. I eyeballed the offbeat contents—rabbit foot keychains (hope those are fake), tarot cards (didn't realize they made so many different types), voodoo dolls (could use one or two of those), holy water for gamblers (that's a new one), lucky blue balls (since when are they lucky?).

A couple of elderly Latinas roamed the narrow aisles filling their baskets

"¿Dónde está Don Pardo?" Lupe called to the ladies.

"En el trastero," the one closest to us answered. "Volverá a la deracha."

Lupe turned to me. "He's in the storeroom. It should just be a moment."

"I'm going to look around a bit," I said.

Walking toward the far wall I passed shelves lined with oils, lotions, powders, and herbs. Some were labeled only in Spanish, some only in English, and some were in both languages. On a tiered rack at the back of the shop a display of candles, in all shapes and colors (including a three-foot high, thick, red, phallic one), burned brightly. Nearby a collection of books with titles such as, *Sex Magic Made Easy, Satanic Sex Rituals,* and *Celtic Coitus for Neo-Pagans* sat beneath a large sign: BUY NOW, READ LATER.

Lupe called out to me. "Don Juan Pardo is ready to see you, Roberta."

I made my way back to the front of the store. Standing behind the counter was a short, balding man in his late sixties—dressed in a rumpled black suit, a pair of wire-rimmed spectacles perched on his nose. The man looked more rabbi than brujo. Not quite what I was expecting.

"Señorita Lopez tells me you are in need of a curse removal," he spoke with an Eastern European accent.

Time to put my investigator cap on. "May I ask what part of Mexico you are from Don Pardo?"

"Spain," he said in a matter-of-fact tone, "by way of Poland. I'm a Sephardic Jew, descended from a long line of Kabbalists. Now that we have my pedigree out of the way, it's my turn to ask the questions. Do you know which type of curse has been cast on you?"

Taken aback by his abruptness, I could not find the words to answer.

Lupe whispered, "Madame Mestral says the evil eye has fallen upon her and she needs something stronger than an egg cleansing."

Don Pardo nodded his head and took a long pause while giving me a visual appraisal. I half wondered if he was putting a hex on me. "Do you know whose path you have inadvertently crossed?"

What's he think I am, a black cat? "Hard to say. Los Angeles is a big city and I meet a lot of different people in my line of work."

"What is your profession?"

"She hypnotizes people," Lupe said enthusiastically.

"So you're an entertainer," Don Pardo shook his head, "probably a dissatisfied patron."

Everybody's a critic. "I'm a hypnotherapist, not a stage hypnotist."

"Even worse," he said.

Tough guy to please.

Don Pardo continued, "You may be the victim of a psychic backfire. Perhaps one of your clients came to you for help with a problem they believed to be of mental origin."

"That's usually why people come to me."

"But what if the problem was placed in their mind by another mind?"

"I'm not following you," I said.

"A sorcerer or sorceress invokes the power of an external, invisible being to do their bidding in the internal world of another. If you interfere with this process, you may be unknowingly transferring your client's problem—which is really a curse—to yourself. Once unbound from its original host, the dark force seeks out a new victim."

This guy's got to be putting me on. "I didn't realize curses were contagious."

"Not so much contagious, but easily transferrable in your line of work." Don Pardo turned and parted the green curtains behind him. "I believe I have what you need in my private stock." He exited from behind the counter.

Lupe looked thrilled, like we were on a shopping spree for new shoes. "Don Pardo has a cure for everything."

We must get his coordinates to the Centers for Disease Control.

"This is my treat." She pulled a roll of hundreds out of her purse.

"Put that away," I said.

"No, I insist. You're practically familia."

"You shouldn't be carrying so much cash on you, Lupe." Out of the corner of my eye, I surveyed the store. An unsavory looking biker type had joined the other shoppers. "It's dangerous."

East Hollywood wasn't the safest part of town. Especially for a tiny woman in her eighties (I wasn't about to bring up the "A"—age—word with Lupe), packing a wad of cash.

Don Pardo walked back through the curtains. "I want you to go right home and take a bath using these salts. You must soak your body completely for at least thirty minutes." He handed me a glass apothecary jar filled with tiny black crystals.

"Do they come in another color?" I didn't fancy cleansing myself in black water.

"No. I mixed them especially for you. There's Dead Sea Salt in there, along with Black Lava Salt, some essential oils, and a few of my secret ingredients. It's quite aromatic, open it up and take a whiff."

Taking the top off the container, I passed its contents under my nose. It had a spicy-sweet, intoxicating aroma—slightly citrus, slightly floral. "Is that Jasmine I detect?"

"Yes, and Bergamot. Here," Don Pardo passed me two small straws, "you'll need these."

"You don't expect me to drink this stuff too?"

"Those are for your nose, so you can breathe. Total immersion is required." Bending down beneath the glass display case, he unlocked a hidden drawer, removed a royal blue jewelry box and handed it to me.

On top, embossed in gold script, were the words:
PARDO'S FINE JEWELRY - Beverly Hills, California.

Lupe had mentioned something about him owning a jewelry store. I opened the lid. Inside a small black fist hung from a silver chain. The tiny thumb protruded slightly from between the index and middle fingers.

"The hand is onyx and the chain's sterling silver. I made this piece myself," he said. "You must put it on immediately after you finish the cleansing ritual."

"What an unusual design." I removed the necklace from its case.

"That's a Mano Fico," Lupe said. "It's a powerful protection against the evil eye."

"Don't forget to wear it at all times," Don Pardo cautioned. "That'll be two hundred dollars." He handed an invoice to Lupe."

This guy was quite the operator. He was trying to make a sale for both of his businesses in one fell swoop. "Let me think it—"

"I'm paying for it." Lupe handed two crisp bills to Don Pardo.

"Two hundred dollars?" I said.

"That's including the bath salts and a case of my holy drinking water for Lupe."

"Still sounds kinda steep," I said.

"You're right, Roberta," Lupe said.

Thank god, she's finally coming to her senses.

Lupe handed Don Pardo a plastic card. "You forgot my frequent shopper points."

How much money is she spending in here? Louie's going to throw a hissy fit when he gets wind of this.

"You're right," Don Pardo stamped the card with a red penta-gram. "No charge for the water this week."

I felt a presence looming behind me. It was the biker guy. He was dressed all in leather; a black and white, scull-studded ban-dana covered his head. A pair of wraparound Oakley sunglasses concealed his eyes and an unkempt salt and pepper beard obscured the rest of his face.

"Can I get one of those discount cards?" He threw two sex manuals down on the counter, then reached for the chain in my hand. "Nice fistin' necklace ya got there, Roberta."

CHAPTER TEN

I'm Gonna Wash That Curse
Right Outa My Body

"JACK?" I GAVE THE biker a closer inspection.

He took off his bandana and placed the sunglasses on top of his thinning head of hair. "The one and only, babe."

I hadn't seen Jack Hensler in a while. One time bassist for the now defunct Seventies band, Sound Squadron, the fifty-something musician had gone from rock star glitter to blue-collar drab. When I met him, he was working as a service technician for a local utility. Despite his coarse expression, deep down he was really a sweetheart. Even those ridiculous looking whiskers couldn't hide his Nicholson-esque bad boy appeal.

"What's with the beard and duds?" His middle age paunch was barely noticeable beneath the black leather jacket.

"Doin' some extra work down the street."

"Aren't you working for the gas company anymore?"

"Gone with the wind—make that noxious fumes—darlin'."

I introduced him to the others. "Jack Hensler, this is Lupe Lopez."

"Any relation to Louie?"

Hmm, there's a tricky one to navigate. I didn't want to violate the unwritten Lopez family rule and introduce her as his aunt.

"I'm Luis' niece," Lupe answered, rescuing me from my predicament.

That's right. She's his eighty-year-old niece.

"Nice to meet ya," Jack said. "Don't think I've met Louise, though."

"Louie is Luis," I said.

Jack looked rather surprised. "Did he get a sex change or somethin'?" He grabbed hold of his crotch. "Youch!"

"Luis, L-U-I-S," Don Pardo interjected. "It's Spanish for Louie. And I, sir, share a moniker with you." He put his hand out to Jack. "I am Juan Pardo."

Jack shook his hand. "Sure man, whatever."

"Now we've dispensed with the 'Who's on first?' business," Don Pardo handed Jack a customer loyalty card. "How would you like to pay for your purchase?"

"Cash." Jack opened his wallet. "Is this sex magic stuff like the Kama Sutra?"

"Yes and no. The Kama Sutra is primarily about pleasure-based, monogamous, heterosexual intercourse—usually involving a married couple. Of course, it was hijacked by swingers a long time ago." Don Pardo gave Lupe a lascivious wink.

TMI, #fingersinears #imnotlistening.

"Sex magic, on the other hand, is about generating energy in a group setting for the purpose of gaining special powers or spiritual enlightenment." Don Pardo put the books in a bag. "That'll be thirty-two dollars and sixty-nine cents."

"Sixty-nine cents." Jack laughed. "Funny, how that worked out." He handed two twenties to Don Pardo.

"Are you looking to join a ceremonial magic group?" Don Pardo deposited the money in his register.

"Sure man, sounds kinda wiggy."

Don Pardo gave Jack his change. "Where do you live?"

"In The Valley," Jack looked my way, "not far from this stunning babe."

"If you don't mind a short drive," Don Pardo rifled through a dog-eared Rolodex, "there's an Aleister Crowley group that meets in Pasadena."

"Roberta's reading a book by him," Lupe said.

Don Pardo stopped what he was doing and looked up at me. "Still waters do run deep."

"Maybe we can be study buddies." Jack nudged me. "Work through that book of yours together."

"I'll write the number down for you." Don Pardo pulled a card from his file. "They like to clear all outsiders beforehand. Are you planning on attending alone?"

Jack took the slip of paper from Don Pardo. "I don't know." He turned his attention back to me. "Whaddaya say, Red? Two's company, but three's a party."

Sometimes it was hard to tell if Jack was kidding. His overtly licentious nature starkly contrasted with Ben's self-restrained abstinence. He'd had the hots for me since day one and, frankly, it scared me a bit. "Think I'll pass, I'm flying solo these days."

"Say it ain't so, babe! Don't go paddlin' the pink canoe alone when we could be partin' the red sea together."

"If you two wouldn't mind taking your plane and your boat outside to play, I'd appreciate it." Don Pardo rang up another sale. "I do have other customers to serve."

"And I'd like to get home and check on Madame Mestral," Lupe said.

On our way out of the store Jack whispered in my ear, "Louie's niece lives in a bordello?"

"No," I said. "She lives in a church."

* * *

I dropped Lupe back at her place. It was reassuring to see the yellow Corvette parked where it was supposed to be, in front of her house.

"Thank you for the lift, Roberta. Don Pardo really seemed to like you."

"He did?" Was it me he liked or the prospect of another cash cow to milk?

"I know he can come off un poquito gruff. He's really nothing but a big teddy bear inside. Like that friend of yours, John."

"John?"

She brushed her cheeks with her right hand. "The one with the barba tupida."

"Oh, Jack! I agree, that beard looks stupid on him."

Lupe laughed. "I said 'tupida'—bushy. But your right, it does look stupid. I don't like it when men hide behind their whiskers. My Tommy didn't have one."

"Lupe, why do you always call him 'Tommy'?"

"Because it's his name."

"Yes, I know. But you call my brother, Danny, Daniel. And you referred to Jack as John. Why Tommy rather than Thomas?"

"The same reason I go by Lupe. Guadalupe Lopez disappeared the night I was first pushed onto a stage to sing. I was transformed from a simple country girl into a star. Thomas Forrester disappeared the day he was pushed off a cliff to die. He was transformed from a simple soldier boy into a star, too. Only his star is in the heavens above and it is an angel that watches over me. An angel named, Tommy."

What an imagination! It's a wonder the woman didn't go into screenwriting.

Lupe opened the car door. "Are you sure you won't join us for dinner? Sheila O'Hara promised to make Daniel's favorite dish tonight. Afterward, I'm having my first private sitting with Madame Mestral."

"What happens if Sheila O'Hara decides to stick around for the entire evening?" The comings and goings of Mestral's various entities intrigued me.

"That rarely happens. Most of the spirits are very respectful of her schedule."

Convenient. "But it does happen on occasion."

"There are times she has spells so bad she can't remember anything. Not even where she has been, or who she has channeled."

"You mean like a blackout?"

"I guess so, but I don't think she passes out or anything."

First sleepwalking, now blackouts. I thought back to all the pill bottles I had seen on her nightstand. "She really needs to be checked by a proper doctor."

"I'll see what I can do to convince her." Lupe stepped out of the car. "She's very headstrong."

Though I wasn't fond of the idea of Lupe having a private sitting with Mestral, I didn't have any idea of how I could possibly stop her. But I did tell Louie I'd look out for her while he was in Vegas. "Will you call me later, let me know how your sitting went?"

Lupe gave me a sly look. "I'll report back to you, Natasha—so you can report back to Boris—on one condition."

Oh, no, here it comes. Something about our impending imaginary nuptials, no doubt.

"You have to promise me you'll take a bath in Don Pardo's salts."

Easy peasy. They smelled great and I could use a nice long soak. I nodded my head.

She wasn't through. "Performed to his exact specifications."

Not so easy peasy, but doable. "Okay."

Still not done. "Then you must put on the Mano Fico and never take it off." Lupe was very insistent on this last point.

Do I really want to spend the rest of my life wearing a tiny black fist around my neck? What if it does have some kind of kinky sexual connotation like Jack suggested? Then again, Lupe is eighty. She's not going to be around forever. Going with the "what you don't know, can't hurt you" theory, I crossed my fingers behind my back and looked right at Lupe. "Deal."

* * *

After feeding Lex and myself dinner, I prepped for my first—and hopefully last— bathing ritual. Wanting to make it as enjoyable as possible, I needed to set the appropriate mood.

Scrounging around my house, I managed to come up with ten candles—a few pillars, some tapers, and a pair of Frosty the Snowman and Santa Claus ones left over from last Christmas.

Next up, my playlist. I plugged some mini speakers in to my iPod and scrolled down to my "I'm in the Mood for Love" playlist.

I filled the tub to the brim with steamy water, added two cups— as directed—of Pardo's Curse Killing bathing salts.

Went into my bedroom, shimmied out of my clothes. Walked back into the bathroom. Shut the door and gently eased myself into the bath.

"Damn, I forgot the nose straws." But do I even need them? Come on, Roberta, are you really going to fully submerge yourself for thirty minutes?

Coming to a compromise with myself, I soaked my body up to my neck. Eyes closed, water warming the cockles of my heart, I sang along with my tunes and let all my cares float away.

In the midst of "gettin' it on" with Marvin Gaye, the bathroom door slowly creaked open.

"How may I help you, Lex?" I waited for the familiar snout to peek in on me.

The door stopped moving, no sign of my nosy beagle.

I sat up. "Lex? Are you there?"

A cold draft filled the bathroom.

Standing up, I reached for a towel. Wrapping it around me, I stepped out of the tub and into the hallway.

"Where are you, Lexie?" I walked into the living room. My front door was wide open. Running to the vestibule, I looked outside. "Lex! Lex!" I reached for my coat—a hand firmly grasped my left shoulder.

"Where do you think you're going?"

CHAPTER ELEVEN

Get Out-A My House

"WHAT ARE YOU DOING in my house? You're supposed to be in Vegas." I turned to face Louie, Lex was by his side.

"My client twisted her ankle during rehearsal. The doctor ordered her to stay off her feet for at least a week. I caught a Southwest flight back to Bob Hope Airport. Since I was so close to your place, I thought I'd swing by and see how everything went with my aunt."

"How'd you get in and why did you leave my front door wide open?"

"I didn't come in this way. When I pulled up I noticed your office door was ajar, I came in through there. As I got nearer the door, a shadow moved across the room and exited into the living area of the house. Wasn't that you?"

A shiver ran down my spine. "No, whoever it was must have gone out this way." I closed the front door and bolted it tight. My eyes fell upon Lex. "At least he's okay. Though you're a lousy watchdog. Not a peep."

"Looks like he was bribed." Louie handed me a gigantic beef-scented femur. "He was curled up on the recliner in your office gnawing on this."

"I need to get out of this towel and into some clothes."

"Aren't you going to call the police?"

"Let's see if anything's missing first."

Louie nervously surveyed my typical, mid-fifties, San Fernando Valley, ranch house living room.

It still has the original hardwood floors and vaulted ceiling. One side is completely windowed with a set of French doors in the center, which open onto the patio. Across the room, a chocolate brown sofa sits underneath twin double-hung windows and faces a matching settee. Two yellow, brown and orange paisley armchairs flank either side of the sofa/settee combo; a mahogany coffee table rests in the middle. The back wall has a built-in entertainment center, which houses my flat screen TV, books, and DVDs. The entrance to the bedroom area sits between the built-in and a fieldstone fireplace with a love seat in front. Nothing fancy, just practical and comfy.

"Think I'll play it safe, turn on all the lights and the TV," Louie said, picking up the remote.

I headed into my bedroom. All told, I was gone no more than five minutes. Still, upon my return, I discovered Louie enthralled by some sort of crime reenactment program.

"Okay, let's check out my office."

Louie hit the pause button on the remote. "I'm watching the Investigation Discovery channel. Have you ever seen this show? It's called *A Stranger in My Home*."

"Nope. Haven't seen or heard of it."

"I'm adding the series to your queue." Louie programmed the DVR before accompanying me to the other room. "You never know, it might give us some leads on your mystery visitor. Tonight's episode was 'The Killer Clown.' "

I flicked the light on in my office. "Well, I don't see any confetti or seltzer bottles. Guess it's safe to scratch 'clown' off our list of suspects." I went over to the door that led outside and checked it for any signs of tampering. Everything seemed in order. "There's no way I didn't lock this."

Louie pointed at my desk. "Taking a walk down memory lane with one of your clients?" He picked up a copy of the Beatles' *Sgt. Pepper's Lonely Hearts Club Band* album.

"That doesn't belong to me."

"It should. It's a classic." He examined the album. "Too bad someone's defiled it." Louie pointed to the top left corner of the front cover. The second head in—a rather intense looking bald-headed man, standing next to Mae West—had been circled with a red marker. A red arrow went from this man's head to the head of another man directly below Mae West.

"Who are those guys?"

Louie shrugged.

"I can't believe it. The king of trivia is stumped."

"The only trivia I know about this album is that back in the day it was at the center of the whole 'Paul is dead' frenzy." Louie opened the gatefold record jacket and three rectangular cards fluttered to the floor.

I knelt down to pick them up. "They're tarot cards. I've not seen this particular deck before." I passed the cards to him for inspection.

"Neither have I," Louie handed me the album, "but I recognize the names—The Fool, The Devil, and Death—doesn't strike me as a winning combo. Why are they even in here? There were a few promotional gifts included with the original release. From what I remember there was a sheet of cardboard cutouts which had a stand-up picture of the band, a fake moustache, and some sergeant stripes. Never heard anything about any tarot cards."

"There's another special bonus in this copy." I showed Louie the interior foldout photo of the Beatles. A snapshot of Tommy Forrester had replaced Paul's face.

"You've got to call the police now."

"And tell them what? Somebody broke in to my house and left presents for my dog and me? There's no evidence of tampering with the lock or forced entry. You saw a nondescript shadow and I didn't see anyone at all."

My home phone rang.

"I better get that, I'm expecting a call from your aunt." My landline and answering machine sit on an antique roll top desk situated between my sofa and front foyer. We headed back to the living room.

"How'd it go today?" Louie asked.

"Not well. I'll bring you up to speed as soon as I find out what Mestral told her tonight." I picked up the receiver. "Hello."

"Tommy is the walrus," a mechanical sounding voice spoke.

I looked down at the Caller ID—"Unknown Caller." "Who is this?" The line went dead. "This is getting annoying and a touch creepy."

"What's the matter?" Louie asked.

"Someone using an electronic voice changer told me Tommy is the walrus, whatever that means, and then they hung up."

"That's another Beatles' tune reference. In the song, 'I Am the Walrus,' John says he is 'the walrus.' But on the White Album, which was released a year later, in a song called 'Glass Onion' he says Paul is 'the walrus.' "

"I don't see how any of this ties in with Tommy Forrester."

"Someone did put his face over Paul's."

"Come on, you don't really think Paul McCartney is dead do you?"

"Maybe it means Tommy Forrester is alive."

"That's kinda hard to swallow too."

"Why? We don't really know much about the guy. Maybe he faked his death for some reason. If he is alive, The Madame's claim he was murdered is totally bogus."

The phone rang again. My heart skipped a beat. "Unknown Caller" flashed on the display.

Louie reached for his cell. "That's it, I'm getting the police."

"Wait." I picked up the phone. "If you keep calling here, I'm going to get law enforcement involved!"

"But you asked me to ring you after my sitting with Madame Mestral," Lupe huffed.

"Please forgive me, Lupe, I thought you were someone else."

"Man troubles?" she asked.

"In a manner of speaking."

"You better not let Luis know you're playing the field. Latin men have fiery tempers when it comes to their women."

"I'll keep that in mind," I said, biting my tongue. "How did it go tonight?"

"How did what go?" Louie whispered.

I put my hand over the receiver. "I'll explain it all to you in a minute."

"Tommy desperately needs my help. He got himself mixed up with some very dangerous people."

"Where? On the other side?" I asked.

Louie strained to hear the conversation. "Other side of what?"

"The people are here on Earth, in this plane of existence."

I tried to reassure her. "No one here can hurt Tommy anymore."

Louie's voice rose. "Is she still on that Tommy business?"

I shushed him with my hand.

"He's worried about his eleven year old sister." Lupe sounded upset. "She was there when it happened—the child saw his killer."

"This happened almost fifty years ago."

"We must help the poor girl."

"She's probably a grandmother by now." I hesitated before making my next statement. "It's also possible she's no longer with us."

Louie looked like he was about to crawl out of his skin at this point. "What are you talking about?"

"Is that Luis I heard?"

"Yes, he came home from Vegas early."

"Awww, he missed you. What a lovesick pup. Put the call on speaker."

I pointed at Louie. "You're up at bat." Pressing the speaker button, I put the phone back in its cradle.

"Hello, Lupe."

"Welcome home, Luis. Were you able to find any bookings for me?"

Louie rolled his eyes. "It's not that easy. They're looking for more contemporary acts nowadays, like Cirque du Soleil and Blue Man Group."

"I have only two words for such hooey—Donny and Marie."

"They've been in the business for over fifty years."

"And I haven't?"

"Not if you're claiming to be thirty-nine years old!"

"Fair enough. Maybe you should look into Laughlin?"

"I'll look into Laughlin, Reno and Atlantic City, but you have to promise me you're done with Madame Mestral and her church."

"Fine."

Louie and I exchanged surprised glances.

Lupe continued, "As soon as I find Tommy's baby sister and make sure she's safe and happy."

"How did his sister get involved with all this?" Louie sounded exasperated.

"Ask Roberta. She'll fill you in. It's getting late, I have to get my beauty rest. Goodnight, Luis. Goodnight, Roberta." Lupe hung up.

"Another fine mess you've gotten us into, Ms. Law."

"Me?"

"You were supposed to look out for her while I was away. She's in even deeper than she was before I left. What happened?"

"After jumping through hoops to rearrange my schedule, I brought Ben over to check out her house and then I escorted her to Don Pardo's shop. I kept my word to look out for her, but I can't control her. She's a grown woman and a mighty stubborn one I might add."

"I'm sorry, Roberta." Louie slumped down onto the sofa. "Guess I'm tired and frustrated."

"I know." I sat down and put my arm around him. "It shouldn't be too difficult to find out what happened to this guy's sister. Maybe we can track her down through the newspaper. She may be the one putting those notices in there every year."

Louie gave me a peck on the cheek. "Thanks for the help, pal."

The phone rang once more. I reached over and hit the speaker button. "Hello."

"When the fool tries to cheat the devil his punishment is death," the electronically distorted voice crackled.

The line went dead.

CHAPTER TWELVE

Party In The S.F.V.

"HELLO! HELLO!" I STOOD up and depressed the switchhook several times—all I got was a dial tone.

"Who the hell was that?" Louie asked.

I checked the Caller ID log. "My old friend, 'Unknown Caller.' Which reminds me, why was the call from Lupe listed as 'Unknown Caller'?"

"She has Caller ID blocked on her phone. You don't think she's the one calling you, do you?"

"Of course not, but the culprit could be using her phone."

"Lots of people in this town have a block on their phones. Hollywood loves unlisted phone numbers and my aunt is no exception. She's a legend in her own mind."

I repeated the ominous message from the caller, " 'When the fool cheats the devil his punishment is death.' What in the world is that supposed to mean?"

"Sounds like some kind of threat. I'm calling the police."

"No." An idea popped into my mind. "Wait right here." I left the room and returned with the *Sgt. Pepper's Lonely Hearts Club* album. "I think the message has something to do with these."

Louie took the three tarot cards from my hand. "The Fool, The Devil, and Death. You may be on to something."

"The first phone message from our mystery guest was about Tommy being the walrus, which connects with a Beatles' song from a different album. You said the *White Album*, right?"

"Yes, if they're referring to the song, 'Glass Onion.' But the actual tune, 'I Am the Walrus,' is from *Magical Mystery Tour*.

"Okay, either one is a possibility. Now what do those tarot cards have to do with the Beatles? Do they tie in with any other songs they recorded?"

Louie studied the cards in his hand. "The Fool automatically brings 'The Fool on the Hill' to mind. Which is also on the *Magical Mystery Tour* album." He pulled out his iPhone. "We need to write this down!"

"What about The Devil?"

"All I can think of is 'Devil in Her Heart.' "

"Which album is it from?"

"I'm pretty sure it's from their second studio album, *With the Beatles*."

"Did they write any songs with 'Death' in the title?"

"No. Although, 'A Day in the Life,' the final song on *Sgt. Pepper's* is about someone dying in a car accident and figures into the whole 'Paul is dead' business."

I plopped myself down on the sofa next to Louie. "Let's face it, we're grasping at straws. None of it makes any sense. I can't figure out how any of this connects to Tommy, or why it even matters.

None of us knew this guy, not even your Aunt Lupe. Maybe we're going about this in the wrong way."

"What do you mean?"

"We need to start in the here and now, not the past. Tommy died a long time ago, but whoever left this stuff in my office is still alive and kicking. First let's figure out who that person is, then we have a chance of finding out what they are trying to tell us. If we take it backwards from there, hopefully the trail will lead us to Tommy's sister; Lupe will get some closure; and The Madame, along with her band of entities, will fade off into the sunset."

Louie got up and headed for the front door. "Get your guest bed ready, I'm staying the night. My bag's in the car."

"You don't have to do that." I lied. The recent strange happenings around my home had me spooked. Why was I the recipient of all these arcane messages? Did the blonde stranger in Lupe's Corvette fit into this puzzle? Or was she Carl Jenkins patient?

"Since you refuse to call the police, I have no choice. As the old saying goes, there's safety in numbers." Louie opened the front door—then slammed it shut and locked it. "I just thought of a better adage—run for the hills! A mean looking bear is headed our way."

I went over to the door and put my eye to the peephole. A lumbering figure was coming up my walkway. "You're safe, my fearless protector." I unlatched the door. "What brings you here at this time of night, Mr. Hensler?"

"Jack? Is that you underneath all that hair?" Louie asked.

"The one and only, man. I was in the hood and thought I'd drop in on Red to personally invite her to my upcomin' Hell's Papas gig. We'll be playing at the CIA on Devil's Night."

Hell's Papas was an old school rock and roll band. Jack formed it with some other flamed out musicians during a stint in a local rehab.

"The Central Intelligence Agency is booking concerts now?" I had no idea what he was talking about.

Jack laughed and handed me a flyer. "Different CIA, babe. I'm talkin' the California Institute of Abnormalarts in North Hollywood. We're headlinin'. It's a marriage made in Hades—who better than Hell's Papas to be whalin' away on Devil's Night?"

"I'm free on the thirtieth," Louie said. "I'd like to go too."

Jack passed him a flyer. "The more, the scarier!"

For the first time it struck me as odd that Jack was a member of a band called Hell's Papas. And then, out of the blue, I bump into him at Pardo's Potions earlier in the day. Plus he took the info from Don Pardo about the Crowley ceremonial magic group in Pasadena and invited me to check it out with him. Now he just happens to show up at my place with flyers for a concert on Devil's Night? Was it possible he was behind all this recent weirdness in my life? Was this some strange elaborate ploy to get me into the sack? Create a damsel in distress and then show up at the most opportune moment to send her running into your waiting arms? We'll see about that, Mr. Hensler!

"Do you have time for a quick drink?" I asked.

"Babe, I'm always up for a quickie with you." Jack made his way into the living room and sat down on the love seat.

Louie raised an eyebrow at me and mouthed the words, "Should I go?"

I nodded and mouthed back at him, "Go get your bag."

Louie gave me a quizzical look and went out to his car.

I sidled up next to Jack. "What can I do you for?"

"Red, if I didn't know better, I'd think you're comin' on to me."

Remembering what Ben had told me about Crowley's Law of Thelema, I bit his earlobe and whispered, " 'Do what thou wilt shall be the whole of the Law. Love is the law, love under will.' "

"You been readin' *Fifty Shades of Grey*?"

"No." I stood up and grabbed the three tarot cards from the coffee table. "You been readin' Aleister Crowley." I threw the cards at him.

"What are you talkin' 'bout, Red?"

"Like you don't know, Mr. Hell's Papa. 'When the fool cheats the devil, his punishment is death'—ring any bells?"

"Huh?"

"How'd you get into my house?"

"You let me in. Don't ya remember?"

Louie came back through the front door, rolling his suitcase behind him. "Did I miss anything?"

"You're just in time. Jack's about to fess up to being the one who was trying to spook me tonight."

Jack turned to Louie with a look of desperation in his eyes. "Red's freakin' out on me, man. Somethin's not copacetic 'bout her."

Louie reached for the *Sgt. Pepper's Lonely Hearts Club Band* album. "This is a travesty." He pointed to the Sharpie marks on the cover. "And you call yourself a musician."

Jack stood up and put his hands in front of him. "Whoa, I don't know what you two are trippin' on." He backed his way to the door, "But just in case it's 'bath salts'," he reached behind himself, fumbling for the doorknob, "I'm hightailin' it outta here before you work up an appetite!" He opened the front door and backed right into Ben.

"Hey, watch where you're going." Ben was decked out in some sort of martial arts outfit—loose fitting white satin pants and matching shirt with frog closures, a pair of black Chinese slippers were on his feet.

Jack turned around. "I never thought I'd be glad to see you."

"Thanks." Ben pushed past Jack. "Are you okay?" He wrapped his arms around me. "I came straight from my Tai Chi class."

"You better take a look at these two, Doc." Jack tapped his head. "Somethin's not right with 'em."

"Sorry, I'm not that type of doctor."

"I am," Danny's voice answered. He was headed up my walkway in a saffron-colored Irish kilt, dark green jacket with matching vest, white shirt, and black tie. A green felt tam was perched on his head. A pair of wool knee socks and silver-buckled brogue shoes were on his feet.

Jack looked at Danny. "No offense, buddy, but aren't you kinda nutso yourself?"

"Takes one to know one," Danny beamed. "Is everything all right, Roberta? I didn't have time to change out of my bagpiping outfit." He entered the foyer. "Louie, what are you doing here? I thought you were in Las Vegas."

"What's everyone doing here? It's half past ten, I don't recall throwing an impromptu Come As You Are Party. And could one of you please close my front door, it's chilly out there tonight."

"I'll close it on my way out," Jack said. "Catch ya later, babe."

"Not so fast, Hensler!" I walked over to the door and closed it myself. "Please make yourselves comfortable in the living room. No one's going anywhere till I get to the bottom of what's happening."

"You're acting very enigmatic tonight, little sister." Danny sat down on the paisley easy chair in the corner. "First the phone call, now this."

"How do you know about the phone call?" I turned to Louie, who had positioned himself on the opposite end of the sofa—close to Danny. "Did you call him and tell him?"

"You called me," Danny said.

Ben put his hand in the air. "And me, too."

I looked over at Jack sitting next to Ben on the settee. "And I suppose you're going to claim I called you as well."

Jack looked dumbfounded. "No, I just dropped by to give ya a flyer. He waived the papers in his hand and then gave one to Danny and Ben. "Everyone's welcome. Might be time to add a little ginkgo to the diet, Red."

Lex ran to the front door barking.

"Come here, boy," I said.

The barks grew more insistent.

"Sounds like more guests are on the way," Danny said.

I walked over to Lex and took a quick look through the peephole. A yellow Corvette pulled up in front of my house.

CHAPTER THIRTEEN

Stalker, Do Lose My Number

THE DRIVER'S SIDE door of the Corvette swung open. Out popped Lupe Lopez, awash in a sea of magenta-colored fabrics—her journey away from her signature color of red still a work in progress. She wore a pair of gold-sequined harem pants, topped with a chiffon peek-a-boo blouse and bolero jacket. Her head was covered with a turban and her feet were clad in a pair of genie slippers, all made of leather.

Lupe scampered down my front walkway. "I was getting into bed and rushed over as soon as I got the message."

This is what she wears to bed? "Oh, Lupe, I'm so sorry. Someone's playing a very bad practical joke on all of us."

Lupe entered the foyer. "What do you mean?" She looked into the living room and saw the gathering of males. "My, my—you are a popular girl."

"Too popular for my liking. Come on in and join the rest of the gang. Can I get you anything?"

Though there was plenty of room on the sofa, Lupe squeezed herself in-between Ben and Jack on the settee. "I am a little parched." She held up two fingers.

Louie translated. "She wants Two Fingers, straight up."

"Two fingers of what?" I asked.

"Two fingers of Two Fingers tequila," Lupe said.

Jack was impressed. "Now that's my kinda woman,"

They would make an interesting couple. "I've never heard of that brand. Is it the one with a worm at the bottom of the bottle?"

"No self-respecting worm would hang out in there, " Louie said.

"They don't put worms in bottles of tequila," Lupe smirked at Louie, "only mezcal."

"Would you settle for some Patron?" I asked.

Lupe shrugged her shoulders. "I can make do if I have to."

"You can hit me, too," Jack shouted, as I headed for the liquor cabinet.

I felt like hitting someone right about then.

"A pot of chamomile tea would be nice," Danny said.

"Be my guest." I motioned toward the kitchen. "Anyone else in the mood for a refreshment?"

"Do you have any Mountain Dew or Dr. Pepper?" Louie asked.

"No, Diet Pepsi only. It's in the fridge." I poured some tequila in a glass. "Nothing for you, Ben?"

"A glass of fresh wheatgrass juice might be nice," Ben said, yanking my chain.

"Aw, shucks, I'm fresh out. Could I interest you in some newly mowed crabgrass?"

Ben stifled a laugh. "On second thought, maybe I'll just get in on that pot of tea with Danny."

* * *

After everyone had settled in with their various beverages, we got down to business.

"I still don't understand why you summoned us here, Roberta," Lupe said.

"That's what I've been trying to explain. I didn't ask anyone to come here tonight. It's every bit as baffling to me as it is to all of you."

"Ya didn't call me," Jack said. "I was in the neighborhood passin' out flyers for the band's Devil's Night gig."

I eyed Jack suspiciously. "Who would you be handing flyers out to in a residential neighborhood this late on a Tuesday night?"

Jack looked round the room. "Everybody here, who else? Babe, ya really need to call your doc first thing in the mornin' and get yourself looked at."

I decided to eliminate Jack from my list of potential suspects; he definitely wasn't "the brains" behind such an elaborate operation.

"You didn't call me either," Louie added. "I dropped by on my way home from the airport."

"You discovered the outside door to my office ajar and noticed somebody snooping around inside."

"Yeah, but I spooked her and she took off before I got a good look."

"You didn't mention it was a female before."

"It only dawned on me now." Louie scratched his head. "Though I'm not a hundred percent sure."

"Someone broke in here tonight?" Danny said.

"Yes," I said.

"Did you call the police?" Ben asked.

"No," I answered.

"Did you bathe in Don Pardo's bath salts?" Lupe queried.

"Yes."

Lupe continued her interrogation. "Are you wearing the Mano Fico?"

"No."

"Tch, no wonder you were burglarized!" Lupe scolded. "The evil eye is still upon you. You'll have to repeat the bathing ritual as soon as possible."

"I'd be willin' to help with that," Jack interjected.

"Calm down everybody! Especially you, Jack. I didn't put the Mano Fico on because my bath was cut short by the intruder episode. And I didn't call the police because nothing was taken." I pointed at my coffee table. "That record album and those tarot cards are what they left behind for me, plus a couple of disturbing telephone calls. Not counting the ones made to Ben, Danny and Lupe."

"It certainly sounded like you on the phone," Danny said. "You mentioned something about an accident and to get over here as soon as I could. You hung up before I had a chance to say anything."

"The call I received was somewhat similar," Ben added. "I don't recall anything about an accident, but you did sound frantic and in need of immediate assistance."

"Did my name come up on anyone's Caller ID?"

"I didn't really notice." Danny took his cell out of his pocket. "No, and I don't recognize this number."

Ben compared his phone with my brother's. "My call came from a different number altogether, but it's not one I'm familiar with either. I suspect our culprit is using burner phones or some sort of app which disguises the identity of the caller."

Everyone shifted their focus to Lupe, patiently waiting to hear what had been said in the call she received from the impostor.

"Did I smear lipstick?" Lupe self-consciously passed her tongue over her top front teeth. "I hate rushing to put my face on."

Judging by the amount of face paint she had managed to trowel on, coupled with the *I Dream of Jeannie* getup she was wearing, I suspected she slept encased in a crypt somewhere—ready to rise up and go at a moment's notice.

Louie was first to break the stalemate. "We're not looking at your makeup, though you are looking rather Divine-ish this evening."

Lupe batted her eyelashes, not at all aware her nephew was referencing the iconic movie drag queen.

"What did Fake Roberta say when she phoned you?" Louie continued.

"It wasn't a call over a phone," Lupe said.

"Did the hoaxer Skype with ya?" Jack asked.

"What's dancing got to do with it?" Lupe snapped.

Louie shook his head. "You're confusing it with twerking." He turned to Jack. "She doesn't own a computer or a smartphone."

"I received the message from Samir. He told me you were in grave danger." Lupe grasped my hand and gave it a tight squeeze. "You must promise to wear the Mano Fico necklace I bought for you."

"What did old Samir have to say for himself this time?" Louie sounded less than pleased.

"It was odd, yet familiar." Lupe opened her handbag. "I wrote it down." She pulled out a small slip of paper and read it to us. " 'The time has come to talk of many things: Of devils and demons - and ceremonial magicians - of Forresters and fools.' I thought it had something to do with my Tommy, but Samir was adamant that I head over to Roberta's immediately."

"And what were you supposed to do once you got here?" Louie asked.

"He said all would fall into place in due time under the heavens."

"Of course, more of his rambling vagaries." Louie cast out an imaginary fishing line. "Just enough to keep you on the hook, until The Madame is finally ready to reel you in."

"Bite your tongue, Luis!"

Ignoring the bickering Lopezes, Ben picked up the *Sgt. Pepper's Lonely Hearts Club Band* album and the tarot cards from the coffee table. "The reason Samir's message sounded familiar to you Lupe is because it's a bastardization of Lewis Carroll's narrative poem, 'The Walrus and the Carpenter.' It's from his novel, *Through the Looking-Glass*. I suspect the references have something to do with these items. By the way, these cards are from the Aleister Crowley Thoth Tarot deck."

"That also ties in with the two weird phone calls I received tonight," I said.

"Did ya get calls from yourself, too?" Jack asked.

"No, whomever called me used an electronic voice changer. In the first call they said, 'Tommy is the walrus,' and the second message was 'When the fool tries to cheat the devil his punishment is death.' "

"Okay, so call number two references each of these tarot cards. And Samir's message mentions The Devil and The Fool, but not Death." Ben threw each of the cards back down on the coffee table. "And call number one connects Tommy to The Walrus, and Lewis Carroll is pictured on the cover of this album."

"Is Lewis Carroll one of the guys circled in red?" I asked Ben.

"No, Aleister Crowley and Aldous Huxley are the only ones marked up."

"Aleister Crowley's the one who wrote the book left outside my office door."

"Right," Ben said. "He was a practitioner of ceremonial magic and was co-editor of the *Lesser Key of Solomon*, a demonology focused spell book."

"That takes care of the rest of the allusions in Samir's message," Danny noted.

"How does Aldous Huxley fit in to the mix?" I asked.

Ben continued, "I've heard it rumored that some time around 1930, H.G. Wells—who's also on this cover—introduced Huxley and Crowley to each other in Berlin. Supposedly, it was Crowley who initiated Huxley into the use of peyote."

"Now you're gettin' into my neck of the woods," Jack chimed in. "Crowley and Huxley were big deals with a lotta rockers back in the Sixties and Seventies. Gary Valentine, one of the foundin' members of Blondie, wrote a great book about it, *Aleister Crowley: Magick, Rock and Roll, and the Wickedest Man in the World.* Some people even say the Stones tune, *Sympathy for the Devil,* was a tribute to Crowley. Jagger denies it though."

"Is that why your ears perked up when Don Pardo told you about the Crowley group in Pasadena?"

"When I heard you were into Crowley, it was a no brainer, babe."

"I'm not into Crowley." I took the album cover from Ben and handed it to Jack. "Can you identify all the people on here?"

"Sure, can't everybody?"

Lupe looked frustrated. "I don't understand what any of this has to do with my Tommy."

"Jack, will you open up the cover?"

"Sure." Jack complied with my request. "Who the hell is this guy?"

"Please pass the album to Lupe."

Jack handed the record to her.

"Tommy!" Lupe cried. "I didn't know he was a member of the Beatles."

"Don't be ridiculous," Louie barked. "Someone stuck his head over Paul McCartney's."

"But why?" I asked. "What does any of it even mean? It makes no sense."

"It makes perfect sense to me," Lupe said. "Tommy's leading us to his killer. He made the phone calls and left these things in Roberta's office."

"Wouldn't it be easier to give us a name," Louie snipped.

"Madame Mestral says the spirits have their own ways of doing things." Lupe stood up. "I must go home and apprise her of what has gone on here tonight."

To paraphrase Dickens, there was more of *grifting* than of grave going on here. "Where is Madame Mestral?" I asked.

"She was feeling under the weather again, so she retired early. I was surprised when she came into my bedroom with the message from Samir."

"Be careful driving home." I escorted Lupe to the foyer and opened the front door.

"¡Hijo de la puta!" Lupe screeched. "Some pinche pendejo stole my car!"

CHAPTER FOURTEEN

Louie/Louise

EVERYONE RAN outside. There was no sign of Lupe's car anywhere.

"Whatcha drivin'?" Jack asked.

"A 1970 yellow Corvette convertible," Lupe said. "I'm the original owner."

"Oooh, that's a sweet ride." Jack shook his head, "Too sweet for a neighborhood like this."

"I beg your pardon," I said. "This is a perfectly safe neighborhood."

"Didn't ya have a break-in earlier?"

Louie pulled out his cell phone. "Okay, now we're calling the police."

"Do you think the incidents are related?" I secretly hoped they were, it was more comforting to believe there was only one bad guy or gal out there who had to be apprehended.

"It's hard to say," Ben sounded worried. "Car thefts are on the rise in The Valley and Lupe's car is a classic. But it's rather unusual both these events occurred within the same evening."

I was relieved to find out Officer Sanchez was on duty that night. He drove the LAPD squad car assigned to my neighborhood and was a real no-nonsense type when it came to local crime. He was my go-to guy the last time I had some perplexing criminal activity going on at my house. His boyish looks belied the fact he was really quite a seasoned patrolman. Normally this type of report was filed over the phone, but when I mentioned the intruder Louie scared off earlier in the evening, he said he'd swing by as soon as he had a chance and requested everyone hang around until he arrived.

After Officer Sanchez showed up, we reconvened in my dining room. Situated at the front of my house, next to the foyer, the room opens up onto the kitchen. A small but cozy space, made for a woman and a beagle. Sitting round the maple table I inherited from my grandmother, we gave our statements and answered Sanchez's questions. I was seated on the left side of the table, between Ben and Jack. Lupe sat across from me, between Louie and Danny. Officer Sanchez sat at the head of the table, facing my front windows. I left the shutters open, so he could see where Lupe's stolen car had been parked

"Do you have any sort of tracking device on your vehicle, Ma'am?" Officer Sanchez asked Lupe. "Like LoJack?"

"I suppose there is a jack in the trunk, but I have no need for such inconsequentials. I'm a Premier member of Triple A." Lupe flirtatiously placed her hand on Officer Lopez's forearm. "And please call me, Lupe."

"That's not what I meant," Officer Lopez cleared his throat, "Lupe."

"She doesn't have any anti-theft gadgets on her car," Louie interjected. "But she should. Maybe you can convince her to have some installed if she ever sees her car again."

"Well, on the bright side, a classic auto isn't the usual candidate for car thieves. They prefer something they can haul into a nearby chop shop and turn into instant cash. Unloading a car like this takes some criminal know-how. They require a counterfeit VIN to be able to sell in this country or ship overseas. I'll issue an alert, patrol the surrounding neighborhood, and check in with my source at the local 818-1320 Sports Club to see if the car turns up at any illegal drag races."

"People are still drag racing?" I said.

"Oh, yes. It's still quite popular," Lopez said. "There are 1320 clubs all over the state."

"How *American Graffiti* of them," Louie said.

"What does 1320 stand for?" Ben asked.

"It's the number of feet in a quarter mile, usual distance of a drag race." Jack looked over at Officer Sanchez. "So I've heard."

"And 818 is the area code identifier for The Valley," Sanchez added. "Let's hope the car isn't on its way to Mexico, that's a whole other ballgame."

"Have you put out the Amber Alert yet?" Lupe inquired.

"Ahhh…no, Ma'am…I mean, Lupe. Those are only issued when a child has been abducted."

"My chiquita banana is my baby," Lupe protested.

"Was the birth natural or did you use an epidural? Please excuse my au…Owww!" Judging by his sudden yelp, I surmised Louie had received a less than gentle reminder about family protocol from the genie seated next to him. "My niece is high-strung," Louie gritted his teeth, "and can be overly emotional when she's under stress."

"So there is a minor involved?" Officer Sanchez reached for his radio. "I'll put out an alert immediately."

"That won't be necessary," I said. "Lupe *is* Louie's niece."

Sanchez scrutinized the two Benjamin Buttons he had unwittingly stumbled upon.

Jack jumped into the muddle. "Ya ain't heard nothin' yet, copper. Louie's not gonna be her uncle much longer. He's gettin' a sex change. Gonna call himself, Louise."

Lupe stood bolt upright. "Have you lost your mind, mijo? What about Roberta? Are you calling off the wedding?"

"Enough with the wedding business already!" I shouted. "Louie and I are never going to get married."

"Of course not," Lupe said in defiant agreement.

Looks like she's finally clued in. All it took was a phony gender reassignment.

Lupe pinched Louie's cheek. "You will walk down the aisle with my dear, Aunt Louise. I will arrange for one of those new gay marriages for the two of you. A Lopez family first!"

"You're forgetting about Uncle Ramón and his drag queen lover, again," Louie sighed.

Lupe put her hand up. "We'll discuss the guest list later. Officer Sanchez is a busy man."

I looked at Ben, he seemed to be quite entertained by the whole affair. Jack, on the other hand, looked stupefied.

"Are we almost done here?" Danny asked. My brother appeared distracted and worn. "It's getting late, I'd like to get Lupe and myself back home and into bed."

Jack winced.

"You're getting the wrong idea," I said to Jack.

"Your bro must be really steamed about this weddin' business between you and Louie/Louise," Jack said out the side of his mouth. "It's driven him from the gay side to the gray side at warp speed. Have to admit I'm kinda pissed myself, Red. Keep my number in case things don't work out."

Officer Sanchez flipped through his notes. "I think I have all I need about the phone calls and the break-in. I'll have them run prints on these items down at the station." He bagged the Beatles' album, tarot cards, and Crowley book. "It's a long shot since so many people have been handling them. Like I said the last time I was here Ms. Law, a security system might be a worthwhile investment."

He was referring to the time someone forced their way into my house via the living room window. After rifling through my office, they stole a confidential client file. But the person had been apprehended long ago. That experience was unusual and, for the most part, I felt pretty safe living in the Big Orange.

"Maybe you should give it some more thought, Roberta," Ben sounded worried.

"I'll be fine." We all made our way to the front door. "Lex was slightly off his game tonight, cut the poor beagle some slack," I joked.

"Stalking is not to be taken lightly," Officer Sanchez opened the front door and stepped outside. "I'll make some extra passes down your street when I'm on patrol. In the meantime, stay aware of your surroundings and call me if you notice anything the least bit suspicious, you have my number. Good night, folks."

Sanchez was the first to leave, followed by Danny and Lupe, then Jack.

"I don't feel right leaving you alone here," Ben hovered on my threshold, "maybe I should stay the night."

Bingo! Looks like I am tonight's lucky jackpot winner. Winner, winner, chicken dinner! Then I remembered Louie had already made the same offer, albeit minus the simmering sexual tension. I looked around, where was Louie anyway?

"Everyone step aside, step aside. Make way for a busy talent manager." Louie rolled his suitcase through the foyer and out onto the walkway. "Almost forgot about my meeting with the folks at the Lawrence Welk Resort Theater in Escondido. I have to be up bright and early in the morning. Ben, could you do me a favor and stay with Roberta tonight? I had promised, but I think I'll head down to San Diego County tonight and avoid the morning rush hour traffic."

"Sure," Ben said. "I was thinking the same thing,"

"You know what they say about great minds." Louie looked back and winked at me. "Bye-bye, my loves. Don't do anything I wouldn't do—which leaves you a ginormously wide berth." Louie hopped into his black SUV, started the engine, and tore off into the night. I owed him one.

"Let's get you settled in," I said to Ben. It was late, but the revamped sleeping arrangements had given me my second wind. "Can I interest you in a nightcap?"

Ben followed me into the living room. "Sure, why not?"

"Really?" His affirmative response caught me off guard. Ben's Zen cool was running a tad hotter than usual.

"I'd love a hot chocolate almond milk."

Not quite what I had in mind. "Would you settle for a decaf coffee with a shot of Bailey's?"

"Do you have any cognac?"

At this point I had to pinch myself. It was after midnight and Ben Cohen was having an alcoholic libation at my place, plus he was planning to spend the night. Was the Booty Call Fairy finally paying me a long overdue visit?

I fished an old dusty bottle of cognac out of the back of my liquor cabinet. "Will Rémy do?"

"Perfect." Ben walked over to the fireplace. "Mind if I start a fire?"

You already have.

"Did you say something?" Ben picked up a piece of wood.

Stay out of my mind. "A fire would be great." I grabbed a pair of brandy snifters, poured our drinks, and headed back into the living room.

"Do you have any kindling or newspaper?

"Today's paper is on the desk in my office." I handed Ben his drink. "I'll get it for you."

"Relax. Make yourself comfortable. I can find it."

While Ben went to retrieve the *LA Times*, I nestled myself into the love seat and contemplated what the evening might have in store.

"Roberta!" Ben called out. "Come here, there's something I need you to see."

Naughty boy. Wants to get into some sultry role-play in my office, does he?

"Should I slip into something more comfortable?" I teased.

Ben was standing inside my office; the outside door was ajar.

"What's going on?" I asked.

Ben pointed at the recliner.

Behind the chair, wrapped in a fetal position, Madame Mestral was fast asleep on the floor.

CHAPTER FIFTEEN

Talk Like An Egyptian

"**W**HAT THE HELL is she doing here?" I marched over to the power-napping prowler. "I'm getting to the bottom of this business once and for all." I reached down to shake Madame Mestral out of her slumber.

"Wait." Ben caught hold of my arm. "Don't shock her."

"She's the one going around shocking people."

"You mentioned she's a sleepwalker. She's probably having an episode right now."

I looked through the open door for any sign of Lupe's missing Corvette. Nothing. "She must have walked all the way from Echo Park."

Ben and I went outside to survey the rest of the street. No unaccounted for vehicles anywhere in sight.

"Maybe she took a cab," Ben said.

"Asleep?"

"Stranger things have happened."

"Help! I'm being eaten by a wild animal!" Mestral shrieked.

We rushed back inside and found Lex showering The Madame with sloppy wet kisses.

I got a hold of Lex. "Sorry, he's not usually so demonstrative with strangers." Why am I apologizing? I didn't break into her place.

"Where am I?" a dazed Mestral pulled herself up off the floor. She was wobbly on her feet, so Ben helped her into the recliner. "The last thing I remember was turning in for the night. What time is it? What day is it?"

"It's Wednesday, October nineteenth," Ben said.

"Who are you?" She started to hyperventilate.

"He's Dr. Ben Cohen," I said. "You met him yesterday at Lupe's. Remember?" She still looked confused. "It's Roberta Law. You're in my office."

"How did I get here?" Mestral struggled to catch her breath.

"I was about to ask you the very same thing."

Ben turned to me. "She needs a paper bag to breathe into."

"How about plastic?" I pulled a poopy scoopy bag out of the bottom drawer of my desk.

"Has to be paper."

"All I have is a Medium Brown Bag from Bloomie's."

"Pinch one nostril and breath slowly through your nose," Ben instructed Madame Mestral. "I'm going to keep counting to five and I want you to time each breath to my rhythm."

Ben's trick worked in no time and Mestral seemed to relax some. "My sleepwalking has returned. When I went to bed it was Tuesday, the eighteenth. I've lost an entire day again."

Again? Sounds like an awfully long time to be asleep.

"It's half past midnight," Ben reassured her, "you've probably been asleep for only a few hours."

"Don Pardo will have to concoct something new for me to take."

"Don't you think you need to see a real doctor?" I said.

"Roberta's right," Ben agreed. "This could be caused by some underlying medical condition. You should get a full work-up as soon as possible."

Mestral dismissively waived her hand. "I don't trust Western practitioners, they are a bunch of stooges for the pharmaceutical industry."

I thought back to the extensive collection of pill bottles I had seen in her room. Maybe she was some sort of addict in a heavy state of denial. "I'm sure there are other treatment options available."

"Do you remember how you got here?" Ben asked. "We didn't see any car out front."

Mestral shook her head.

"How did you manage to get into my office?"

"You must have left the door unlocked."

I knew this was impossible after the shenanigans that went on in there earlier.

Mestral looked truly bewildered. "I don't even know how I knew where your office is located."

"Lupe must have mentioned it," I reasoned.

"But why would I come here?" Mestral sounded perplexed.

If this is an act, it's a good one. "Something to do with Tommy Forrester maybe? Somebody's been leaving a lot of weird stuff in here lately."

"Tommy Forrester?" Mestral paused. "That's the last thing I remember before drifting off to sleep—Tommy Forrester's face. I must tell Lupe. Is she still here?"

Even in the direst of circumstances, she was still fixated on her mark.

"No, Danny drove her home." I was curious to see her reaction to my next statement. "Someone stole her car."

"What terrible news!" Mestral seemed genuinely surprised. "She must be heartbroken, she treats that vehicle like it's her own child. Perhaps one of my spiritual guides can locate it for her."

Boy, she really knows how to turn every human misfortune into a latent business opportunity.

"The police are looking into it," I said. "You wouldn't happen to have any leads for them, would you?"

"I already offered to consult my conduits." The Madame appeared flustered by my question. "What more can I possibly do?"

Hoping to back her into a corner, I decided to continue with my impromptu interrogation. "You never loaned Lupe's car to anyone, did you?"

"Why in the world would I ever do such a thing?" There was a defensive edge to her tone. "I'm rather parched, may I have some water?"

Ben gave me a don't-push-your-luck nudge.

Determined to press my advantage to the limit, I looked at Ben. "Would you mind going into the kitchen and fetching a glass for her?"

Ben reluctantly agreed.

With him out of the way for the moment, I went for the gold. "Who's the blonde you've been letting drive Lupe's Corvette?"

Mestral clutched her head between her hands and glared at me with a transfixed stare.

Fearing she had slipped into a catatonic state, I bent down and placed my right hand on her left shoulder. "Madame Mestral, are you all right?" I gave her a gentle shake.

Before I had a chance to react, Mestral's right arm shot up and grabbed me by the wrist of my free hand. "Shall we dance, mistress?" she thundered.

"Ow!" I recoiled, breaking free of the lusty grip.

Ben bolted back into the room. "What's the matter?" He passed the water tumbler to Mestral.

The Madame took a whiff of the liquid. "Do you have any stronger libations?" Samir's familiar laugh erupted. "It has been a rather long journey to get here this evening."

The ancient entity's abrupt appearance was too well timed for my liking. "My line of questioning wasn't sitting well with Madame Mestral, Ben. So presto change-o," I snapped my fingers, "good old Samir has come to the rescue."

"I'm sorry if I caused you any discomfort, mistress. It can be difficult to gauge the muscular abilities of a host body."

Spare me the otherworldly apologia. I rubbed my wrist, "To what do we owe the dubious pleasure of your company?"

"Who is your gentleman companion?" Samir asked.

"That's right, you two haven't met. Dr. Benjamin Cohen, this is Samir—I'm sorry I never caught your last name. Or do you just go by one name like Cher?"

"I'm afraid all I have to offer you is 'Samir.' My existence predates the advent of surnames." Mestral let out a deep belly laugh. "There weren't quite so many of us around in my day, one name usually sufficed."

"Right, I forgot." I turned to Ben with a sardonic smile. "Samir lived in ancient Egypt."

"What sort of medical man are you Dr. Cohen?"

"Please call me, Ben. I'm not a medical man, I hold a Ph.D. in parapsychology."

"How intriguing. I would love the opportunity to pick your brain—so to speak—sometime."

"Madame Mestral is scheduled to come by my office this week. She's consented to take part in a study I'm doing on electromagnetic fields and paranormal phenomena. You're welcome to drop in on us if you like."

"I just might take you up on that offer." Mestral's body shifted awkwardly in the recliner. Samir's voice dropped to an almost inaudible whisper, "But let's not tell Madame Mestral, she isn't overly fond of surprise visits."

This last remark had me wondering if The Madame was being sincere when she said she didn't know how she had arrived at my place. "How did you get here tonight, Samir?"

"The usual channels, if you'll pardon the pun." Samir chortled and then immediately shifted gears. "Did Lupe deliver my urgent message to you?"

"Yes, but what does it mean? What kind of danger am I in?"

"All matters will be revealed in their appointed time under the stars. Wear the Mano Fico and remember," Samir's voice was fading, "I'm looking through you, girl. You won't see me drive my car, run for your life!" Mestral's head dropped to her chest.

I pointed my index finger at my temple and twirled it. "You see the kind of cray cray I'm dealing with here, Ben. What the hell is that drivel supposed to mean anyways?"

Ben shook his head. "Maybe I can get some more info out of Samir when Mestral drops by my office."

The Madame appeared to be sleeping again. I signaled for Ben to follow me into the kitchen, safely out of Mestral's earshot. "Do you think she is legitimately going into a trance state? Or is she a seasoned con artist? I'm having a heck of a time trying to decide."

"I think she's being sincere. When I do some testing of those off the chart EMF readings she's emitting, we'll have a clearer picture of what's going on inside her."

"When's she coming by?"

"Day after tomorrow." Ben looked at his wristwatch. "It's getting late, I think we better call it a night."

I knew he meant a hit-the-hay rather than a romp-in-the-hay kind of night. Foiled again. Though to be honest, I was absolutely exhausted by this point. "I don't have the energy to drive her back to Lupe's."

"Neither do I."

"Will you help me set up the hide-a-bed for her?"

Ben nodded and gave me a reassuring hug. "Give her the guest room, I'll take the hide-a-bed."

"You could bunk down with me."

Ben's eyes twinkled. "I know, but I'm afraid I'll never get any sleep if I do."

We went back into the office to rouse my uninvited guest. The recliner was empty and Mestral was gone.

CHAPTER SIXTEEN
Mestral's Little Helpers

I PUT IN A CALL to Officer Lopez at one a.m. He said he'd keep an eye out for Madame Mestral, but that was about all he could do at this point. It was too soon to file a missing persons report. And it was still possible she was on her way back to Lupe's place. I wasn't about to get Lupe all worked up by phoning her at such an early hour.

"Do you think someone came by to pick her up?" I asked Ben.

Ben looked at his cell phone. "There are a couple of Uber vehicles in the neighborhood right now, she could be in one of them."

I grabbed an extra blanket from the linen closet. "Flake or not, I don't like the idea of her roaming around alone out there at this time of night."

"So you've given her an upgrade from fake to flake." Ben followed me into the guest room.

"Her trances are unusual, but I think they're legit. I suspect all those meds she's taking are causing them."

"Did you run them by Danny?" We turned the bed down together.

"No, he's too close to the whole situation. He and Lupe are convinced she's the real deal. I did call an old colleague of Danny's about it, but I haven't heard back from him yet."

"She could be both. Drug addiction and psychic ability are no strangers to one another."

"In what sense?" I threw the extra blanket on the bottom of the double bed.

"A powerful gift like that can scare people. Drugs and alcohol are used as a sort of refuge—a convenient escape route from the barrage of voices and/or images coming at them 24/7. While under the influence, mind altering substances will suppress their abilities completely. In the case of someone with a particularly potent talent—which might explain the EMF activity emitting from Madame Mestral—the drugs may only dampen her acute faculty." Ben picked the blue blanket up from the bed. "Do you really think I'll need this?"

"It's gonna be mighty cold in here without me to cuddle up to, Mr. Cohen." I ran my fingers through Ben's hair. "Last chance to upgrade your room."

Ben gave me a hug. He looked exhausted. "Rain check?"

"Yeah, I'm pretty wiped myself." I gave Ben a deep, penetrating, toe-curling kiss. "That's in lieu of a chocolate on your pillow."

On my way out the door, I switched off the light and bumped up the air.

* * *

I was up at the crack. Showered, dressed, and ready to rock Ben's world with how fabulous I looked in the morning. This was no simple feat. Two early mornings in a row required breaking into my stash of makeup from my days on the boards. A little greasepaint can create an amazing illusion under the right lighting conditions. After adjusting the shutters and curtains in my kitchen, I set about preparing a breakfast feast worthy of Martha Stewart—freshly squeezed OJ, crème brûlée French toast, crispy bacon, and a steaming pot of Kona coffee.

When Ben hadn't surfaced by eight o'clock, I gently knocked on the guest room door. "Good morning, sleepyhead. Breakfast is ready."

No one answered.

I put my ear up against the door, but couldn't hear a thing. I rapped a little louder. "Don't let the smell of bacon scare you away. It's nitrate free and compassionately raised."

Still not a peep.

I turned the doorknob, "Are you okay?" and went inside the room.

The bed had been stripped and Ben was gone. There was a note on top of the pile of sheets, "Sorry, didn't have time to throw in the laundry. Forgot I had an early meeting and didn't want to battle rush hour traffic to the Westside. Was too early to wake you to say goodbye. Will call later. Love, B."

So much for wowing him with my prowess in the kitchen—or the bedroom. I was a two room loser. Later—while noshing on my four star breakfast—I googled "Home Security Systems" on my iPad, finally convinced there were far too many people making surreptitious entrances and exits at my home.

I settled in behind my office desk by nine. Five minutes later the phone rang, it was Dr. Carl Jenkins returning my call.

"I apologize for not getting back to you yesterday, Roberta. The day got away from me. If you were checking back in about Angela

Fowler, I'm pleased to report she has resurfaced and would like to meet with you today if at all possible."

"Will one o'clock work?"

"Let me run it by her, if there's a problem I'll let you know. She promises not to run away again."

"So she *is* the blonde woman I saw watching me from the yellow Corvette?"

"Possibly. She mentioned something about a friend loaning her a vehicle, while hers was in the shop, and having to get it back in a hurry. I forgot to ask what type of car it was though."

Would The Madame really have the chutzpah to reloan Lupe's Corvette to someone else? Why would she betray her benefactor's trust this way and risk losing her cushy living arrangements?

"Carl, I called you for another reason yesterday. I wanted to run some meds by you and see if you could come up with a possible diagnosis for such a combo."

"I'll try, what are they?"

"Valium, Thorazine, Dexedrine, and Prozac."

"Quite a potent and dangerous mix. How are they are being administered? I need dosage strengths and frequencies."

Darn! I didn't get a chance to take that down. "I'm not sure, but they've each been prescribed by a different doctor. I saw a bunch of different patient names on the bottles, though I suspect they're all being used by the same person."

"I'd say it sounds like a classic case of pill shopping, though you usually see that with painkillers. Those meds are psychotropic and anti-psychotic. It doesn't surprise me they're not all from the same physician. Any decent MD would be hard put to give such a combo to a single patient. Are you sure just one person is taking them all?"

"Not a hundred percent."

"Is there any way you can get this person to set up an appointment with me?"

"That would be a challenge, she claims not to trust Western doctors."

"She may be suffering from latrophobia?"

"Latrophobia? I'm not familiar."

"Plain old fear of doctors."

"Then how did she get all those meds prescribed to her?"

"You mentioned seeing various patient names on the bottles, were any of them in her name?"

I was pretty sure I hadn't seen Mestral's name on any of the meds. But I closed my eyes and took a moment to revisualize her bedroom nightstand. "Not a one."

"Well, that makes sense if she truly is latrophobic. Whatever's ailing her, she's treating it by self-medication using black-market drugs."

"You may be on to something."

"It's not uncommon for people with severe mental illness to be non-compliant with their meds. Many don't like the way they feel, they miss the natural highs and grandiose fantasies brought on by their condition. And if they need cash, selling their pills on the street is a convenient way of getting money fast."

Somehow I couldn't imagine The Madame hanging around MacArthur Park trying to make a score with some random stranger. But I could see her turning to her beloved Don Pardo for help. I was guessing his potion and jewelry stores provided him with both a viable cover and a steady stream of clientele.

"I'm sorry I can't be of more help, Roberta."

Then it hit me! "Maybe you can be, Carl. Since there's no way of getting her to make an appointment with you, would you be willing to make an appointment with *her*?"

"I'm not sure I'm following you. What kind of appointment?"

I took in a deep breath before plunging ahead with my ridiculous proposal. "She's a medium, as in 'I see dead people.' What if you booked her for a private sitting? Of course, I'd pay for the whole thing." Not. This one's on Louie's tab. "Maybe you could get a read on her? Conduct an evaluation, without her even knowing what's going on."

Carl cleared his throat. "You want me to read the reader?"

I laughed. "She's not a reader, exactly—more of a channeler. There's a whole cast of characters holed up inside her head."

"I must confess, you have me intrigued. Give me a day to think it over, I need to work through any possible ethical implications of such an encounter."

"Thanks so much, Carl. If this works out, I owe you one."

"Tell you what, try not to scare off my patient again today and we'll call it even. I'll give you a call back tomorrow with my answer. And to see how things went with Angela Fowler."

After I hung up, I added Angela Fowler's one o'clock to my calendar. "Good god, I hope she actually makes it in here today."

I was about to give Lupe a call to see if Madame Mestral had made it home safely, when I heard a faint knock on the outside door to my office.

It was quarter past nine. My first client wasn't scheduled until eleven. Did I forget about someone?

The knock grew more insistent.

"Just a minute!" I headed over to the door and opened it. "Yes, may I help you?"

A frazzled looking old woman stood on my doorstep. "Are you Roberta Law?"

"Yes, I am. Sorry, I don't accept walk-ins. If you'd like to make an appointment…"

"I'm Bonnie Lawson. You phoned me at home last night and asked me to meet you here at nine-thirty. Forgive me, I'm a little early. I could hardly sleep after receiving your call."

I looked at the frail woman and shook my head. "You must have me confused with someone else."

"You said you had some vital information about the death of my son, Tommy Forrester."

CHAPTER SEVENTEEN

The Little Old Lady From Altadena

I STOOD IN THE doorway, simultaneously flabbergasted by what Bonnie Lawson had just said and still not sure I had actually heard it. "I beg your pardon?"

The old woman appeared quite shaken. Clutching an embroidered lace hanky in her left hand, she gently dabbed her forehead. Her right hand shakily rested on the derby handle of a carved, black, wooden cane—which resembled a gnarled branch. "I'm feeling somewhat faint. Would you mind if I sat down for a moment?"

"By all means." I took hold of her arm and escorted her into my office.

She was a tiny woman, barely five feet tall and slightly hunched over. I guessed her weight to be no more than ninety pounds. Her hair was a yellowish white and pinned up in a tight bun. The powder blue, floral print dress she wore was slightly threadbare.

"Would you like some water?" I asked, easing her into the recliner.

"Yes, that would be wonderful." She fished around in her lacquered wicker handbag. "I can't seem to find my glucose monitor. Do you have any fruit juice?"

"I have some freshly squeezed orange juice in the fridge."

"That'll do the trick, but just a small glass."

I went into the kitchen and returned with the juice and a jug of water. "Here you go." I handed her the OJ and placed the water on my desk.

"Thank you." She took a series of small sips from the glass before lying back in the chair, closing her eyes, and letting out a deep sigh.

For a minute I thought she had fallen asleep, or even worse—passed away. I was rummaging through my desk drawers, looking for a mirror to hold underneath her nostrils, when I heard her softly sobbing. "Are you all right? Do you want me to call a doctor?"

She took a tissue from the box I kept on a small round table next to the recliner. "Never mind me, dear. I'm just a foolish old woman grasping at straws and reaching for shadows. My son's been dead for decades, I don't know what I'm expecting to hear from you." She reached for the water jug.

"Let me get that." I jumped up from my seat and poured her a glass.

"You look too young to have known Tommy. How did you stumble upon this information of yours?"

"You said you received a call from me last night, about what time?"

"It was somewhere around ten o'clock. I'd fallen asleep in front of the television; the ringing of the telephone jarred me awake. I was tuned to KCAL 9 and the last newscast of the evening was on."

"I'm afraid you've been the victim of a prank caller."

"The person sounded just like you."

"I know. She also called some of my friends last night. The police have been alerted." I picked up the phone. "I'll call Officer Lopez and add your name to the list of complainants."

"Oh, dear! I don't want to get anyone into trouble."

"Whoever it is, they brought this upon themselves." I started to punch in the number for Officer Lopez's cell.

"Please leave me out of this." A distressed look came upon her face.

Not wanting to be the cause of this sweet elderly woman's heart attack or stroke, I hung up the phone. "You're too kind a person, Mrs. Lawson. It is Mrs., isn't it?"

She relaxed back into the chair. "Yes, I remarried after Tommy's father passed. Unfortunately, my second husband is also deceased."

"I'm so sorry to hear that, Mrs. Lawson."

"Please call me, Bonnie." The color had come back into her face and she appeared more relaxed.

"Bonnie it is then." I wanted to get as much info as possible about Tommy and his sister without unduly upsetting the woman, or alerting her to the fact I did know a few things about her son. If lucky, I could put this entire mystery to rest and help Louie get Lupe past all this business. "You mentioned your son, Tommy, had passed away a long time ago. Was he ill?"

"No, quite the contrary. He was hale and hearty, just shy of his twentieth birthday when he had his accident."

"Accident?"

"We lived in Altadena at the time. Tommy had returned from Vietnam and was at loose ends about what he wanted to do with the rest of his life. He spent most of his free time up in his room listening to music and reading." She had a wistful look about her as she remembered her son. "When he wasn't home or driving around in his new car, he liked to go for long rides on his motorbike. That darn thing always made me nervous. He'd managed to come home in one piece from that godforsaken war, I was not in the mood for losing him on a California freeway!" She appeared agitated.

"You don't have to continue if you don't want to, Bonnie"

She took a gulp of water and resumed her tale. "I remember feeling relieved when he told me he was going to be spending the day hiking. Out in nature, getting some exercise—nothing could harm him there! What a cockeyed fool I was then." She let out a sigh, which sounded like a low moan. "He had no business staying out there past dark. If only he hadn't lost his footing on his way up to The White City in the Sky."

Is this her euphemistic way of saying she thinks her son fell short of heavenly expectations and plunged into hell? "White City in the Sky? I haven't heard that term before."

"It was quite the destination in its day. My mother had a framed picture of my grandparents up there. I never had any interest in making the journey myself. There isn't much left of the place anyway—a pile of rubble and some debris from the funicular that would transport people up into the sky."

I've heard of a stairway to heaven, had no idea there was once a cable car, too. "Are you talking about heaven?"

Bonnie laughed. "It was to some. I take it you're not a native Californian."

"East Coast transplant, but I've been here long enough to put down some roots."

She laughed again. "Honey, we're all too close to the shifting sands of the Los Angeles Basin to put down any real roots. The remains of the Echo Mountain Resort and the Mount Lowe Railway can attest to this fact. Hike up there one day and see for yourself."

Good, she's talking about an actual place on Earth. What a relief! Mental note—google "White City in the Sky" after she leaves. "Was there ever any suspicion of foul play in your son's death?"

She gasped. "Where in the world would you get such an idea?" Her milky blue eyes fixated on me. "You do know something about Tommy's death."

I wasn't ready to tip my hand. The last thing in the world I wanted to do was tell Bonnie Lawson about Madame Mestral and her otherworldly communications. I had no intention of feeding The Madame and Don Pardo any new dupes. "Excuse me, I didn't mean to upset you. It's just the way my mind works, I'm a bit of a mystery buff."

She sat there quietly, seeming to evaluate my explanation, before reaching for her cane. "I should be on my way, I've taken up enough of your valuable time."

I couldn't let her go without finding out something about Tommy's sister. "Here, let me help you." I got up from behind my desk and offered her my arm as a support.

"Thank you." She steadied herself on me as she rose up out of the recliner. "Oh, what I wouldn't give to be young and able-bodied again."

"Do you have any other children or grandchildren around to assist you with errands and such?"

Her grip on my arm tightened. "There's just the three of us."

"Three?" I opened the door.

She gave me a sly smile. "Me, myself, and I."

"I can see you to your car, if you like. Which one is it?"

"A friend drove me here. My eyes aren't what they used to be." She looked down at her wristwatch and then held her arm up to me. "What time does it say?"

"Nine-forty."

"She said she had to run a short errand and would be right back." Bonnie waived her hand in the air. "There she is now."

A vintage, yellow, Corvette convertible pulled up in front of my house.

CHAPTER EIGHTEEN

Wife Of A Preacher Man

I COULD HARDLY believe my eyes. Was this Lupe's stolen car? Did the thief actually have the audacity to return to the scene of the crime driving the nabbed vehicle?

Bonnie Lawson turned to me. "Thank you, Miss Law. I can make it to the car without any assistance."

"Are you sure?" I was stalling—desperate to come up with an excuse, which would allow me to get a look at both the license plate and the driver.

The driver's side door opened. A dark-haired, statuesque woman stepped out of the car and headed our way. "Are you ready to leave, Bonnie?" She spoke with a trace of a British accent.

"Yes, I'm all done here. It turns out the whole thing was some sort of prank. But this lovely lady standing next to me really is a hypnotherapist named Roberta Law."

The woman gave me a searing inspection. "I'm Lilith Darvell." She appeared to be somewhere in her early thirties. And looked nothing like the mystery blonde I had seen driving Lupe's car.

"Lilith is a close friend of mine—the daughter I never had. She's married to Rev. Lucious, the pastor of my church."

This woman did not look like your stereotypical minister's wife. She wore a black Donna Karan pantsuit, sans blouse. The outfit was cinched around the waist by a gold metallic belt with a buckle that looked like a tricked-out Star of David—a six-pointed star containing a five-petalled flower at its center.

"I see you're a classic car fan," I said.

"Not really," Lilith replied. Her curtness highlighted the icy aloofness of her demeanor. "It belongs to my husband."

"I'm guessing it's a 1970?"

"Close," Bonnie said, "1966. It belonged to Tommy. My husband and I gave the Stingray to Lou after the accident." The confused look on my face must have cued her next response. "That was Rev. Lucious' nickname back in those days, he and my son were best friends."

Best friends? How old is this guy? I tried to maintain a neutral look on my face.

"My husband is seasoned like a fine wine," Lilith said.

Since Tommy would have been somewhere in his late sixties if he had lived, I assumed Rev. Lucious' season was the winter portion of this May-December romance.

"A friend of mine drives a car just like this one," I said. "Except hers is a 1970. Mind if I take a look?

"Be my guest," Lilith said.

On closer examination, I realized the two cars were not quite the same. This one was a paler shade of yellow than Lupe's and did not have as sleek a line. It did have a specialty plate though. "What does M A G U S stand for?"

"It's biblical," Lilith said.

"Doesn't ring a bell," I said. "Though I wouldn't call myself a religious scholar."

"You must be familiar with the three wise men, also known as the Magi?" Bonnie asked me.

"Sure."

"Well," Bonnie continued, "magi is the plural of magus."

I smiled at Lilith. "So your husband's a wise guy."

My lame attempt at humor was lost on her. "He's a highly respected and very learned man." She shifted her focus to Bonnie. "We better be on our way, I promised Lucious we'd be home before lunch."

"Do you all live together?" I asked.

Lilith glowered at me. "You certainly are a curious sort."

I was caught off guard by her hard-eyed response to my innocent question.

Bonnie broke the ice. "They've set me up in a charming little guest house at the back of their estate in San Marino."

Who knew the ministry compensated so well? San Marino is the third richest area to live in Los Angeles County, according to a recent *LA Weekly* article. A starter home in the neighborhood would set you back at least a million dollars. Maybe I should check out this church one Sunday.

The two women got into the car and Lilith started the engine.

I spoke to Bonnie through the passenger window. "What number can I reach you at, in case there's a break in the case?"

"What case?" Lilith asked.

"Bonnie isn't the only victim of this prank caller who's been impersonating me."

Lilith shut down the engine. "Why didn't you tell me this?" she sternly asked Bonnie.

"I haven't had a chance," Bonnie timidly answered. "Besides, what does it matter? It was only a stupid trick."

"Seemingly innocent tricks can sometimes have far-reaching consequences." Lilith's words had a cryptic air. "You may contact me, if the need arises." She handed me a business card and restarted the engine. "Emphasis on the words *me* and *need*." The car pulled away from the curb.

I looked down at the card she had given me: LILITH C. DARVELL GALLERIES - Antiquities, Artifacts & Appraisals. The phone number had a San Marino area code.

This explained it all. No wonder the preacher and his wife were living in such a high-end locale. I didn't know much about the line of work Lilith was in, but I did know it was an extremely lucrative vocation.

Heading back into my office, I sat down at the computer. Still intrigued by Bonnie Lawson's mention of Tommy "loosing his footing" on his way up there, I googled "white city in the sky." The top result was an LA hiking site. Turns out it was this amazing Victorian resort which once sat atop Mt. Echo, overlooking Altadena. Dance hall, observatory, bowling alley, tennis courts, zoo, 40-room chalet and dormitories all painted in a brilliant white to reflect back the dazzling California sunshine to the peons below. Its heyday was brief, about six years in the late 1800s, before falling prey to a series of man-made and natural catastrophes. The ruins of the hotel, and railway which serviced it, were taken over by the US Forest Service and promptly declared a hazardous nuisance. They blasted away most of what remained with dynamite about four years prior to Tommy's visit. Hikers can access it from the Sam Merrill Trail via The Haunted Forest.

"There's a Haunted Forest in LA?" I said to myself.

My fingers flew over the keys, typing the words "haunted forest" into the search engine box. The first two results were for

Halloween attractions in Utah and Vermont, but the third hit was for Pasadena. Since Altadena sits directly north of Pasadena, I clicked on the link. It took me to a paranormal investigation web page. Apparently, The Haunted Forest is a local nickname for the old Cobb Estate, which sits at the entrance to the Sam Merrill Trail. The place has long been rumored to be a hotbed of paranormal activity, with numerous reports of people believing they were being watched or followed while walking in the area. The unexplained activities have been attributed to everything ranging from teenage pranksters, to aliens, to demonic forces. I glanced at my watch. It was ten a.m. Time to put in a call to Lupe and check on the whereabouts of the elusive Madame Mestral. So I bookmarked the page, and several others I came across, to read at a later date.

Lupe's phone rang and rang. I knew this was an early hour to be calling Louie's aunt, but I had to find out if The Madame had made it home safely. I was about to give up after the tenth ring, when someone finally answered.

"Hello," Danny said.

"Hi, it's me. Is Madame Mestral there?"

"Calling to set up an appointment?"

"Very funny."

"She's not here."

"If she doesn't show up soon, I think we may need to file a missing persons report."

"Whatever for? She and Lupe left less than an hour ago."

"They couldn't have gone very far, Lupe doesn't have a car."

"I loaned them mine. Lupe was informed her Corvette had been abandoned in Altadena. It's parked at the end of Lake Avenue, near some place called the Cobb Estate."

CHAPTER NINETEEN

The House Of The Dying Son

"T HEY'VE GONE TO The Haunted Forest?"

"I didn't say anything about a haunted forest," Danny retorted. "It's rather early in the day to be drinking, Roberta."

"Did the police apprehend anyone?"

"How would I know?"

"Was it Officer Sanchez who called to tell her about the car?"

"No one called. Lupe did an early morning sitting with Samir. He told her where she could find it."

"Listen to yourself, Danny. That's ridiculous!"

Or is it? Why did Mestral really show up at my place last night? I already suspect she's secretly loaning Lupe's Corvette to some friend of hers. It's possible she and the mystery blonde were involved in last night's car theft. And if The Madame is an accomplice, it stands to reason she would know where to find the stolen vehicle.

"Why don't you reserve judgment until they return from their destination?" Danny sounded annoyed.

"Did you at least notify the police?"

"Samir advised against it."

Figures. "Why didn't you go with them?"

"Patañjali charged me with another assignment."

"Who the hell is he?"

"Honestly, Roberta, you can be so pedestrian at times. He's arguably the greatest yogi who ever lived. His *Yoga Sūtras* are the foundation of Raja Yoga. I'm honored he has agreed to take me under his wing."

"We're talking angel wings, aren't we? He's dead, right?"

"Of course he's dead! The man lived around the second or third century CE. He'd be over two thousand years old by now."

Funny how my brother viewed this as being more preposterous than the idea of having a deceased guy teach him yoga. "Did you at least let Louie know what Lupe is up to?"

"He's right here, if you would like to speak with him," Danny snapped. "Now if you'll excuse me, I have to work on my yamas."

Louie came on the line. "What's up?"

"Shouldn't I be the one asking you that?"

"I'll be with you in a minute, Danny!" Louie spoke in a rushed tone, "Sorry 'bout that, I promised to help him with his Brahmacharya. He called me early this morning and asked me to come by."

"What are you talking about?"

"It's his celibacy yama."

"Wouldn't your not being there be the best way to help him out with that one?"

"Ya'd think! But this Patañjali dude told him he had to go to his room, take off all his clothes, and sit there in the nude for one hour—meditating on the virtue of sexual self-restraint."

"So his challenge is to resist the temptation to play with himself?"

"That's the easy part. I'll be sitting across from him—naked as a jaybird. Or should I say gaybird?"

"I thought you had an early morning meeting at the Welk Resort."

"It was a ruse to leave you and Ben alone together. Did it work? Did you *voulez-vous coucher*?"

"Yeah, in separate rooms. Madame Mestral made an unannounced appearance and put a damper on the mood."

"What?"

"I'll fill you in some other time. Why'd you let your aunt take off with Mestral?"

"They left before I arrived. But don't worry, I put in a call to our cute cop."

"What did Officer Sanchez say?"

"There wasn't much he could do with the information, considering the informant was a dead Egyptian guy. He said to get back to him if the car actually did show up somewhere. Look I gotta go, Danny's waiting for me. Keep your fingers crossed he fails his chastity challenge."

Why are all the men in my life such sexual extremists? "Call me when Lupe and Mestral get back."

"Will do. Bye"

It seemed obvious to me The Madame had cooked up this entire Patañjali business to keep my brother occupied, while she took Lupe on this bogus vehicle recovery mission. She'd been around Danny long enough to know he had a predilection for all things spiritual. These religious delusions were one of the symptoms of his schizophrenia. Lupe's Achilles' heel was her romantic flights of fancy, which up until this point had been relatively harmless. There most definitely was a genius to Mestral's grifting skills. What her end game was, and the identity of her blonde-haired cohort, still eluded me. But I suspected getting her hands on someone else's money was going to play into it sooner or later.

I reflected on my recent encounter with Bonnie Lawson and Lilith Darvell. Were they just innocent bystanders caught up in the wake of this scam? Or did Mestral have her sights set on them, too? What I knew at this point about Tommy Forrester and his tragic demise didn't amount to much. But it did seem odd Lupe's car—which looked a lot like Tommy's car—was abandoned so near the location of his death.

There was nothing much I could do about any of this at the moment. My instinct was to chase after Lupe and Mestral, but the rest of my day was filled with clients. I gathered together the paltry amount of info I had on Tommy—notes I had jotted down from the Samir sessions, the "In Memoriam" clipping from the *LA Times*—and placed it all in a manila folder.

As I was about to put the folder in my desk drawer something popped into my mind—*Didn't Lupe's newspaper clipping mention Tommy was not only a son, but a brother and a fiancé as well?*

I checked this year's "In Memoriam" clipping. All it contained was another strange poem. It dawned on me to take another look at the "Tommy Forrester Page" on the legacy website I had come across yesterday. Browsing through the Photo Gallery, I noticed in many of the snapshots Tommy was with a little girl who looked about twelve years old. Was this his sister? Bonnie Lawson said she had no other children when I asked. So who is this girl in all the photos? And who is Cissy, the sponsor of the site? His tragic bride-to-be? Or someone else? I clicked on the Obituary tab. The page was blank.

I needed to know what was written in the clipping Lupe kept on the fridge, so I rang Louie on his cell. The call went directly to voicemail. Guess he was still tied up in his naked yoga endurance test with Danny. *LA Times* obituaries prior to 1985 were not available online. I didn't have time to hustle over to the library and look through the archives, so I followed up my call to Louie with a text. With that out of the way, I turned my attention to the workday ahead.

* * *

My eleven a.m. was the culmination of a five-session Stop Smoking Package. I offered this to people who dreaded the idea of going cold turkey in three sessions or less. The client was a good subject and had managed to quit after our second meeting, but he cherished the security blanket of the full package of hypnotic visits. We wrapped up at ten minutes before the hour. He booked himself one more session, what he referred to as a "safety," in six months time. I should have taken the opportunity to offer him a package of trust building sessions, but I've never been an adept practitioner of the art of upselling.

I grabbed a quick bite of lunch at my desk while prepping for my upcoming appointment with Carl Jenkins' phobic referral. At the top of my To-Do List was a reminder to double-check the outside of my house for any stray Halloween decor. Everything looked okay at my place, though the same couldn't be said for my neighbors. My entire block looked like it was taking part in a Scariest Haunted House competition. There wasn't much I could do about it, so I said a prayer and hoped for the best.

By quarter past one it looked like this was turning into another no-show for the elusive Angela Fowler. I was about to apprise Dr. Jenkins of the situation, when I heard a soft knocking sound.

"Be right with you!" I walked over to my office door and opened it.

No one was there. And there wasn't a single person in sight.

Sitting back down behind my desk, I assumed I had mistaken some other sound— like the rustling of a tree branch—for the soft knock. I picked up the phone to call Carl, when I heard the exact same sound again. Rushing to the door, I pressed my ear against the wood. It was very quiet, but someone was definitely standing on the other side. Not wanting to scare the person off, I slowly turned the knob. The door was opened about a quarter of the way—when a figure darted past me.

I stepped outside. Pressed between the olive green stucco exterior of my house and a tall cedar bush was the Corvette driving mystery blonde, though the car was nowhere in sight.

I was abrupt. "Who are you and what are you doing here?"

The woman's voice was faint and barely audible. "My name's Angela Fowler, I have an appointment."

CHAPTER TWENTY

Twitchy Woman

S O ANGELA FOWLER *was* the mystery blonde I'd seen lurking around my house Monday afternoon and evening. She was also the woman Madame Mestral had been letting drive Lupe's car, though the Corvette was nowhere in sight today. And she was Carl Jenkins' patient, my new client referral. There were so many confusing angles to this encounter, I barely knew where to begin. But I did know I needed to get some answers.

"I've been waiting for you," I said. "Please, come inside."

"Sorry I'm late," her voice trembled. Most of Angela's face was hidden behind a pair of oversized Jackie O sunglasses and a floppy black hat. Her blonde hair framed her face in a shoulder length bob reminiscent of Doris Day's perky do from the late Sixties/ early Seventies.

I waited for her to move from her hiding spot behind the cedar, but she didn't budge. "I think you'll be more comfortable inside," I said in an attempt to coax her out.

"Do you own a cat?"

"Just a lazy old beagle. Do you have allergies?"

"No, I don't like cats. They can't be trusted."

Sounds like another of her irrational phobias. Carl told me about her fear of meds and her fear of death, I wonder if he's aware of this one? I decided to apply some reverse logic. "You're a lot more likely to run into a cat out here, than you are in my office."

She bolted out from behind the bush and into my recliner.

I followed right behind.

Angela Fowler shifted nervously in the chair. Her khaki green trench coat was buckled and wrapped tightly around her.

California was in the midst of a multi-year drought, I couldn't even remember the last time we had seen any rain. "Would you like to hang up your coat?"

She shook her head and I noticed a slight twitch in her upper lip. Whether it was caused by nerves or something else altogether, I couldn't really say at this point.

"How about your hat and sunglasses?"

"If you don't mind, I prefer to leave everything on. I have a mild case of Tourette's that makes me very self-conscious. It affects my eyes the most." She cleared her throat. "And sometimes it makes me do that."

Funny, Carl never mentioned anything about this.

"I don't have any Coprolalia symptoms, so you don't have to worry about me cursing you out," she tittered.

This would be a challenge. When hypnotizing someone I like to be able to see their entire face so I can monitor the various physical signs, which accompany the onset of the trance state. Of course, one of those signals is eyelid fluttering which would be difficult to gauge in this case. Then again, was I even going to be able to accept this woman as a new client? She seemed to be stalking me, although she did only show up twice—once for her appointment, when my decorations scared her away—and later, in the evening. Her second appearance could be chalked up to a skittish personality desperately trying to overcome the limitations of their affliction. As far as Lupe's Corvette was concerned, she only borrowed a car from a friend. Angela probably has no idea the vehicle belongs to someone else.

I handed her a clipboard with some papers on it. "This is preliminary paperwork I need you to fill out. You can skip over the part about requesting a referral from your psychologist, Dr. Jenkins already faxed it over to me."

She stared at the forms.

I handed her a pen. "Here you go."

Her eyes were still glued to the papers. "Didn't Dr. Jenkins give you all my information?"

"This is for my files. We each keep our own set of client records. It's mostly general intake info like your name, address, etcetera. Along with a background questionnaire to help give me some insight in to your issue, plus an informed consent document with an acknowledgement of fees."

"This is t-t-too much," she stuttered. "I c-c-couldn't possibly." She handed the clipboard back to me.

Suspecting she might be suffering with some learning disabilities, I reframed the request. "Would you prefer if I asked the questions verbally and wrote down the responses for you?"

She nodded.

"All right, I already know your name." I wrote down "Fowler, Angela" in the respective boxes. "Address?"

"I'd rather not say."

"Excuse me?"

"You can reach me on my cell." She rattled off the number.

This was unusual. I'd not dealt with anything like this before. Was she homeless and embarrassed to admit it? Is this the reason Mestral loaned her Lupe's car from time to time?

"I've had problems with people following me in the past, so I'm very hesitant to give out my specific coordinates."

Sounds like she has a touch of paranoia. I'll get the address from Carl when I confer with him. "E-mail?"

"None, I'm a Luddite."

"Emergency contact?"

Visibly uncomfortable, she shifted in her seat.

"It doesn't have to be a relative, a friend will do." Maybe this is where I'll be able to make a definitive tie between her and Mestral.

She took a moment before answering. "Dr. Carl Jenkins."

I'd never met such a secretive client; her trust issues were deeply entrenched. "Birthdate?"

"Ten, sixteen, sixty-six."

"That was three days ago, happy belated birthday," I said.

"Thanks, I don't consider it a cause for celebration. My childhood was not a happy one, and I've always found that particular day dredges up a lot of unpleasant memories."

"Sorry, I didn't realize…"

"No need to apologize," she said, flicking her hand. I couldn't tell if this was an intentional cavalier gesture, or an involuntary nervous reaction. "As long as those people can't find me, they can't hurt me anymore." Her upper lip quivered.

"By *those people*, do you mean your parents?"

"Among others. Next question."

Her deflection seemed like a reflexive avoidance tactic, so I decided to get through the rest of the questionnaire before pushing any further. "Occupation?"

"I'm a visual artist. Painting mostly, sometimes sculpture."

"Have you ever been hypnotized?"

"No…yes…maybe." She hesitated for a minute. "Can children be hypnotized?"

"Children are wonderful hypnotic subjects. In many ways they already are in a sort of trance state, fueled by their vivid imaginations and guileless natures. Where do you think you were hypnotized?"

Angela was still and non-responsive.

Sometimes people who've attended stage hypnosis shows are unsure whether or not they have been hypnotized. "Did you take part in some sort of act?" I asked, hoping to prod her out of her inertia.

She brought her hands up next to her face, made two fists, and let out a wail worthy of a banshee.

I jumped in my seat—her visceral response catching me totally off guard.

Lex showed up in a nanosecond, howling and scratching outside the office door adjoining the living quarters of my house.

Angela stopped screaming. "Is that a cat I hear?"

"That's my dog, Lex. Cats don't howl," I said matter-of-factly, "they yowl."

"What's the difference?"

I shrugged my shoulders. "You replace the 'H' with a 'Y'?"

Angela broke out in hysterical laughter. "I like you. You're funny. Will you let Lex in so I can meet him?"

I glanced at the clock on my bookshelf. Though I always booked clients in for an hour and a half, rather than one hour, for their first session—to allow for the filling out of paperwork—we weren't making much headway. "Maybe if there's some time left when we finish."

"Pleeeeeease," Angela pleaded like a young child. "I love doggies."

I was struck by the rapidity of her shifts in mood and temperament, wondering if I might be out of my league. Carl Jenkins had faith in me. And it wasn't in my nature to let people down, if I could help it. So I went with the flow and let Lex in for an impromptu meet-and-greet. "He can stay till we're ready to put you into trance."

Tail wagging, Lex made a beeline for Angela. She leaned forward and gave him a big hug, while he planted a series of sloppy wet kisses on her face.

Next to the question about previous hypnotic experiences, I penciled in a question mark. Though based on what I'd seen so far, my instincts told me the real answer was most probably—YES. I checked off the Referral Box and wrote in the name, Dr. Carl Jenkins. "Marital status?"

She was still focused on Lex. "That depends."

"Depends on what?"

"On whether or not this delicious beagle of yours will have me for his bride."

I checked off SINGLE. "The rest of this form outlines payment options. We can discuss that at the end of today's session."

"I'll be paying in cash." She reached into her coat pocket and plunked a wad of bills on my desk. "Take out what you need."

There goes my homeless theory. "Now let's get to the heart of the matter. Since you are adverse to taking any meds, Dr. Jenkins has asked me to assist you in getting your panic disorder under control." I noticed her lip twitching had ceased since Lex entered the room. He was acting as an environmental hypnosis trigger, shifting her focus away from her fears and onto him. "Do you recall when you had your first panic attack?"

"They started when I was a child."

I felt confident the panic episodes were linked to her Tourette's syndrome and knew there were studies out there, which had shown self-hypnosis techniques had been very effective in symptom relief. "Can you pinpoint it more precisely?"

She shook her head. "Most of my childhood memories are Swiss cheese. And the holes have only grown bigger over the years."

Age regression would be the best approach. If I could get to the root cause and isolate one or two early incidents, there was a good chance I could minimize the overall effect they had on her impressionable childhood psyche.

"Okay, that's all I need for now. If you're ready, I'd like to move to the hypnosis portion of our session. We'll start with a couple of suggestibility tests, to give me an idea of how responsive you are to the trance state, and from there move directly into the induction. Would you mind taking off your hat and sunglasses?"

Angela's upper lip spasms returned with a vengeance.

I mentally debated whether or not to allow Lex to stay in the room with us. Part of me reasoned he might aid in soothing her. On the other hand, if some random scent or street sound provoked a barking spree, his presence would ultimately serve to be more distracting than helpful.

"Will you excuse me for a moment, while I escort my canine associate back into the house?" I got up and grabbed hold of Lex's collar. "Be right back."

It wouldn't suffice to open the door and send him on his merry way. Having been allowed entree into the forbidden inner sanctum, he was bound to hang around pawing at the door and whining to get back in. We walked to the back of the house. I set him up in my bedroom with a fresh bowl of water and the radio tuned to the cool jazz song stylings of 94.7 The Wave. With that piece of business out of the way, I was ready to tackle the challenging assignment that lay ahead of me.

"Do you need to use the restroom before we begin?" I asked, re-entering my office.

Angela didn't answer my question. To be more exact, she *couldn't* answer my question. Ms. Fowler had flown the coop.

CHAPTER TWENTY-ONE

50 Ways To Leave Your Hypnotherapist

I COULDN'T BELIEVE it! Once again, Angela Fowler had managed to slip away from me. Even my most hypnophobic clients managed to stick around long enough to experience the trance state firsthand. The thought of having to ring Carl Jenkins and let him know how—for the second time this week—I had managed to scare off his referral was a chore I dreaded. The phone rang before I had a chance to place my call.

"Roberta Law, speaking."

Nothing but the sound of anxious breathing.

"Hello, who is this?"

More breathing, then the sound of a weak voice struggling to find words. "P-P-P-Please for…give me."

"Angela, is that you?"

The call went dead. I immediately hit *69 on my phone. The line was busy. I couldn't be one hundred percent certain it was Angela, but my gut told me it was her. I hit the Caller ID Log button to see if there was a name. The display read "Wireless Caller" and the number wasn't one I recognized. Reluctantly, I dialed.

"Dr. Carl Jenkins' office," the flat voice on the other end answered.

"It's Roberta Law, may I please speak with Dr. Jenkins?"

"The doctor is at lunch. This is his service. Would you like to leave a message?"

Who knew answering services still existed? "When do you expect him back?"

"He didn't leave a time."

"I'll try him later. Thank you. Goodbye."

My iPhone barked, signaling I had a new voicemail. It was Louie reading back the Tommy Forrester "In Memoriam" clipping from Lupe's fridge. Everything I needed to know was in the first line of his message, "In loving memory of Private First Class, Thomas (Tommy) Forrester, a devoted son, brother, fiancé, and friend."

Louie's words rang in my ears, "a devoted son, brother," followed by Bonnie Lawson's response to my question about her having any other children, "There's just the three of us…Me, myself and I."

Though I didn't think so when she said it, her answer was rather evasive. Not a yes or a no, but a verbal dodge. True, she might not have any children around to help her at the moment. Of course, this didn't necessarily mean Tommy was an only child. Her children might not live nearby. Or maybe they're not involved in her life for some other reason. Of one thing I was certain—Bonnie intended to leave me with the impression Tommy had no siblings. Why she wanted to mislead me was a mystery I felt compelled to unravel.

* * *

The rest of my day played out in a routine manner—no surprise appearances or disappearances. Louie sent a text letting me know Lupe did indeed find her missing Corvette abandoned at the end of Lake Avenue in Altadena, outside the entrance to the

Cobb Estate aka The Haunted Forest. I called him back as soon as I read the message.

"Hi, it's me. Did you contact Officer Lopez?"

"Yeah," Louie said. "He wasn't too pleased Lupe drove her car home before the police had a chance to check it out."

"Did he come by to look it over?"

"He wants to wait till The Madame gets back, so he can question her about the info she received from Samir."

"More like the info she received from her accomplice." I sincerely hoped Angela Fowler wouldn't turn out to be her fellow conspirator. "Where is Samir's sweetie anyway?"

"Mestral told Lupe she had an errand to run and would catch up with her later. I should check to see if she's returned yet, Danny needs his car tonight. He's meeting up with Jack."

"Jack?"

"Jack Hensler. They're going to some kind of meeting in Pasadena."

I thought back to Jack's conversation with Don Pardo yesterday. "Does it have anything to do with Aleister Crowley?"

"No, it was some kind of magic club meetup. I told him he didn't have to go that far afield to see some magicians. One of my clients is a member of the Magic Castle and will get me passes anytime I want."

"We're not talking Vegas style magic, this stuff has something to do with sex orgies. That's why Jack's so gung ho."

"I want to go, too," Louie whined.

"What happened to Danny's celibacy pact with his guru, Patañjali? That certainly didn't last very long."

"Maybe he's testing himself again?"

"I just hope he's not off on another one of his religious tangents. The last thing we need is to have him get mixed up in this Thelema business—it gives me the creeps."

"Church sure has changed a lot since my days as an altar boy."

"I'm going to give Jack a call and see what's up with this magical rendezvous he has planned." I said goodbye to Louie and dialed Jack's number.

"Well, hello there, my luscious lovely. What can I do ya for?"

"Why didn't you tell me you were dragging my brother along to this sex cult meeting tonight?"

"Come on, don't be all jealous like, babe. Ya know I'm not a fudge man, it's seafood all the way with me."

I wasn't in the mood for Jack's colorful sexual euphemisms. "You know how susceptible he is to anything with even the slightest religious overtone."

"Ya don't take this stuff seriously do ya, Red?"

"No, of course not! But Danny certainly does." I hesitated for a moment. "You have to take me with you."

"Your wish is my command. I'll pick ya up at seven."

"This isn't a date, Jack. I thought Don Pardo said you have to call these people up and get permission to attend one of their meetings."

"I already got permission for me and Danny. The guy on the phone told me I could bring along as many women as I wanted. Looks like they currently have a shortage in the chick department."

Why was I not surprised? "Did Danny mention to you why he was so interested in tagging along?"

"Some guy named Sam told him he should check it out."

"Did he say, 'Sam' or 'Samir'?"

"Come to think of it, the guy's last name was Ear."

I couldn't help but laugh; Jack's crude innocence was one of his more endearing qualities.

"I remember laughin' when I heard it, too. Hey, he's the guy Lupe was talkin' about last night. Sam Ear, what a weird name."

"Thanks, Jack. I'll see you at seven. Is there a dress code? Should I wear anything special?"

"The less, the better, babe. I'm hopin' by the end of the night nobody has a stitch left on. Catch ya later."

I wanted to keep a watchful eye on my brother, plus find out more about Aleister Crowley and Thelema, but if the price of admission was strutting around in my cellulite dimpled birthday suit I wasn't so sure I was up to the task. Since it was a cool evening, I opted for lots of layers. If any of my clothes were destined to come off, I wanted to make sure it would be a slow, arduous process trying to get to any of my bare assets. My entirely black ensemble—in honor of my excursion into the belly of the beast—was comprised of a pair of leggings, long skirt, turtleneck jersey, blouse, shawl, and knee-high boots.

Jack arrived fifteen minutes early—obviously eager to get a jump on the evening's festivities. He honked the horn of his cherry red Thunderbird convertible.

"What's the rush?" I said, jumping into the passenger seat.

"Looks like we're gonna have to swing by Angelino Heights and pick up your bro. He lent his wheels to some gypsy woman."

"Mestral hasn't returned?"

"Nope. Hope we're not late to the meetin'. Wouldn't wanna miss anythin'."

"Do you mind putting the top up? It's kind of chilly tonight."

Jack reached over and put his arm around me. "I was hopin' we could snuggle together for warmth."

"Nice try," I extracted myself from his clutches, "but how do you expect to shift gears?"

Jack hit the switch for the hood.

"What year is this car, Jack?"

"It's a 1966, fourth generation, Ford Thunderbird." He put the car into gear and peeled away from the curb.

"Hmm, that year keeps popping up. Maybe I should do some research on it."

"Sure was great for music." Jack smiled. "Brian Wilson started working on the *Smile* sessions—the Beatles were more popular than Jesus Christ…How's it keep poppin' up for ya?"

"Well, it's the year Tommy Forrester died. And a woman was picked up at my house earlier today by someone driving a 1966 Corvette."

"Was it a yellow convertible?"

"Yes, how'd you know?"

"It took off from in front of your place when I pulled up."

CHAPTER TWENTY-TWO

Smokey Satan's Cafe

I WAS FLUMMOXED by Jack's revelation. "Did you get a look at the license plate?"

"Yeah, I remember thinkin' M A G G O T S was an odd sort of thing to put on a vanity plate."

"The word was M A G U S."

"Even weirder."

"It's the car I told you about, the one that was here earlier. Maybe we should go back and check it out."

"Nothin' much to check out, Red. Like I said, they hightailed it when I arrived."

"Did you get a look at the driver?"

"Naw, it's too dark out. Why not ask the gal that was here earlier who picked her up?"

"I met the woman who picked Bonnie Lawson up, her name is Lilith Darvell. Maybe her husband was driving it tonight, the car belongs to him."

"Or he could have loaned it to somebody like Danny did. Speakin' of cars, any news on Lupe's?

"It turned up in Altadena at the end of Lake Avenue."

Jack merged onto the Hollywood Freeway. "If it got dumped at The Haunted Forest it was probably some kids out for a joyride."

"You're familiar with The Haunted Forest?"

"Sure, I grew up in Glendale. No self-respectin' teen in my neighborhood didn't know about the legend of the old Cobb Estate, or Gravity Hill, or Devil's Gate. There's a whole buttload of spooky shit up in that neck of the woods. My pals and I were always darin' each other to do some crazy thing or other in those places. That's why I think it was kids prankin'."

I envied Jack's easygoing attitude. With all the uncanny happenings of late, I wished I could be as carefree. "What kind of mischief did you get up to in those days?"

"One summer a coupla buddies and me headed over to Gravity Hill in my dad's Chevy Impala. The old man had no idea I'd absconded from the house that night with his car keys. So we're sitting there on Loma Alta Drive, I throw the car into neutral like your supposed to, and we wait for the car to start rollin' uphill. One of the guys jumps out of the car screamin' 'bout how we forgot the baby powder. He runs to the rear, starts sprinklin' the stuff over the trunk, and the car backs up right over him."

"Oh my god! Was he okay?"

Jack laughed. "Larry was fine. After fallin' he stayed on the ground—straight as a board—with the tires on either side of him. I put the parkin' brake on, then the other guys got out and pulled him from underneath the car. But here's the interestin' part, we found fingerprints in the baby powder on the back of the car."

"They were Larry's, weren't they?"

Jack shook his head. "Nope, swore he never put his hands on the trunk."

I rolled my eyes. "He probably had a mild case of shock and forgot he touched the car as he fell."

"Nice theory, except those prints were way smaller than Larry's and there were lots of 'em. It was the spirits of the kids who died in the school bus accident on that hill. They're the ones who push your car up the hill when you put it in neutral—just like the legend says—to avoid another tragedy."

I still wasn't buying his story. "Were any of you stoned when this occurred?"

"Of course, we were always stoned back then. It still happened though." Jack had a dejected look on his face. "No point tellin' ya my Cobb Estate and Devil's Gate stories."

"There, there, big boy." I patted him on the shoulder. "It's not that I necessarily doubt your story, I just want to put it into the proper perspective. What exactly is Devil's Gate?"

"It's part of the Arroyo triangle, which also includes the Cobb Estate and Suicide Bridge." Jack looked over at me. "And it's one of the seven portals to hell."

I tried my best to keep a straight face. "Good to know."

"Look, babe, I'm not the one comin' up with this stuff. I'm just bringin' ya up to speed."

"And I appreciate it."

"This legend goes back to the days when only Native Americans lived in these parts. There's some kinda vortex down there."

We were approaching the exit for Angelino Heights. The traffic had been surprisingly light. "You can get off the freeway here," I said.

When we arrived at Lupe's, Danny was standing on the street waiting for us. I got out of the car to let him in the backseat.

"Good evening, fellow seeker—and Roberta," Danny pushed the front seat forward.

"Ha, ha, ha," I said. "So I see The Madame is still missing in action."

"I'm sure Madame Mestral will return as soon as she finishes whatever business she's transacting. The woman has my utmost trust." Danny fumbled around looking for his seat belt.

"Classic car, man," Jack said. "It's a retractable lap belt."

"Yes, of course. I, myself, am a classic car owner."

"Did ya get rid of that purple Gremlin of yours?" Jack asked.

"No, that's the vehicle I'm referring to."

Jack shrugged. "To each his own, man."

We made our way past Dodger Stadium and Jack merged onto the 110 northbound. About fifteen minutes later he stopped in front of a quaint looking coffee shop, housed inside a red brick building, on Mission Street in South Pasadena.

"Everybody out, we're here," Jack announced.

"This is it?" I looked up at the sign on the cafe. "The Satan worshippers are holding their meeting in It's All About The Bean?"

"Satan worshippers," Danny shouted. "Take me home right this instant!"

"What's going on? You're the one who asked Jack to let you tag along in the first place. The only reason I'm even here is because of you."

"I need to consult with Samir. Perhaps I misunderstood his instructions."

"Samir is MIA, remember? I don't even get why he told you to come here in the first place."

"It had something to do with Tommy Forrester, I felt I owed it to Lupe to come."

"I'm surprised Samir didn't send Lupe instead, it's his usual MO."

"I know why she isn't here," Jack interrupted our sibling banter. "She's too old."

Even Samir was afraid to deflate Lupe's youthful delusions.

I looked at Jack. "There are age restrictions on this meeting?"

"No one under eighteen and no women over forty."

"That's totally sexist. And ageist, I might add. What am I even doing here?"

"Don't get all worked up, Red. You look smokin' hot for your age, I told 'em you're thirty."

Despite my raging feminist ire, Jack's assessment of my physical attributes flattered me. "It's still not right. This is the twenty-first century and women are no longer considered chattel—at least not in this country."

"Whoa, babe! No one said you're a cow."

"She said *chattel* not *cattle*," Danny piped in.

Jack looked perplexed. "Huh?"

"Never mind, take me away from this wretched place."

It seemed my brother and I had somehow mysteriously switched viewpoints about participating in this expedition. The innocuous location, the finicky requirements for admission, and Samir's directive piqued my curiosity. What the hell—no pun intended—was going on inside this otherwise breezy looking bistro? "Why so much resistance, Danny? Don't you trust Madame Mestral and her cast of characters anymore?"

"Of course, I still trust her. I'm just not very comfortable with demon-focused movements."

"Don't know about any demons," Jack said. "I'm here for the group sex."

"Group sex, as well?" Danny wiped his forehead with a tissue. "This is all too much to take in. What if Patañjali finds out about this?"

I made a feeble attempt at lightening the mood. "Maybe Samir is trying to play a practical joke on Patañjali, he does seem to enjoy a good laugh."

Danny's hands trembled.

"Jack, are you sure the meeting is taking place in there? It looks like your typical trendy coffee joint." Inside, I could see a barista drawing an espresso shot from a large copper machine, the requisite writer sitting at a corner table, and a handful of teenagers hogging the comfy chair section—ignoring each other while merrily texting away. "Would you mind checking to see if we're in the right place?"

"No problem," Jack exited the car.

Danny was doing deep breathing exercises by this point.

"Why did Samir want you to come here tonight?"

"He said, 'In the beginning was the Word, but in the end the Word was distorted.' Then he asked me to accompany Jack to the temple and 'separate the wheat from the chaff.'"

"And this made sense to you?"

"Well, it did in the heat of the moment. Now that I'm here in the flesh, I don't get it. Where's the temple?"

"Oh, Danny," I let out a sigh, "how did you expect to carry out this bizarre assignment, even if this place had been a temple?"

"Samir said I would know once I was inside. This is the starting point to finding the key to Tommy's death and Cissy's disappearance."

"Cissy?"

"Yes, Tommy's sister. Apparently, she vanished not long after he died."

CHAPTER TWENTY-THREE

San Gabriel Valley O.T.O.

"LET ME GET THIS straight, Danny. Madame Mestral told you Tommy had a sister named, Cissy."

"*Has* a sister, she's still alive. And it wasn't Madame Mestral who told me, I received the information from Samir."

Mestral, Samir—what difference does it make? They're both sharing the same body. "Where is this Cissy?"

"Like I said before, she went missing back in 1966, a few weeks after Tommy died. She was last seen in the vicinity of the Devil's Gate Dam."

Devil's Gate? That's one of the places Jack mentioned earlier. Better not tell Danny it's rumored to be one of the seven portals to hell, he's worked up enough as it is. "You have to go to this meeting with Jack and me."

My brother adamantly shook his head.

I needed to appeal to his conscience. "How old was Cissy Forrester when she disappeared?"

"I believe she was twelve."

"What about her family? Don't you think they would get a great deal of peace if we were able to locate her?"

"Tommy's dead, he was her only sibling. And I'm sure her parents are long gone."

"I met her mother today."

Danny eyed me curiously.

I crossed my heart. "God's honest truth. She showed up unannounced on my doorstep this afternoon. Seems she received one of those phone calls last night from my vocal doppelgänger. The woman told her I had crucial information about Tommy's death."

"We must get her to set up a session with Madame Mestral."

"No!" I snapped. "I didn't let on I knew anything about her son. And I don't want to quite yet."

"Why?"

Danny already knew I wasn't a fan of Mestral's, but I wasn't sure how he'd react if I revealed my suspicions about her involvement in Lupe's car theft and the recent spate of prank calls. "I have my reasons, please just trust me on this one."

Jack opened the driver's side door. "The meetin's takin' place in a room at the back of the coffee shop. It looks like a gatherin' of accountants in there."

"Did you hear that, Danny? I'm sure everything will be fine. What sinister event could possibly take place in a coffee shop called It's All About The Bean?"

"I'm not so sure I want to go back in," Jack said.

"Why? What did you see in there?" Danny asked with a slight tremor in his voice.

"Nothin'. It's what I'm afraid I'm gonna see—naked accountants."

Jack's prurient segue lightened the mood in the car. I burst out laughing and heard Danny chortle under his breath.

"What's so funny? You haven't seen 'em yet."

I reached out for my brother's hand. "Will you reconsider your position on this? If not my for my sake, will you do it for Cissy's mother?"

Danny let out a deep breath. "All right. But the minute I see or hear anything the least bit devilish, I'm heading for home."

I squeezed Danny's hand and then turned to reach for the door handle. A face—grotesquely distorted by the glass—was pressed up against the passenger side window. I shrieked.

Danny gasped.

"What the hell..." a startled Jack yelled. "Step away from my car, buddy!"

"It's only me." Louie laughed as he pulled his face away from the glass.

I rolled down the window. "What are you doing here?"

"Thought I'd crash the orgy and check it out for myself."

Jack leaned over me. "Sorry to disappoint ya, pal. It looks more like a Chamber of Commerce meetin' than an orgy in there. I think that Don Pardo guy gave me a bum lead."

"We were about to go inside." I opened the door and stepped out of the car. "How'd you know where to find us?"

"I followed you from Lupe's."

"Don't know if they'll let ya in, buddy. I noticed a check-in table with a list of names. Wait a minute!" Jack snapped his fingers. "Are ya still plannin' on gettin' a sex change? Chicks don't need to be on the list."

"Once and for all, he's not becoming a woman!" I insisted. "And even if he was, he'd still be banned because he's over forty."

"What's this about my age?" Louie sounded offended. "I'm barely past forty and I look fabulous."

"That you do, my darling." Danny gave Louie a peck on the cheek.

"Can we please go in before this event is over?" I held open the door to the coffee shop.

Once inside, we made our way past the glass pastry counter to the small room at the rear of the cafe. The sign on the door read: "SAN GABRIEL VALLEY O.T.O. - MEETUP IN SESSION."

"Should we knock?" I asked.

"Dunno," Jack answered. "The door was wide open when I came in before."

"What time is it?" Danny asked.

Louie looked at his watch. "One minute past eight."

"We're late." Danny turned around. "Let's go."

"Not so fast!" I caught hold of my brother's arm. "A minute after the hour doesn't qualify as late in my books." I rapped on the door.

"Come in," a male voice responded.

Huddled together, we entered the room like Dorothy and her band of over-the-rainbow denizens when they first encountered The Wizard.

The room was painted a dull beige color and the walls were bare except for a couple of coffee bean posters. A handful of ordinary-looking people, quietly sitting on wooden chairs, faced an empty blackboard standing at the front. Right inside the door, two middle-aged men—one wearing a gray business suit and the other dressed in navy—sat behind a rectangular folding table.

"Please sign in." The man in gray handed Louie a clipboard. "And give your name to Earl," he pointed to the man in navy, "before taking a seat."

Louie scribbled his name on the paper. "Louie Lopez," he whispered.

"Sorry, I didn't catch that," Earl said.

Louie cleared his throat. "I'm not sure if my name made it onto the list, Lopez—Louie."

Earl scanned his sheet of paper. "You're right, it didn't."

The man in gray looked at Louie. "I'm afraid you'll have to leave, sir. No one is admitted unless they're on the list."

Jack intervened. "Don Pardo referred us. I forgot to include Louie when I called."

"I'm sorry," Earl said. "We have a very strict policy, all names must be cleared prior to entry."

I tapped Louie on the shoulder. "Come on, let's get out of here. We can grab some coffee while we wait for Danny and Jack."

The man in gray stood up. "You're welcome to attend, ma'am."

It always irks me when someone calls me "ma'am," makes me feel like some old maiden aunt. "It's Roberta. And I'm not on the list either."

"Women are always welcome," Earl said.

Provided they're between the ages of eighteen and forty. "I find your system sexist. If my friend here is not welcome, then I'd rather take a pass."

Danny looked like he was about to join us. I caught his eye and silently signaled him to stay put. Hooking my arm in Louie's, we turned to exit.

"Wait!" Earl called out. "I'm sure we can work something out."

My gamble paid off. There was only one other woman in the room beside myself, I was hedging my bets they weren't willing to lose any potential female recruits. After check-in was complete, we set up camp in four empty seats near the back.

While Earl arranged a series of pamphlets and books on the registration table, the gray-suited man positioned himself in front of the blackboard. "Good evening. Thank you all for coming out tonight. My name is Samuel." He looked at his wristwatch. "It appears our scheduled guest speaker has been delayed, so Earl and I will attempt to entertain you until his arrival. How many of you are familiar with Aleister Crowley?"

About half the room raised their hands, including Louie, Danny, Jack and myself.

Samuel pointed at me. "Roberta, can you tell us what you know about Crowley and your reason for attending tonight's meetup?"

Why was I being singled out? Was this his way of punishing me for getting Louie into the room? "Not much, really. I know he's on the cover of the *Sergeant Pepper's* album. He created his own tarot deck, wrote a number of books, and started a religion called Thelema. Guess I came here to find out more."

"So you're a seeker, good. You're in the right place to begin your journey and believe me—should you prove worthy—you're in for a wild ride." Samuel flashed a lascivious smile.

My skin crawled.

Danny raised his hand.

Samuel nodded at my brother. "It's Danny, right?"

"Yes. I have a question. Is this a satanic theology?"

Samuel sighed. "That old bugaboo has plagued us for years. Do Earl and I look satanic?"

A ripple of nervous titters moved across the room.

Louie spoke out, "No more so than little Damien did in *The Omen*." Judging by the look on his face, I think his sudden outburst surprised him.

Samuel and Earl glared at Louie. I was expecting them to kick him out when they were distracted by a knock on the door. Samuel looked down at his smartphone and appeared to be scrolling through texts. He nodded at Earl, who rose from his seat and opened the door a crack.

My view was obstructed, but I overheard a familiar-sounding voice. "My husband's attending to an urgent matter at the temple, he asked me to come in his stead."

Earl stepped aside and Lilith Darvell strode into the room.

CHAPTER TWENTY-FOUR

Cruella Darvell

SAMUEL AND EARL scurried about the room like a couple of lackeys. Earl took Lilith's red cashmere cape. Underneath, she still wore the same basic black Donna Karan ensemble from earlier in the day. Samuel hurriedly filled a glass tumbler with water.

Lilith appeared accustomed to deferential treatment. She walked over to the blackboard at the front of the room and picked up a piece of chalk. "My name is Lilith C. Darvell. I'll be filling in for my husband, Rev. Lucious Darvell, this evening." She turned and wrote "MINERVAL DEGREE (0°)" on the board behind her. "This is who you are," she said, pointing at what she had written. "Minerval Initiates at the degree of zero. Or as I prefer to say—you are nothing. Those of you whom we choose to accept will be given the opportunity to become *SOMETHING*—something greater than you ever imagined."

She certainly doesn't beat around the bush. I was expecting at least one or two people to be offended by her harshness and walk out. A glance around the room proved the complete opposite to be true. Most of the attendees, including my trio of males, appeared enraptured. It was obvious to me she was playing to a crowd of highly suggestible subjects.

Lilith continued, "Though it took only one sponsor to admit you to this gathering, two members will be required for full admittance—with the exception of the women in the audience. I will personally evaluate and refer all female initiates on the path."

Earl took Lilith aside and whispered in her ear.

"Mr. Louie Lopez, please come to the front." Lilith peered out into the room.

"I think this is the end of the road," Louie whispered as he made his way past me.

"Samuel will be passing out membership applications and fee schedules, while I attend to some business with Mr. Lopez."

Lilith and Earl took Louie aside. After a brief confab, Lilith sat Louie down in one of the chairs behind the table filled with reading materials.

"I would now like to speak with Ms. Roberta Law," Lilith announced.

Jack and Danny looked at me like I had been called to the principal's office.

I got up from my seat. "Wish me luck, guys."

"Good evening, Ms. Law." I could feel Lilith scrutinizing me. "We can't seem to get enough of each other today."

"It does look that way," I said.

"I understand two members of your party," Lilith looked down at the reservation list, "a Mr. Hensler and a Mr. Law, were sanctioned by Don Pardo."

I nodded my head.

"Is Mr. Law your husband?"

"No, he's my brother."

Lilith looked over at Danny and Jack—then Louie—then me. "If it helps any, I *do* know Don Pardo."

"How did you come to know him?"

"We met at his shop, Pardo's Potions." I pointed at Louie. "His aunt introduced us."

She took out her smartphone. "So if I was to text Don Pardo right now, he'd know who you are?"

"Well, we only met once. But if you tell him I'm the woman Lupe Lopez bought the Mano Fico for, I'm sure he'd remember." I pulled the necklace out from underneath my turtleneck. "It looks something like yours."

Lilith touched the red hand-shaped charm hanging from the gold chain around her neck. Though similar to my black onyx amulet, there were noticeable differences. The index and little fingers of her piece were extended, while the middle and ring fingers were curled in to the palm. My Mano Fico was more of a fist shape, with the thumb thrust between the curled index and middle fingers.

"This is a coral Mano Cornuto—a wedding gift from my husband. It appears we have more in common than a penchant for black outfits."

"I'm not sure I know what you mean."

Lilith tapped her Mano Carnuto against my Mano Fico. "Our mutual interest in the darker side of life." She gestured at Samuel. "Mr. Lopez may stay. Please make sure he receives a membership application."

Louie took the form he was handed and returned to his seat.

"Guess I'll rejoin my party," I looked at Lilith, "if that's all right with you."

"Just a minute, I'd like you to have something." She picked a book up off the sign-in table. "I'd like you to read this as soon as possible."

I took the volume from her; it was a copy of Crowley's *The Book of Lies*. "Thank you, but I already have a copy." Sure, if you want to get technical, it was currently in the possession of the LAPD.

Lilith was pleased to hear this. "Wonderful, you'll be my protégée." She handed me another book. "*The Book of the Law* is the central scared text of Thelema. It was dictated to Crowley by a discarnate entity."

Enough with the discarnate entities, already. "I'm not really much of a joiner."

Lilith looked insulted by my remark. "Then why are you here?"

I had to tread lightly, so as not to alert her about our search for clues to Cissy Forrester's whereabouts. "To keep an eye on my brother, he has mental health issues."

"You think only crazy people would come to this meeting?"

Didn't tread quite light enough. "No…no…I didn't mean to imply…Look, Danny only came here tonight because some imaginary Egyptian guy sent him."

"Your brother hears voices?"

"Yes, he's schizophrenic. Don't get me wrong, though. He's got things under control these days. I just want to keep it that way."

Lilith appeared confused. "You said a figment of his imagination brought him here."

"Actually, a figment of someone else's sent him," now was my chance to see if she was in cahoots with Lupe's resident medium, "an ancient Egyptian called Samir, via a trance channeler named Madame Mestral."

I waited for even the slightest telltale reaction from Lilith. If she did know The Madame, she was certainly adept at concealing the fact. "How fortuitous, I deal in rare artifacts and antiquities. Egypt is of particular interest to me..."

Earl broke into our conversation. "Most Holy, Most Illuminated and Most Worshipful Mother..."

"Can't you see I'm in the middle of something?" Lilith snapped.

"Please forgive me," Earl pointed to a clock on the wall, "we have to be out of the room by nine. A Toastmasters group is scheduled to meet in here right after us."

"Well, la-di-da. Am I supposed to be impressed by the imminent arrival of those suburban bores?"

Earl bowed his head submissively. "No, it's just that it's a quarter to nine and everyone has finished filling out their applications..."

"YES, spit it out!"

"You haven't told them much about the tenets of Thelema."

"Excuse me, Roberta." Lilith walked over to the blackboard, picked up a piece of chalk, and wrote something underneath her name. She turned to face the people seated in the room. "This is all you need to know." She underlined the quote on the board. " 'Do what thou wilt shall be the whole of the Law' is the message imparted from the ether to our founding prophet, Aleister Crowley. Simple and to the point, yet how many of you here tonight have the will to discover exactly where your will may lead?"

The hands of all the men shot up in the air. The lone female in the sea of male limbs sat there motionless, hands folded in her lap. I hadn't paid much attention to this woman when I first walked in, now I couldn't take my eyes off her—shortly cropped red hair, bright blue eyes framed behind Harry Potter style glasses. Seated directly behind Danny, she wore a green cable knit sweater with mom jeans and a pair of tan riding boots. It didn't take long for her lack of enthusiasm to register on Lilith's radar.

"Any man or *woman* afraid of exploring the limitless possibilities of their own power is free to leave, the rest of you should purchase a copy of *The Book of the Law* to read in preparation for your Initiation Ritual. We will review your applications and contact the candidates we have chosen by phone. Good night."

The men rose, making their way up front to turn in applications and purchase the Crowley text. The woman headed for the exit. Curious to find out what had brought her to tonight's meeting, I tried to catch up with her before she left, but was blindsided when Lilith took hold of my arm.

"You must come by the house for lunch tomorrow and be formally introduced to my husband."

"Could you give me a moment, I need to speak with the woman over there before she leaves." Careful Roberta, don't reveal your hand. "She asked for one of my business cards."

Lilith squeezed my arm even tighter. "Let her go, she's not right in the head. She shows up here every now and again, sits there and doesn't say a word. I should have the old cow banned, but I'm a softie at heart."

Yeah, like a steel marshmallow. "Isn't she past the expiration date for admittance to your organization?"

"I'd give her somewhere between fifty and death, but she never fills out an application so I haven't had to burst her bubble." Lilith let go of my arm and handed me a form. "Don't forget to turn in yours."

I took the paper and made a beeline for the door. The redhead was nowhere in sight.

Danny walked up beside me. "Looking for someone?"

"Have you seen the woman who was sitting behind you?"

"She was in an awful hurry to get out of this place." Danny pulled a flyer out of the inside pocket of his coat jacket. "She handed me this, it's about some Halloween show."

I unfolded the paper. It was a flyer advertising Wicked Lit's annual outdoor theater production on the grounds of the Mountain View Mausoleum and Cemetery in Altadena. They were doing a compilation of short macabre pieces—adaptations of classic stories by Edgar Allan Poe and H.P. Lovecraft—along with some original pieces based on local legends. One title popped right out at me: *Magic & Mayhem: The Haunted Forest Murders* by Caroline Foster.

CHAPTER TWENTY-FIVE

I Wonder What The Magus Is Doing Tonight

COULD THIS FLYER be the clue to Tommy's murder and Cissy's disappearance as foretold by Samir?

I ran up to Samuel. "Can I see the sign-in sheet?"

He gave me a suspicious look.

"I think I wrote down the wrong contact number."

"I love to see a woman eager to join our ranks." Samuel flashed a smarmy smile and pulled the list out of his briefcase.

The fifth name from the top was Caroline Foster.

"Is it correct?" Samuel asked. "Do you need a pen to change it?"

"Yes, a pen would be great!" I turned my back to him and scribbled Caroline's phone number on the palm of my hand. "Thanks." I handed him the paper and pen.

"You didn't change anything," Samuel said.

I feigned a laugh. "Silly me, I forgot to bring my glasses. Looks like I gave you the right number in the first place."

"Is that a cell number?" Lilith appeared at my side.

"Yes."

"Good. I'll text you my coordinates for lunch tomorrow."

"I have a pretty heavy schedule on Thursdays."

"Then dinner it is!"

This woman was not easy to shake. Of course, this might be a blessing in disguise—an opportunity to find out more about Cissy Forrester and why her mother acts like she never existed. "Will Bonnie Lawson be there?"

"I can arrange for her to be there if you wish."

Bingo! I played down my inner reaction in front of Lilith. "She seems like a sweet woman, such a tragedy the way she lost her son." I decided to test the waters. "And then for her daughter to disappear so soon afterwards."

"She told you about Cissy?" Lilith's sharp response had a defensive air.

I didn't think it would be so easy to trip her up. Now what do I say? If I tell her Bonnie told me, she'll be able to check back with her and discover my deception. Best to stick with an unverifiable white lie hidden in a half-truth. "No, she mentioned Tommy hiking up to The White City in the Sky. Since I'd never heard of the place I googled it and ran across some old newspaper articles about Tommy's accident. One of them mentioned Cissy."

"Well, aren't you the resourceful one?" Lilith appeared to be mulling over my story to see if it would pass muster. "Yes, it is a tragic tale." Then she switched gears and brushed the whole thing off. "Best to let sleeping sorrows lie. She has Lucious and me now."

I doubt Lilith's brand of warmth is much consolation. Hopefully, her Magus husband is the touchy-feely half of the duo. "Where is your husband this evening?"

"Unavoidably detained at the temple."

"There's an actual temple?"

"Of course! You don't think we're going to initiate people into The Solar Lodge at the back of a java hut, do you?"

"Solar Lodge? The sign on the door says San Gabriel Valley O.T.O."

"It's both. Think of it like the structure of the Roman Catholic Church—a parish within a diocese. Oh, I've said too much already." Lilith took me aside and spoke in a hushed tone. "Don't forget to bring your application with you tomorrow. It's just a formality. Barring any unforeseen circumstances, you're as good as in—my husband has a long-standing penchant for redheads."

Earl gave Lilith a cautious tap on the shoulder.

She turned to face him. "Yes, what is it?"

"Sorry to interrupt you again, Most Holy, Most Illuminated and Most Worshipful Mother." Somehow the title didn't quite fit the personality. "The Magus has sent a car for you."

"It better be an UberBLACK car, I told him I don't do UberX."

Earl draped Lilith's red cashmere cape around her shoulders. She waved one of her black lacquered talons at me. "I'll see you tomorrow night at eight sharp." Samuel and Earl breathed sighs of relief as she swept out of the room.

I rejoined Danny, Louie and Jack at the book table. They were the last ones making purchases.

"Aren't ya gonna buy any?" Jack asked.

"Don't have to." I reached into my handbag and took out the paperback Lilith gave me. "Our illustrious instructor gifted me this one."

"Look who's teacher's pet," Louie teased.

"More like creature's pet," I said half under my breath and out of earshot of Samuel and Earl. "Can we go now?"

"I wouldn't mind a coffee and a pastry," Danny said.

"Okay," I said, "but not here."

We reconvened out on the street.

"How about The Pie Hole? It's nearby—just over on Colorado." Louie smacked his lips. "I could go for a piece of their Bacon Buttermilk Coffee Pie."

"Is that a wise idea?" I looked at the Crowley book in his hands. "Don't you have an orgy to train for?"

"Judging by the other candidates in the room tonight, I don't want to make the cut. They weren't exactly my caliber of orgy participant."

"Why'd you turn in an application?" I asked Louie.

"Only to be polite. And I didn't want to have as much trouble getting out of the place as I did getting in."

Jack scratched his head. "I don't even know why I turned in mine. They seem kinda short on chicks. Though that Lilith broad's kinda hot—in a wrap-me-up-in-latex-and-whip-me kinda way." He shot me a look. "Not that you aren't, too, babe."

"Thanks, I'm allergic to latex."

"I'll go get my car," Louie said. "Jack, you can follow me to the restaurant. Anyone want to keep me company? Anyone meaning—Danny."

"We need to do a touch base first." I wrapped my arm around my brother; his stoic melancholy eluded the men. "You can drive him back to Lupe's later."

Jack got behind the wheel of his Thunderbird. I climbed into the back seat with Danny.

"Red, don't be sore 'bout that Lilith remark I made. Ya know I think you're da bomb."

"You're forgiven." I turned to Danny. "Are you all right? You were pretty shook up before we went in there."

"My mission failed. I didn't find out a thing about Cissy or Tommy."

"Don't be so sure." I pulled out the flyer the red-haired woman had given him. "This is the clue you were hoping to find."

Danny took the paper from me. "I don't understand."

"If my hunch is right," I pointed to the third title on the bill, "this play, *Magic & Mayhem: The Haunted Forest Murders,* is about what happened to Tommy the night he died. And the writer of this piece is using a pseudonym—Caroline Foster is Cissy Forrester."

Danny's mood changed in an instant—from forlorn to irate. "Why didn't you tell me any of this before I handed in my membership application to those fiendish people—and bought this vile book?"

"I was surprised you filled out an application, but you did look enthralled by Lilith's spiel."

"That was an act, dear sister. You're not the only one in the family with thespian tendencies. My plan was to play along until I received Samir's promised tidbit and then hightail it out of there."

Louie's SUV pulled up alongside us. "Ready to roll?"

"As soon as I get my shotgun gal back," Jack said.

I was relieved to get back in the front passenger seat, away from Danny and his impending snit.

Jack trailed the SUV as it headed south on Fremont Street. We'd gone about half a mile when Louie pulled over in front of a church.

I rolled down my window to see what was up. "Planning on getting in a late night confession?"

"Very funny. I think we're headed the wrong way, you know I have a lousy sense of direction. Give me a second while I look up the address."

"I remember this church," Danny said.

Danny and I were raised Roman Catholic. "Of course you do, I think you referred to it as the Whore of Babylon during your Holy Roller days."

"No, I recognize it."

"Maybe you attended Mass here when you became a Charismatic Catholic."

"I've never been here in person, but I know I've seen this place of worship somewhere."

Oh, no. Here we go. Another one of his hallucinations.

Danny tried to push the front seat forward.

"Hey, what are you doing?" I said.

"I need to get out."

"Well, wait a second. Let me get out first." I opened the door and exited the car.

Danny bolted out of the backseat.

"What's goin' on?" Jack said.

"My brother's having one of his episodes. I shouldn't have pushed him so hard earlier. The pressure's made him snap."

"Does he spit or vomit durin' one of these fits? Cause I had the T-Bird detailed this mornin'."

"Your prized possession will make it through in one piece. Though I'm not so sure I can say the same thing about Danny." I went to check on my brother's condition.

"This is Holy Family Church," Danny said.

I looked at the sign next to him. "So it is."

"You don't understand." Danny was getting worked up. "It's coming back to me...Lupe has a photo of this place. They held the funeral here."

I gently rubbed my brother's back. "I'm sure the person is now at peace."

"No, they are not!" Danny knocked my hand off of him. "For god's sake, Roberta, this was Tommy Forrester's parish!"

CHAPTER TWENTY-SIX

Babalon With An "A"

WEDNESDAY, OCTOBER nineteenth had been a whirlwind—jam-packed with surprise comings, goings, and serendipitous encounters. Starting right after midnight with Madame Mestral sleepwalking her way into my office—then Tommy Forrester's mother, Bonnie Lawson, making an unexpected appearance on my doorstep in the morning—followed by an encore performance of Angela Fowler's disappearing act—news of Lupe's Corvette being abandoned outside the Cobb Estate aka The Haunted Forest—a second encounter with the imperious Lilith Darvell, this time chairing the San Gabriel O.T.O. meeting—a brush with Caroline Foster, who might very well be the disappeared Cissy Forrester, at the very same meeting—and capping off the evening by stumbling upon Tommy Forrester's former parish, within spitting distance of the aforementioned meetup. I'm exhausted even thinking about it.

Though my appointment roster was tight on Thursday, it was a welcome change from the previous day's happenings. Before taking lunch, I checked my voicemail to see if anyone had tried to reach me while I was in session.

Dr. Jenkins had called. "Hi, Roberta. It's Carl. I just got off the phone with Angela Fowler, need to speak with you ASAP."

Damn it, I forgot to try him back yesterday and let him know she had given me the slip again. I wanted him to hear it from me first, rather than from a distraught Angela or a message left with the service. So much for any future referral business coming my way. I immediately rang his office.

"Dr. Jenkins, speaking."

Not accustomed to him answering his own line, I was momentarily dumbstruck wondering how I could finesse the situation.

"Hello? Is anyone there? Is this you again, Angela?"

I cleared my throat, "It's Roberta Law," and waited for the anvil to drop on any future client prospects.

"Oh, I'm so glad you caught me. I was about to head out to lunch with my secretary, it's her birthday."

Such a nice man. "Please forgive me, Carl. I did call about Angela Fowler yesterday. Your service answered and I didn't want to leave the message with them. I meant to call back, but I got caught up in…well, it doesn't really matter…there's no excuse for my unprofessionalism."

"There's no need to apologize, Roberta. Angela loved you."

"She did?"

"She sounded like an entirely different woman when I spoke with her today. I don't know how you did it. One thing's for sure though—hypnosis obviously agrees with her."

Except I never hypnotized her.

"You can expect to see a lot more referrals coming your way."

Thank you, Angela Fowler.

"It was a stroke of genius bringing in a therapy dog to work with her."

"Are you talking about Lex?"

"He's a beagle, I forget the name she mentioned."

"That's my Lex."

"He's your dog? Interesting idea—never thought about owning a therapy dog for my practice. I wonder how one would get along with my guide dog, Hank?"

Hmm, Danny never mentioned anything about Carl being blind. "I wouldn't call Lex a therapy dog, per se, though he has soothed the waters with a few clients here and there."

"I've got to go, we're running late for lunch. Keep up the good work!"

My next call was to Angela Fowler, I was curious to hear this sudden change in attitude for myself. "Sorry, I can't come to the phone right now. Leave a message," the voice was weak and hollow.

"Hello, Angela. It's Roberta Law calling. Dr. Jenkins told me about your rapid progress. Please call as soon as you get this to set up your next appointment with Lex and me." Maybe if I act like nothing unusual happened, so will she.

After retrieving some leftovers from the fridge, I ate lunch at my desk. Lex joined me in his usual spot—the blue-green oval rug that sat between my desk and the recliner.

Digging into my chicken salad, I watched Lex contentedly gnaw on a rawhide bone—his reward for helping me save face with Dr. Jenkins. "Keep up the good work, fella, there's more where that came from."

Lex stopped chewing, cocked his head, and looked up at me—as if to say, "Lady, it's going to cost you a lot more than some two bit bone from Costco."

"How about a possible promotion—a chance to get your name on the door?"

Lex barked twice and went back to his treat.

Taking that as a "yes," I doodled "ROBERTA LAW & LEX" on a notepad. I pondered the imaginary shingle for a moment, then crossed it out and wrote "ROBERTA LAW & SON." That beagle's not the only tough negotiator in the family.

The next item on my agenda was to contact Caroline Foster, the redhead at last night's O.T.O. meetup. I phoned the number she had written on the sign-in sheet. Turned out it was the box office for Wicked Lit. I bought two tickets for Friday night's performance of *Magic & Mayhem: The Haunted Forest Murders,* the play she had written—on the off chance I might run into her. Then I called Ben.

"California Center for Parapsychology and Paranormal Research. How may I help you?"

"Hi, Nancy. It's Roberta. Is your fearless leader around?"

Nancy Perkins was Ben's assistant. Her quintessential California blonde, surfer babe body belied the scientific proclivity of her mind—think Cheryl Tiegs meets Stephen Hawking.

"He's due back from lunch in about five minutes. Do you want me to check his calendar and see if he's available to go to the play with you tomorrow night?"

Oh, did I forget to mention she's also psychic? Think Cheryl Tiegs meets Stephen Hawking meets Nostradamus.

"If I was free, I wouldn't mind tagging along. Those Wicked Lit shows are a blast. Where better than a cemetery to get your Halloween spook on?"

"Sorry to hear you can't join us. I'm particularly interested in a piece called *Magic & Mayhem: The Haunted Forest Murders.*"

"Yeah, the old Cobb Estate has quite the checkered past."

Seems like all the natives know about this place. "When did you first hear about it?"

"Can't say for sure. It wasn't really on my radar until college when I did some research on it for a paper. Charles Cobb, a lumber magnet, had the Spanish-style mansion built in 1918. He lived there until his death in 1939. The guy was an active Freemason. In his will he deeded the entire 107-acre estate to the Pasadena Scottish Rite Temple. A few years later, the Masons sold it to the Roman Catholic Church and it was converted into a retreat for the Sisters of Saint Joseph. It went through a series of other owners until it was finally purchased as an investment property by the Marx Brothers in 1956."

"*The* Marx Brothers? As in Groucho, Harpo and Chico?"

"And Gummo and Zeppo. The Brothers left the mansion vacant for a number of years while trying to decide what to do with it. The property went into decline as various miscreants trashed the place. After that, the Brothers had most of the house demolished in 1959. It was auctioned off in 1971 and eventually wound up in the possession of the National Forest Service. Rumor has it lots of weird stuff has gone on there over the years. Everything from becoming a haven for drug addicts and delinquents—to being a favorite gathering site for the Klu Klux Klan and satanic ritualists. Nothing's ever been substantiated though."

"Wow, you sure know your stuff, Nancy. What was the topic of the paper?"

"It was a treatise on Jack Parsons—one of the founders of NASA's Jet Propulsion Laboratory—and his brief association with L. Ron Hubbard, prior to the founding of Scientology. I wanted to see if I could find any evidence of them performing their Babalon Working magic ceremonies on the grounds of the Cobb Estate."

"Babylon, like in the Bible?"

"No, Babalon, like in Mother of Abominations—replace the 'Y' with an 'A.' She's a Thelemic sacred whore goddess. It was a sex magic ritual they developed in their Agape Lodge in hopes of conjuring her up. Hang on a sec, Roberta, I think I heard Ben come in."

Wait! Don't put me on hold now! While I did want to talk to Ben and see if he'd be my date for tomorrow night, Nancy's sex magic dissertation had piqued my curiosity.

Ben came on the line. "Hello, Roberta. How are you doing this fine day?"

"Great. Would you mind putting Nancy back on?"

"She said you wanted to speak with me."

"I do—in a minute. We were in the middle of something."

"I'll leave her a note to give you a call when she gets back."

"Where'd she go?"

"Lunch. It's been so busy around here lately, we've been staggering our meal breaks. I'm testing Madame Mestral tomorrow. Are you still planning to drop by?"

I wasn't about to miss such a momentous occasion. "Yes, but that's not why I called. Will you come to the Mountain View Cemetery and Mausoleum with me tomorrow night?"

"Did someone you know pass away?"

"No...no...nothing like that. I have tickets for an event taking place there—a series of one-act plays. One of the pieces may shed some light on Tommy Forrester's death, I think the woman who wrote it is his sister."

"Looks like it's going to be a busy weekend for us. Mountain View Cemetery on Friday night and Sinai Temple on Sunday afternoon."

I had completely forgotten I promised to accompany Ben to his cousin's wedding. With all the ups and downs in our relationship, it seemed like he had asked me a lifetime ago. "Is that still on?"

"Of course, it's still on. Why wouldn't it be? You forgot."

"No, I didn't." Not wanting to come off as a total space cadet, I scrambled to come up with a plausible reason for my question. "I was wondering because it's been so long since you invited me."

"I asked you two months ago." Ben sounded annoyed.

Okay, Roberta, you may proceed to the head of the space cadet class. When in doubt—laugh. "Come on, Ben. Where's your sense of humor? I'm kidding. How could I forget your cousin Ava's wedding?"

"Aviva."

"Right...little Aviva."

"She's six feet tall."

"And I'm sure she'll make a beautiful bride." Change the topic already and abandon this sinking ship. "Did I mention I went to an O.T.O. meeting last night?"

"Which lodge?"

Subject changed—mission accomplished. "I forget."

"Star Sapphire or Golden Lotus?"

"It might have been Star—I'm pretty sure it had something to do with the solar system. Oh wait...that's it! I was at an introductory meeting for the Solar Lodge."

"Impossible," Ben's voice was somber, "it was disbanded years ago. A number of the members were wanted by the FBI for felony child abuse."

CHAPTER TWENTY-SEVEN

Over At The Darvell Place

F ELONY CHILD ABUSE in the back room of It's All About The Bean? I was having a tough time wrapping my head around what Ben had told me. "There weren't any kids present at the meeting and they have very strict age guidelines. Maybe they adopted the name without realizing its sordid history."

"Also very troubling," Ben said. "Any legitimately sanctioned lodge of the Ordo Templi Orientis would steer clear of the name. The Solar Lodge was never recognized by the O.T.O., it operated outside the confines of Crowley's Thelemic religion."

"Do you really think it could be the same group? When did this happen?"

"It was during the summer of '69, and took place in either San Bernardino or Riverside County. The papers dubbed it the 'Boy in the Box' trial because the Sheriff's Department found a six-year old boy chained inside a wooden box when they raided the group's compound. The whole thing ended up being over-shadowed by the Tate-LaBianca murders and the subsequent Manson Family trial."

"How come you know so much about this case?"

"My mother served as a judicial clerk on the case when she was in law school. It still irks her how so many of them got off with such light sentences or had charges dropped against them due to lack of evidence."

Ben's mother, Barbara Goldberg, is one of the top criminal lawyers in the nation. Her elegant, haute couture exterior conceals a formidable opponent—and not just in a courtroom. She gave me a taste of her take-no-prisoners style of interrogation when we first met and she agreed to represent Louie—innocent and facing a possible vehicular manslaughter charge because of a situation I had dragged him into. Barbara put us through our paces, grilling us until she was satisfied our improbable story panned out.

"I'm sorry, Roberta, I have to get off the line. George Noury's calling me any minute to pre-tape an interview for *Coast to Coast AM*. Promise me you'll stay away from these people until we get a chance to look into this further."

"Sure," I said with fingers crossed. "See you tomorrow."

I felt it best not to mention I was slated to have dinner that evening at the home of the Solar Lodge's Most Holy, Most Illuminated and Most Worshipful Mother—Lilith Darvell, and her Magus husband, Lucious. Lilith wasn't the warmest person I had ever met, but she couldn't possibly have been a part of this atrocious incident—she wouldn't be born for at least another decade. And Bonnie Lawson didn't pose a threat; she was too old and frail. All right, I had yet to meet Lucious. Though if he was Tommy's best friend, he'd be no spring chicken. Bottom line—I needed to find out more about Tommy's death and Cissy's disappearance. This invitation into the devil's lair, so to speak, was the quickest way to achieve my goal. Although, Ben did manage to scare me enough to not want to risk going in there on my own. I reached into the top drawer of my desk, took out Lilith's business card, and dialed the number.

"Lilith Darvell." Clearly she had no time for the frivolous niceties of life—like "hello."

"Hi, Lilith. It's Roberta Law calling."

"I texted my address to you this morning," she curtly responded. "Did you not receive it?"

"Yes, I did. Thank you. The reason I'm calling is to ask if it's all right if I bring a date along with me."

"We could make room for a boyfriend, I suppose." She didn't come across as being overly enamored with my request. "Or a girlfriend, if you're so inclined."

"Boyfriend," I replied.

"I do hope you both like Japanese food."

"Sure do." Louie is a sushi fanatic. We often meet for lunch at one of his favorite West Hollywood haunts, Sunset Strip Sushi. "Is there anything we can bring?"

"Yourselves will more than suffice." Lilith hung up.

Now to get Louie on board. My next client was due to arrive any moment. Figuring I'd save the lengthy explanation for when we were en route—I opted for a text. "R u up 4 sushi 2nite?"

"U r on —," Louie texted back.

"Meet me here @ 7:15," I typed.

"OK, G/F," Louie signed off.

I stared at the text—"Okay, girlfriend"—my old pal had no idea how appropriate his chosen moniker was for tonight's din-din.

* * *

"Where we headed?" Louie asked after I got into his SUV. "Asanebo in Studio City or 4 On 6 in Encino?"

"Neither," I said, buckling my seatbelt.

"Why not? Those are two of the best Japanese places in The Valley."

"We're not eating in The Valley—at least not this valley."

Louie shut off the engine. "I absolutely refuse to eat in Santa Clarita Valley."

I reached over and turned the ignition key. "Calm down, Anthony Bourdain. We've been invited to dinner at a private home."

"Who's private home?"

I plugged Lilith's address into the GPS. "The Darvell's."

"Never heard of them."

"Lilith Darvell is the woman who spoke at last night's meetup. Her husband, Lucious, is some bigwig in the San Gabriel Valley O.T.O.—he may even be the founder."

Louie still had not put the car into gear. "I don't know about this, Cruella didn't appear to be overly fond of me crashing their meeting. And I'm not so sure I want to meet her hubby, Lucifer."

"Tommy Forrester's mother, Bonnie Lawson, is going to be there. It'll give us a chance to feel her out some more about Tommy and Cissy. You're the one who dragged me into this mess in the first place. Remember?"

Louie acquiesced and pulled away from my house.

"There's one more thing you need to know—I told Lilith you're my boyfriend."

Louie slammed on the brakes. "What you do that for?"

"It was the only way I could think of wrangling you an invite."

"Is she some sort of homophobe?"

"I don't think she's too fond of people in general. It made sense to ask to bring along a boyfriend—more difficult for her to refuse."

Louie put his foot back on the gas pedal. "I'll accept that explanation."

"Gee, thanks."

"So what are our pet names for each other?"

"How about Louie and Roberta?"

"That's no fun. I'm going to call you, Toots."

"No, you are not."

"Come on, you gotta love it—it's so retro. You can call me...Cowboy."

"Like in the Village People?"

"You got it, Toots. I'm going to be your very own personal *Macho Man*."

* * *

The Darvell's place was in the estate area of San Marino. We stopped outside the wrought iron, electronic gates at the bottom of the driveway. A camera watched us from atop one of the stone columns, flanking either side of the entrance. Louie rolled down his window and pressed the speaker button on the intercom.

"Darvell residence," a male voice crackled through the machine

"Mr. Vega and Ms. Law," Louie said. "We're expected for dinner."

"I'm sorry, sir, only Ms. Law's name appears on my list."

Louie turned to me with a look of frustration. "I feel like an undocumented immigrant whenever I'm around these people."

I leaned over Louie. "This is Roberta Law speaking, Mr. Vega is my plus one."

"Gracias, señorita." Louie affected an exaggerated Spanish accent. "Will you be my sponsor?"

The towering black gates parted and we proceeded up the long, winding driveway for about a mile—past horse stables, an Olympic size swimming pool, and a tennis court—before reaching the actual house, a stunning-looking sandstone villa.

"I'm in the wrong line of work," Louie said, parking the car.

"Ditto."

As we climbed the curved flagstone steps, the front door opened and a butler—in full regalia—showed us inside. The high-ceilinged, stark white foyer was larger than my living room and kitchen combined. An enormous crystal chandelier hung above a black emblem, inset on the gray marble floor below. It was the same funky-looking Star of David insignia I had seen on Lilith's belt buckle the other day—a six-pointed star with a five-petalled flower at its center. Behind, a double winding staircase led up to a second floor balcony.

"Cocktails are being served in the drawing room, if you'll please follow me." Jeeves escorted us through one of the five doors leading off the entranceway.

I whispered to Louie, "Don't forget, I'm your girlfriend."

"Yes, Toots. Keep on nagging me like this and they'll be none the wiser."

We entered a wood-paneled sitting room. The place had the look and feel of an old British pub.

Bonnie Lawson—wearing a navy-blue, Church-Lady-style outfit with a string of pearls around her neck—was seated on a tan leather sofa. Lilith—in another black, Donna Karan number—was perched atop a stool, in front of the cherry wood wet bar near the back of the room. A handsome, distinguished-looking gentleman in his late sixties, stood behind the bar pouring drinks. He wore a black velvet smoking jacket with a red cravat. I half-expected Miss Marple or Hercule Poirot to waltz into the room and join us.

"Welcome to our humble abode," the bartender said. "You must be Roberta Law. I'm Lucious Darvell. My wife's description didn't do you justice," he scrutinized me in a way that made me feel naked, "and she gave you high marks all round." He poured an amber liquid from an oversized decanter. Something appeared to be coiled up on the bottom of the bottle. "May I interest you in a glass of wine?"

I moved nearer the bar to get a closer look at the wine decanter. "My god, is that a real snake inside there?"

"Yes," Lucious said calmly, "a cobra to be exact. I had a heck of a time getting it into the country. Something or other to do with the endangered species act."

CHAPTER TWENTY-EIGHT

Days Of Wine And Reptiles

WHY WOULD ANYONE want to import snake wine into the country? I mean, why would you even want to bother?

"I had to get a certificate from the manufacturer stating the snakes were farmed—not wild—before U.S. Customs and the Fish and Wildlife Service would let me bring in a single bottle. We Americans can be so provincial." Lucious was, undoubtedly, a determined connoisseur of this unusual libation. "I first sampled it when Bonnie's son, Tommy, and I were in Vietnam. He was starting his tour of duty, as I was completing mine. Poor fellow never developed the palate for it." Lucious held out a shot glass. "Please you must try some."

I surveyed the pale yellow liquid, unable to convince my feet to move any closer. It was difficult getting past the fact that, only a moment ago, my least favorite reptile was suspended in the dubious fluid.

Lucious poured a second glass of serpent slop and walked toward Louie and me. He seemed attuned to my wine sampling heebie-jeebies. "One must never pass up an opportunity which may never come your way again." He handed us the exotic infusion.

Louie and I went to sniff the contents.

"Ah...ah...ah," Lucious shook his head, "I suggest you hold your noses and knock it back as fast as humanly possible."

I could feel Lilith's and Bonnie's eyes on us—watching and waiting. Why weren't they throwing back a couple of these snake shots? Was this a test? Some kind of weird way to weed out inner circle undesirables?

Louie and I locked eyes, almost daring each other to be the first one in the pool.

"One other thing I forgot to mention," Lucious prodded, "this drink is heralded as a potent aphrodisiac in Asia."

That was all it took for Louie to jump into the water. "Wow!" His eyes bulged out of his head. "It sure packs a mighty punch. Your turn, Roberta."

"Yes," Lucious teased, "you don't want to leave your virile lover standing alone at the gates of Eros."

I'd almost forgotten I was trying to pass Louie of as my boy toy. "Here goes nothing!" I knocked back the shot. My body felt a tingling and then a numbing sensation as the alcohol—and quite possibly venom—charged into my blood stream. It was both invigorating and nauseating.

"Bravo!" Lucious shouted, while Bonnie and Lilith applauded. "I'll have the pool boy fire up the hot tub for later. Nothing stimulates the libido more on a cool night than an ounce or two of snake wine, followed by a dip in warm, sensuous waters."

I wasn't in the mood for a skinny dipping session with a group of orgy-prone strangers. Though there was something oddly alluring about Lucious. "Sorry, I didn't bring my bathing suit."

Lilith laughed, "I haven't worn a swimsuit since I was a child."
"I burn very easily."

"At night?" Lilith said with contempt.

I didn't miss a beat. "Yes, I have extremely sensitive skin."

"Touché!" Lucious seemed entertained by our verbal sparring. "Spoken like a true redhead."

A matronly woman in a black and white maid's uniform entered the room. "Dinner is served."

What is this, *Downton Abbey*? Butler, pool boy, maid—how much staff do these people employ?

We were shown into a long, rectangular room with red oak walls and floors. Along one side, four sets of arched French doors—also done in oak—opened onto an outdoor terrace. At the far end of the room, a fireplace blazed. An oil portrait of Lucious and Lilith in fox hunting garb, hung above the mantelpiece.

The Spanish Revival table could easily have sat twenty guests, yet our high-backed chairs were huddled close together at the end nearest the fire. Each place was assigned a name card. Lucious sat at the head of the table, with me on his right, and Bonnie beside me. Louie was seated to the immediate left of Lucious; Lilith was next to him.

"Cook has put together some of my favorite dishes for tonight's menu," Lucious said.

Add another servant to the list.

The maid placed delicate, floral-patterned soup bowls in front of everyone. I should say, they *appeared* to be soup bowls—the contents didn't look like any kind of soup I'd ever eaten. A clump of shiny, white, intestinal-looking matter sat nestled in some type of miso broth.

Lucious picked up a ceramic Japanese spoon. "For our first course we are having Shirako Soup."

Soup it is then! "What does Shirako mean in English?"

"White children," Lilith said with a dry laugh.

"Lovely." It was quite obvious I did not see the humor in her translation.

Lucious intervened, "Stateside it's usually referred to as Cod Milt Soup."

That's better. I liked cod, though I must admit, I'd only ever eaten it encased in batter with a serving of English chips. I dipped my spoon into the bowl. Mmmm—doesn't taste so bad. Creamy and buttery with a slightly sweet, briny note.

Louie appeared to be enjoying his as well.

"This tastes so different from the cod I've eaten," I said in-between mouthfuls.

"You're probably used to eating the flesh of the fish like most Americans," Lilith said.

"What's in this Cod Milk Soup then?" Louie asked.

"Cod *Milt*, not milk," Bonnie answered.

Louie wasn't the only one who had misheard the name of this dish.

"Exactly what is that?" Louie ate another spoonful.

Do we really want to go there?

"It's the sperm sac of a male fish," Lucious replied matter-of-factly.

The impact of those words hit my brain in mid-swallow. As Mr. Cod's nasty bits slid down my throat, it was all I could do to stop my gag reflex from kicking in. I put my spoon down, there was no way I was sampling another bite of the first course.

"Finished already?" Lilith savored another taste of the revolting chowder.

"I want to save room for the main course."

I looked over at Louie lapping up the remaining contents in his bowl. "What?" he said. "It's not like I haven't had worse in my mouth—sure beats menudo."

"It most certainly does, my man." Lucious patted Louie on the back. "Shirako has many health benefits, including stamina and virility." There was something suggestive about the way he let his hand linger on, and then caress, Louie's shoulder. "It doesn't hurt a woman's libido either," he said, turning his attentions to me.

Is all the food and drink in this joint a prelude to a hop in the sack?

Lilith appeared nonchalant about her husband's mealtime flirtations. It was harder to get a pulse on Bonnie. She seemed oblivious to much of what was going on around her. I couldn't tell whether this was due to her advanced age or some other reason.

The maid—I'll call her Hazel, since no one bothered telling us her name—came back into the room to clear away the first course. Can't say I was sad to see it go.

"Roberta," Lilith said, "last night at the meeting you didn't mention Louie is your lover. If Earl and Samuel had known they wouldn't have given you such a hard time of it. As Lucious always says, 'Thelema is for lovers.'"

I felt someone's foot rub against my calf. Judging by the wanton look in Lilith's eyes, I was pretty sure it belonged to her.

"Louie and I don't like to flaunt our affections in public." I moved my leg away from the wayward tootsies.

Lucious nodded his head. "I, myself, am an advocate of public reticence." He winked at me. "Providing it's accompanied by private abandon."

Hazel placed a salad plate in front of me; I carefully scrutinized its contents.

"Sunomono," Lilith said.

I waited for the inevitable stomach turning translation.

Lilith picked up her chopsticks and dug right in. "Cucumber salad."

Louie looked relieved. "I thought you were going to tell us it contained Sumo wrestler or something."

"We're saving that for the main course," Lucious quipped with a smile.

I wasn't sure his witty remark was entirely untrue. It seemed like now was as good a time as any to broach the topic of her missing daughter with Bonnie Lawson. "Lilith and I were discussing Cissy's disappearance last night."

A pregnant hush fell over the table. Lucious gave Lilith a withering look. Bonnie hastened the pace of her eating. Louie and I held our breaths, hoping we weren't about to be forcibly ejected from our seats because I dared to bring up the topic of the forgotten Cissy.

"I'm afraid Lilith may have given you the wrong impression, my daughter is not missing." Bonnie put down her chopsticks and blotted her mouth with a napkin. "Cissy had always been a problematic child. She and Tommy were very close, despite their age difference. My son's sudden death was difficult for the family to bear, but most of all for my daughter. Cissy experienced a complete break with reality at Tommy's funeral—throwing herself on top of the casket after it had been lowered into the ground. She was committed to Camarillo State Hospital and died there shortly before the facility closed in 1997."

"I never brought up the subject." Lilith was defensive. "As I recall, Roberta was the one who mentioned reading about Cissy's disappearance in a newspaper she stumbled upon online."

"Do you recollect the name of the paper?" Lucious asked. "I'm curious to find out, since the entire matter was handled privately by the family."

They had managed to back me into a very tight corner. Good luck wiggling out of this one, Roberta. I scrambled for a reasonable explanation. "You know I've been so busy lately, I don't actually remember. I might have conflated the pictures and obituary on Tommy's legacy web page with some other old news items I saw about missing kids in the area."

"You can blame me," Louie piped up in a misguided attempt to come to my rescue, "I can't keep my hands off her. She's exhausted from my never-ending sexual demands."

"Then you'll be happy to hear Lucious approved your application this morning." Lilith fondled Louie's hair. "I anxiously await your initiation."

Lucious interrupted his wife's budding love match. "Tommy doesn't have a legacy web page." He turned his unwelcome attention to Bonnie. "Does he?"

"Not that I know of." Bonnie looked scared and confused,

I was the next unfortunate to come under his Magus scrutiny. "What is the address of this unsanctioned site?"

Somewhere deep down I knew Bonnie Lawson had spun another tall tale. Cissy Forrester hadn't died inside any mental hospital—and I was the idiot who'd blown her cover.

CHAPTER TWENTY-NINE

Food, Goriest Food

"I REALLY DON'T RECALL the name of the website hosting Tommy's memorial page." And I didn't.

Of course, Lucious was no idiot. All he had to do was enter a few prime keywords and he'd find the site in a flash. I had to get to Cissy before him. My hopes were pinned on running into her at the next night's Wicked Lit performance.

"Does anyone mind if I change the subject from the dead to the living?" Lilith asked.

Bonnie looked relieved. "I'd like it very much."

Me, too.

Lucious nodded his assent, though he appeared mentally preoccupied.

"As I was saying before we went off on that pointless tangent, Lucious has approved Louie's application." Lilith trained her eyes on me. "Did you fill out the form and bring it along with you as I asked?"

Maybe we should go back to the previous topic. "It must have slipped my mind."

Lucious took my hand in his. "Don't worry, my darling. I've never been fond of red tape either." He looked at Lilith. "She more than meets my standards," he rubbed my palm with his finger, "I say we let her in and never let her go."

"Thanks for the vote of confidence," I extricated myself from his grip, "but there's a hungry beagle waiting for me at home." The wandering foot resumed massaging my calf.

"It's hard to resist a woman who's into animals," Lilith purred. "I second your motion, Lucious, and suggest we personally sponsor the two of them."

"Yes, I like the idea!" Lucious grabbed my hand and Louie's. "It's been a while since we've undertaken any couple-on-couple actions. I want them prepped and ready for the next initiation ritual."

It felt like Louie and I were being groomed as Thelemic sacrificial offerings. That was one altar I had no intention of kneeling at or lying on.

The maid returned with a large serving tray.

"At last, our main course has arrived." Lucious took the platter from Hazel and placed it in the center of the table. "Ikizukuri—you can't get sashimi any fresher than this."

A large fish, head intact, was splayed across a mound of crushed ice. Thinly sliced pieces of its pinkish-white, raw flesh were layered on top.

Lilith handed me a serving fork. "After you."

I was about to help myself to a piece or two when the fish opened its mouth and looked right at me. "Oh, my god! It's moving!"

"Of course it is," Lilith said. "Ikizukuri means prepared alive."

Suddenly awash in a sea of nausea, I pushed myself away from the table—Louie followed suit.

Unsteady on her feet as she was, Bonnie Lawson stood up and came to our aid. She scolded Lucious and Lilith. "What is the matter with you two? Why must you keep serving this appalling dish?"

"It's considered a delicacy in Japan." Lucious popped a piece into his mouth.

"Well, it's considered animal cruelty in America! I'm taking these two back to my place for some Pepto-Bismol."

"As you wish." Lilith was as unperturbed as her husband. "I'll be in touch with you two about requirements for the upcoming ceremony."

Bonnie Lawson escorted Louie and me to her peach-colored, stucco cottage behind the main house. Nestled in a grove of California black walnut trees, its cozy charm starkly contrasted with the decadent opulence of the Darvell mansion.

"Make yourselves comfortable, I'll be right back," Bonnie said.

We sat down on the Laura Ashley, cranberry and cream, floral sofa.

"I think that Lucious guy was coming on to me," Louie said.

"No shit, Sherlock. So was his wife. They were coming on to both of us."

Louie nodded his head knowingly. "Suburban swingers. I bet they're both hardcore Republicans."

"Among other things." My stomach grumbled queasily. "Ben will be happy to hear I'm reconsidering my stance on vegetarianism."

"Yeah, I'm with you. No more dining at Sushi On Sunset for me. I'm sticking to meat and potatoes—and I don't mean steak tartare."

Bonnie returned with two spoons and her bottle of bright pink relief. "You'll have to excuse Lucious and Lilith. Those two can get carried away. They've both spent far too much time overseas," she gave us a conspiratorial wink, "picking up strange habits."

I wondered what kind of hold Lucious and Lilith exerted over the fragile-looking, white-haired woman. Why was this embodiment of the traditional American grandma living in a little house behind the castle of Dr. Frank N. Furter and Vampira?

"Can I get you a cup of tea or anything?"

Here was my opportunity to speak with Bonnie, away from the prying eyes of Mr. and Mrs. Magus. "I'd love some."

I nudged Louie. "Me, too," he said.

"Me, three!" Bonnie clapped her hands together. "I think mint and lemon—both from my garden—along with some homemade gingersnaps should fit the bill."

"Can I help you prepare it?" I offered, getting up from my seat.

"Nonsense," Bonnie said, pushing me back down.

I was surprised by her strength.

"I'll be back in two shakes." Bonnie headed for the kitchen.

"Why'd you poke me in the ribs?" Louie complained.

"It was more of a light jab."

Louie rubbed his right side. "I don't care what you call it—it hurts."

"Sorry, but this is our chance to get some background on Cissy."

"She's dead. What more do you need to know?"

"She may have spent part of her life in Camarillo State Hospital, but my gut tells me it didn't end there." I stood up, visually sifting through the framed family photos scattered amongst random, church bazaar tchotchkes. "Either she was released…or maybe she even escaped…but she's out there somewhere and we're going to find her." Lots of snaps of Tommy—Bonnie doesn't seem averse to being surrounded by constant reminders of her dead son. Not a single shot of Cissy—odd. "I'm hoping this Caroline Foster hunch pans out."

"Do you really think she's Cissy?" Louie asked.

Bonnie reappeared with a full tray in her hands. "Think who's Cissy?"

Not wanting to alert her to my intentions, I needed to quickly conjure up a plausible cover story.

"We were gossiping about a trans friend of mine." Louie to the rescue! "Please forgive my pronoun faux pas. I should have said, 'Do you think he's a sissy?' I can't seem to keep up with all this LGBTQRST stuff. Frankly, I find it ridiculous."

Don't lay it on too thick, Mr. Macho.

Bonnie put the tray down on the antique sled coffee table. "A man after my own heart."

My sincerest apologies, Mr. Lopez. The lady *is* buying what you're selling. I sat back down on the sofa.

Louie wrapped his arm around my shoulders and pulled me in toward his body. "My Bobby likes to kid me about my old-fashioned ways."

He knows I hate it when anybody calls me by that name.

"What can I say?" Louie gave me a tight squeeze. "It's the way I was built—all man, through and through."

More like all bull. "Enough about us. Let's give our hostess a chance to tell us more about herself."

Bonnie passed me a cup and saucer. "I'm flattered by your interest, though I'm afraid I'm like your Louie. What you see is what you get."

You ain't seen *nothing* yet.

"May I offer you a cookie?" Bonnie held out a plate of ginger snaps.

Louie grabbed a handful and wolfed them down.

"Pardon my boyfriend, Bonnie. He has the manners of an ape. Must be all the excess testosterone coursing through his body."

Bonnie smiled. "I don't mind, it reminds me of Tommy. He always had a healthy appetite."

There's an inconspicuous opening. "Was Cissy a big eater, as well?"

Bonnie's expression went sour. "I don't recall." She turned pensive for a moment. "She was a silly girl...always getting into trouble."

Louie jumped in, "What kind of trouble?"

Bonnie looked from Louie, to me, and back again. She went to say something, then hesitated. I could almost see the wheels turning in her brain. "She was a terrible flirt, always enticing and teasing the men. It caused a lot of problems in the family, if you know what I mean."

"Wasn't she still a child when Tommy passed away?" I said.

"Old enough to know better. A regular nymphet, my husband used to say."

A very unpleasant picture was forming in my mind. "Her father called her a nymphet?"

"Stepfather—Edward Lawson was my second husband. I told you I remarried after Tommy's father died. Ed was Lucious' uncle. He took both boys under his wing, acting as mentor and role model. Cissy was an entirely different story—he tried to tame her, but she wouldn't submit."

The image in my head came into sharper focus—it was an ugly one.

CHAPTER THIRTY

Electromagnetic Blues

FRIDAY CAME NONE too soon. Bonnie Lawson's unguarded revelations of the previous night left me with an uneasy feeling. It turned out her second husband had been a member of the original Solar Lodge in its heyday. When I put together Edward Lawson's unseemly sexual assessment of Cissy with what Ben had told me about the Solar Lodge's sordid history, it led to only one conclusion—"The Boy in the Box" wasn't the only child victimized by this heinous organization.

I was anxious to see what would be revealed in Caroline Foster's play about The Haunted Forest murders that evening. If lucky, maybe I would even run into the playwright for an impromptu Q&A. And, to my surprise, I found myself looking forward to Ben's cousin's wedding on Sunday. Ben's mom, Barbara Goldberg, was sure to be there and I hoped to pull her aside to get the lowdown on the Solar Lodge abuse trial she clerked on back in the late Sixties.

But first, I was expected at the California Center for Parapsychology and Paranormal Research. I couldn't wait to sit in on Ben's assessment of the inexplicably high level of electromagnetic frequency emanating from Madame Mestral's body.

My Bug rattled into the underground parking at Ben's Westwood Village office without a minute to spare. I hurried upstairs to check in with Nancy at reception, and was surprised to see an unfamiliar face sitting behind the circular glass desk.

"Where's Nancy?" I asked.

"Why is that the first thing out of everybody's mouth?" The pimply-faced, red-haired fellow in his late teens seemed genuinely insulted.

"Forgive me, I didn't mean to be so abrupt." I extended my hand. "My name's Roberta Law, Dr. Cohen is expecting me."

"I'm Cary," he said, shaking my hand.

"Cary?" I probed for his last name, attempting to make up for my brusque first impression.

"The intern."

"Do you have a last name, Cary, the intern?"

He screwed up his face. "Grant."

Poor kid. Either his parents are big movie fans or a pair of sadistic practical jokers.

"There you are." Ben walked out of his office. "Madame Mestral is in one of the testing rooms—wired and ready to go. Nancy's walking her through a questionnaire. Cary, please hold all my calls for the next hour."

"Will do, Dr. Cohen."

"Like I said before, you can call me Ben."

"Okay, Dr. Cohen."

I followed Ben down a short hallway and into a room equipped with a two-way mirror. On the other side of the glass Mestral—seated in a black leather recliner—faced us. A series of electrodes were attached to her body. Nancy stood next to her, marking notes on a clipboard.

Ben positioned himself behind a bank of monitors. He motioned for me to pull up a chair and join him.

I surveyed the equipment lining the walls of the room. "Won't the electricity from all these machines affect Mestral's EMF reading?"

"Not the way I have it set up. The room on the other side of this glass is specially insulated and acts as an electromagnetic shield. That's why all the instruments taking readings are in here with us." Ben flicked the intercom switch on the console. "How's it going in there, Nancy?"

"All finished with the questions."

"Good. Why don't you join me in the control booth? I want to take some preliminary neutral readings before we begin the actual test."

"I feel like Frankenstein's bride," Mestral's lisping Spanish accent filled the room.

Ben chuckled. "Thank you for your patience, Madame Mestral."

"How much are you paying me for this again?"

Back to her favorite topic.

Nancy came into the room. "Fifty dollars an hour." She sat down on the opposite side of Ben.

"In that case, you may take your time." Mestral jerked forward in her seat. "This isn't going to hurt is it?"

Ben turned to Nancy. "Could you run in there and make sure all those wires are still in place?"

Nancy hurried back into the adjoining room.

"You have nothing to worry about Madame Mestral," Ben said, reassuringly. "This is as painless as a routine physical."

I signaled Ben to mute the mic and whispered in his ear, "She's doctor phobic, remember?"

"Why are you whispering? She can't hear you."

"Hello, Roberta," Mestral called out. "So nice of you to come watch my transformation into a guinea pig."

"I thought you flicked the sound off."

"I did."

"Then how come I can hear her and she can hear me?"

"You can hear her because I only shut off the outgoing sound from the booth. There must be a malfunction in the control button."

Nancy re-entered the room.

"Could you hear Roberta and me speaking while you were adjusting Madame Mestral's sensors?"

"Not a word. Why?"

"Don't torment yourselves, my dears," Mestral said. "I can't hear anything you're—" Her head drooped and bobbed, then snapped upward with a harrowing wail. "Of course, I can hear everything you say. The night might have a thousand eyes, but Samir has a thousand ears!"

Great. The Egyptian Henny Youngman is back.

"There goes my neutral reading." All of the needles in Ben's various gauges furiously bounced back and forth.

"She must be intentionally trying to screw up your results."

Ben shook his head. "It's not humanly possible."

I took his remark to mean it was *inhumanly* possible. But I was not willing to accept the premise behind Ben's conclusion. "She must have smuggled some sort of electrical gadget into the room. Did you strip search her, Nancy?"

"You're kidding, aren't you?" Nancy eyed me like I'd taken total leave of my senses.

"I think she's dead serious," Ben said. "Unlike us, Roberta is vested in a particular outcome."

"No, I'm not!"

"Of course you are, madam," a deep male voice with a British accent answered from the other room.

Looks like Ben and Nancy are in for the full Mestral experience. "Dr. Greystoke, I presume?"

"At your service." Mestral was relatively motionless, although Ben's readings were still going crazy. "If I learned one thing in my many years of medical practice, it was never presume anything. To borrow from the Bard—there are more things in heaven and earth, Miss Law, then are dreamt of in your philosophy."

"How many entities manifest through her?" Nancy asked me.

"I've only seen Samir, Dr. Greystoke, and an Irish maid named Sheila O'Hara."

"Were you looking for me, mum?" a soft, lilting brogue came from Mestral's mouth.

She's really on a roll today. "You don't happen to know a young woman named Bridey Murphy, do you?"

Ben was furiously scribbling notes. "Very funny."

"Let me see…I know a Bridey Flanagan…a Bridey Griffin… and a Bridey O'Neill. Don't believe I've ever had the pleasure of meeting a Bridey Murphy. Is she a friend of yours?"

Nancy laughed. "Never mind her, Sheila. She's trying to be funny."

"I'm sorry, Miss?"

"You can call me Nancy."

"I'm afraid I don't understand the joke, Lady Nancy. Begging your pardon, I never got much in the way of a proper school education."

"No need to apologize, Sheila," Ben added. "Do you mind if I ask you a few questions?"

"If it pleases, your Lordship."

"Please, call me Ben."

"Oh…I couldn't possibly…"

There was a camera trained on Mestral. Ben zoomed in on his subject. "Nancy, does it look like she's blushing to you?"

"It sure does."

Ben scratched down another note. "Am I making you feel uncomfortable, Sheila?"

"Do you mind if I call you sir, your Lordship?"

"Go right ahead."

The flush subsided from Mestral's face.

"How long have you known Madame Mestral?"

"It's hard to be precise, sir."

"Why's that?" Nancy asked.

"What seems like a few days to me, could be a few years to you."

"Ask her something we can verify," I whispered to Ben. "Something about herself, like her birthdate and where she was born—the name of her parents—how she died."

"Where were you born, Sheila?"

"Ireland, sir."

Ben anticipated my next request. "Could you be more specific?"

"County Sligo, in the village of Balleygawley."

"Do you recall the year?" Ben inquired.

"I remember death and starvation was upon the land for most of my childhood."

Nancy jumped in, "Was it during the Great Famine?"

"Too much content," Ben admonished Nancy. "You don't want to lead her to any conclusions, let her find them on her own."

"For sure," Sheila continued, "it was during the Great Hunger."

Ben shrugged. "Can't be sure if this is legit info or she's taking a cue from Nancy."

"Sorry, Ben," Nancy sounded contrite, "I should have known better."

"Don't worry, you'll catch on after you do a few more of these. I'll put a question mark next to this section."

"You'll do no such thing! Sheila's veracity is beyond reproach. My father would never have hired a liar or a cheat."

"Whoa," Ben said, "who have we got now?"

"My money's on an encore performance from Dr. Greystoke," I said.

"Dr. Neville Greystoke to be exact."

Nancy looked to Ben for approval before asking another question.

"Go ahead," Ben said. "But tread carefully."

Nancy nodded. "You knew Sheila O'Hara?"

"*Know*," Dr. Greystoke corrected her. "Sheila spent many years in my family's employ, when we were on the other side of the veil."

Nancy continued, "Are you aware of any other entities?"

"Well, there's Samir, of course. We all know Samir. As far as the others go, I've only met the ones working with Madame Mestral."

"Exactly how many of you are there?" I blurted out.

"If you want enumeration figures, I suggest you converse with Samir."

"Can you get him?" Ben asked.

"I'll see if I can find him, be back in a mo." Madame Mestral's body slumped in the recliner.

Ben, on the other hand, had never been so animated. "If we can verify any of the information we gather here today, this could prove to be the most astounding case of mediumship on record."

Nancy reviewed her notes. "I want to find out more about the entities not working with Madame Mestral. Who are they? Did they live on planet Earth? Or are they from some unknown place or other dimension?"

"The only way we can prove any of this is by researching historical records," Ben said. "And see if we can dig up anything on a Dr. Neville Greystoke, who had a family maid named Sheila O'Hara."

"A cousin of mine's a Mormon," Nancy said. "He's a genealogical whiz, I'm sure he could track down some documents for us."

"That's both the answer and the problem," I said.

Ben looked perplexed. "I'm not following you."

"Don't you see? If we can find information confirming the existence of these characters, so can anybody else. All Mestral had to do was memorize a few facts, learn some accents, and develop a vocal trick or two."

"I agree," Ben said. "It's good to be skeptical. But we should always leave the window open a crack for other possibilities."

Mestral's body stirred. "Sorry for the delay," Dr. Greystoke said. "Samir appears to have stepped out."

Precisely where does a disembodied spirit go to step out?

"He's working on a play," Greystoke added.

Is everyone in this town trying to break into the business? "Let me guess, he's starring in a production of *Aida*."

"No, I believe it's a mystery. My father was a friend of Verdi's."

"I was thinking more along the lines of Elton John and Tim Rice."

"Who? Never heard of them. Hold on a tick...What's that, dear?...Righto. Sheila says the piece is about some murders in a haunted forest."

CHAPTER THIRTY-ONE

Kung Pao Dining

THE MADAME MESTRAL Show came to an abrupt close after we were informed of Samir's deft getaway. Ben attempted to continue with his line of questioning, delving for more details and facts to help prove the actual nineteenth-century existence of Dr. Greystoke and Sheila O'Hara. But the entities faded away, as Mestral grew more and more restless.

Ben started shutting down the monitors. "We're going to have to bring this to a close."

"Free at last," Mestral reached for the wires on the left side of her head, "my days as a lab rat are over."

"If you could wait one more minute, Nancy will be right in to help you with those," Ben said.

"How did I do? Did I pass your test?"

"It wasn't designed to be a test," Ben explained. "You're taking part in a scientific study to determine the source of high EMF levels in humans, and if there is any correlation between those levels and an individual's psi abilities."

"Psi?" Mestral looked askance at Nancy. "What am I? Some old tire?"

"Not psi, as in pounds per square inch," Nancy removed the electrodes from Mestral, "psi, as in the unknown factor behind psychic phenomena."

"All I am is an empty vessel—a channel between worlds. I'm not a psychic anymore than you are, my dear."

"Actually, I am psychic," Nancy said. "My gift is ESP based, mostly mind reading stuff."

"So tell me, what am I thinking?"

This'll be interesting—now we'll get the unequivocal lowdown.

"Hmmm," Nancy pondered, "you're not an easy read. It's like listening to a radio hovering between stations. It's difficult to sort out the chatter."

"Tell me about it," Mestral groaned. "Some days I think the noise will drive me mad."

Ben and I entered the room.

"So, Dr. Cohen, which of my companions paid you a visit this afternoon?"

"You don't know?"

Mestral sat up. "I hear them all in my head, but I never recall what goes on once they pop out of me."

When my brother started hearing voices he was diagnosed as a schizophrenic. "So you don't remember anything about Samir working on a play?"

"Dear Samir," Mestral clapped her hands together, "he's quite the Renaissance man. How I would have loved to make his acquaintance back in ancient Egypt."

"Maybe you did in a past life," Nancy said. "Or perhaps you're part of a soul cluster like Jane Roberts and Seth."

Or one of the greatest con artists in history. "It's called *Magic & Mayhem: The Haunted Forest Murders*." I waited to see how she would react—play it cool or feign surprise.

"That's the show Danny and Lupe are going to tonight."

She was cool as a cuke—I was the one caught unawares. My brother never mentioned anything to me about this. "Ben and I are going, too."

"Well, I hope you all have a delightful evening." Mestral got up off the recliner. "I must be on my way."

I couldn't let her get away that easily. After all, she was the one—via Samir—who urged Danny to attend the San Gabriel Valley O.T.O. meeting the other night. She told him he would receive a message about Tommy's death and Cissy's disappearance—then, conveniently, Caroline Foster hands a flyer to him. Could this woman be The Madame's cohort?

"Will you not be joining us?" I asked.

"No, I have a previous engagement." Mestral headed for the door.

"I'm hoping to meet the playwright, Caroline Foster. Funny how she has the same initials as Cissy Forrester, don't you think?"

Mestral stopped in her tracks and put her hand to her head. "Excuse me, I'm feeling faint."

Ben rushed to her side. "Why don't you sit in the lobby and have a glass of water. Sometimes these tests can be overwhelming."

Nancy and I followed them into the waiting area.

"Rest here for a moment." Ben guided Mestral to the blue sofa beside the reception desk. "Cary, could you please fetch a glass of water for this lady?"

"I'll be fine," Mestral said. "It's one of my spells."

Strangely making its appearance when I mentioned Caroline Foster's name in conjunction with Cissy Forrester.

241

Cary returned with the water. "Here you go, ma'am."

"Thank you, young man. You're every bit as chivalrous as your dashing namesake. He and his mother, Elsie, often visit with Samir. They talk about how when Cary was a young boy his father, Elias, wrongfully confined her to a mental institution, so he could take up with another woman. Their precious bond—severed so prematurely in this world—has been reattached and is flourishing under Samir's tutelage."

"I thought the guy was dead," Cary said flatly.

"Is he really?" Mestral downed the water in one gulp. "Perhaps we are the dead ones." She handed the empty glass back to Cary. "Now where's my check? I have to go!"

* * *

After we wrapped with Madame Mestral, Ben followed me home in his silver Tesla. The Wicked Lit production was slated to start at seven-thirty, and we wanted to get something to eat beforehand. Ben suggested we dine vegan again, which was more than fine with me after last night's flailing fish fare at the Darvell's house of gastronomic horrors.

While Lex went for a walk around the block with Ben, I prepped his evening meal by adding some warm water to a fresh bowl of diet kibble. The expansion of the fibrous nuggets when wet was supposed to trick Lex into believing he was receiving a much larger quantity of food. It seemed to be working, the formerly bulging beagle never looked better. Now if I could only come up with the human equivalent of this miracle product, my dieting days would be over and I'd be financially set for life.

I freshened up, grabbed a sweater to wear for the al fresco night of theater, and was ready to go when my two guys returned from their neighborhood stroll.

On the drive to the restaurant, I picked Ben's brain about any conclusions he had drawn concerning Madame Mestral's purported otherworldly visitations. "So tell me is she faking it or not?"

"What took place in my lab today can't be faked."

"Didn't Houdini go around exposing these so-called spirit mediums? He never found one who's tricks he couldn't replicate."

"It isn't quite the same thing. He had firsthand experience like we did, but lacked the equipment to measure any phenomena. Being able to duplicate something doesn't necessarily mean it's a hoax. Why are you being so stubbornly cynical about this?"

I couldn't put my finger on why I was so reluctant to believe The Madame was the real deal. As a hypnotist, this wasn't my first brush with the paranormal. I'd already witnessed one young client spontaneously regress into what, undoubtedly, was a past life. But my gut instincts kept telling me there was more to this situation than met the eye—third or otherwise.

* * *

Real Food Daily in Pasadena was a short hop from the Mountain View Mausoleum and Cemetery in Altadena—where Caroline Foster's play was being performed. Feeling adventurous, I let Ben order for me. The Kung Pao dish he selected was organic and delicious.

Ben nodded at my empty plate. "I take it you liked my pick."

"Tasted just like chicken," I teased.

"What do you think of this dish?" Ben fed me the last forkful of his Lasagna Napoletana.

I savored the satisfying bite. "What can I say? Another winner."

Ben took a long, slow sip of biodynamic Pinot Noir and looked deeply into my eyes. "I think we're ready to take this relationship to the next level."

If I'd known being a good girl and eating my veggies was all it took to kick-start our stalled romance, I'd have jumped aboard the Good Ship Legume ages ago. "I'm game!"

"Good. Cake? Pie? Or pudding?"

I had another type of dessert in mind—non-fattening, calorie burning, and cooked over an intensely hot fire back at my place later. "I'm watching my waistline." Someone has to.

"We could share something."

How about a bed?

"Come on, you know you want to dig into a gooey pot of pudding with me." Ben smiled that annoying, inscrutable smile of his. "The night is young, we may need some extra energy before the evening's through."

Well, if we're swapping clichés. "Hope springs eternal."

* * *

"This is the most amazing chocolate pudding I've ever tasted!" I licked what was left on my spoon. "There's no way this stuff is dairy free."

Ben wiped the corners of his mouth with a napkin. "Oh, but it is my suspicious little omnivore."

"Not possible," I shook my head, "it's too rich and creamy."

"We'll have to make a date to come back, so you can taste their Banana Maca milkshake. It's out of this world."

"Milkshake?"

"Hemp milk."

"No wonder it's out of this world," I laughed. There was something oddly charming, albeit frustrating, about this chaste adolescent mating ritual we were engaged in. Right down to the fact we had slated a soda fountain treat for our next rendezvous.

Ben picked up the check. "Since you bought the theater tickets, this one's on me."

We left the restaurant and walked along Del Mar Boulevard to the Shoppers Lane parking lot.

"What are you going to eat at this wedding on Sunday? Unless your cousin's a vegetarian."

"She's kosher, which is about as exotic as her dietary restrictions get."

"I smell a brisket in your future."

"Don't worry about me, I'm situationally flexitarian."

"Mmm, I'd like to get in on one of those situations."

As we crossed the alley bordering the lot, a car bolted out of nowhere—narrowly missing us. A yellow car—a vintage Corvette—Lupe Lopez's Corvette. I caught a glimpse of the driver before she zoomed off. It was Madame Mestral. She looked panicked and confused.

CHAPTER THIRTY-TWO

Hotel Camarillo

"ARE YOU ALL right?" Ben caught hold of my arm. "That was a close call."

"Did you get a look at the driver?"

"No, I barely saw the car."

"It was Madame Mestral. Do you think she's on her way to the play?"

We jumped into the Tesla.

"Isn't that a bit of a stretch?" Ben started the engine. "I thought she said she had another commitment this evening."

"Perhaps she had a reason to change her plans. You saw how she suddenly fell ill in your office when I mentioned Caroline Foster and Cissy Forrester in the same sentence. She knows I'm on to her clairvoyant confidence game."

"Maybe something else is going on." Ben pulled out of the lot. "I think she's legit."

We headed in the same direction as the Corvette—west on Del Mar and then right on Lake. Though it wasn't much of a pursuit, since Ben wasn't willing to risk life and limb to see if my hunch was correct.

I lost sight of the car long before we hung a left on Woodbury Road. "Where'd she go to?"

"She might have turned at Maple and hopped onto the 210. Either way, if she's going to the Mountain View Cemetery, we'll catch up with her soon enough."

Our arrival at the cemetery coincided with the arrival of Danny, Louie and Lupe. Ben parked next to Louie's SUV.

"I didn't know you were coming also," I said to Louie.

"Lupe loaned Mestral her car again. And I don't like her rattling along the freeway in that purple tin can Danny drives."

"No need to cast aspersions on a vehicle which has acquitted itself quite admirably all these years," Danny said defensively.

I looked at my brother, not sure if his feelings about his car were due to his mental health problems or his innate quirky personality. "It's a Gremlin, Danny, not a Rolls." There wasn't any sign of Lupe's Corvette in the lot. "Is Madame Mestral planning on joining us at some point?"

"I don't think so," Lupe said. "She needed to attend to a personal emergency."

Like tipping off her friend, Cissy Forrester, her Caroline Foster cover was blown?

We followed a stream of other patrons making their way into the staging area for the evening's ghoulish entertainment. The one-hundred-year old, plus change, cemetery, mortuary and crematory was still family owned and operated by the descendants of Levi W. Giddings, an early resident of frontier Pasadena. Its beautiful arboretum-style landscaping, complemented by the surrounding San Gabriel Mountains and stained glass filled stone buildings, was the perfect locale for the macabre line-up of short plays.

Since the three pieces on the bill were performed simultaneously in different parts of the grounds, the audience was divided up. Each party of attendees was given a color-coded ticket. We were in the green group.

Everyone gathered in an outdoor garden, which served as a holding area. Carnivalesque entertainment diversions, designed to keep people occupied between performances, were going on all around us.

While waiting for our group to be called, I looked for Mestral among the roving gypsy fortune-tellers making their way through the crowd. She was nowhere to be found, though I did spot a familiar face working the concession stand.

"Isn't she one of the members of Madame Mestral's Abundant Beings Church of Divine Energy?" I pointed out the Goth girl wearing a skeleton apron and bagging fresh popcorn to Danny.

"Yes, that's Electra." Danny waived to the girl in black. "You met her at the Seers Symposium on Monday night."

"I'm going to get some water. Anybody else want something?"

Danny shook his head. Louie and Lupe were busy getting their palms read. And Ben had gone to find a restroom.

Electra recognized me right away. "You're Danny's sister, right?"

"Yes, I am. How much for a bottle of water?"

"Flat or fizzy?"

"Flat."

She handed me a bottle of Arrowhead Mountain Spring Water. "It's on me. Any sister of Danny's…"

"Is a sister of yours?"

She laughed, "Sure, why not? It's all just one big brotherhood or sisterhood of man."

That line of thinking could rack up quite a tab by the end of the evening. "You didn't happen to see Madame Mestral anywhere around here?"

"Did she come along with the rest of you?" Electra's voice went up in pitch. I wasn't sure if this was a bad thing or a good thing.

"No, I saw her in the area earlier and thought she might have been headed this way."

"Too bad. I wanted her to meet my friend, Caroline. Those two remind me so much of each other. I don't know why, they look nothing alike. Must be a past life or an aura thing."

"Are you talking about Caroline Foster?"

"Yeah, do you know her?" Electra continued filling bags with popcorn and stacking them on a rack next to the big, red popping machine.

"Sort of. We've not been officially introduced. She's the one who told Danny about this show." Okay, she shoved a flyer at him; I exaggerated somewhat. I'm sure my new little sis will forgive me. "Is Caroline here tonight?"

"I saw her coming out of the makeup room before I started my shift."

"Is she in the show?"

"No, she's too shy. She does the special effects makeup."

"A playwright and a makeup artist. She's quite the talented woman."

Electra put down the silver popcorn scoop and drew in close to me. "Can you keep a secret?"

I nodded my head.

"She isn't a writer. A friend asked if she could use her name. No one's ever met the real author. The director would tell Caroline about any dialogue changes he wanted and she would relay the info to her friend. Kinda cool in a creepy kinda way, huh?"

"I don't follow you. What's so creepy about it?"

"Hey, Electra!" a vampire selling raffle tickets called out. "Can you give me a hand over here?"

"What about the refreshments?" Electra shouted back.

"Mandy's on her way over to relieve you."

"Okay, be right there!" Electra turned back to me. "Gotta go."

"Wait," I said. "You haven't told me what the creepy part is yet."

Electra put her right index finger up to her lips, "Shhh!" She took off her apron and handed the popcorn scooper over to a gypsy girl. "Here you go, Mandy. Be careful, the kettle inside that thing is super hot." Electra took me aside before heading over to help the raffle ticket guy. "Caroline told me—except for the names—the play her friend wrote is one hundred percent the real deal. The writer wants to bring the killer to justice, but fears for her own life because she witnessed the entire thing."

"Why not go to the police?" I asked.

"She tried to years ago, but they went all *American Horror Story* on her."

"You've lost me again."

"Nobody believed her and she got locked away in some nut house in Camarillo."

CHAPTER THIRTY-THREE

Graveyard Rock

FROM WHAT I learned from Electra, Caroline Foster's timid playwright friend fit the profile for Cissy Forrester. My dilemma was whether to believe she was the genuine article or a con artist in cahoots with Madame Mestral. If she did pan out as legit, I would have no choice but to admit The Madame was communicating with the dead after all.

Ben came up behind me. "You'll never guess who I ran into in the men's room?"

"Madame Mestral?"

"No, Jack Hensler."

"What's he doing here?"

"He's performing in one of the shows tonight."

"October is a busy month for Hell's Papas."

"The band's not here. He got a last minute call to sub for a sick buddy of his."

"Did he say which show?"

"No, he had to rush into makeup."

"Since we're talking about surprise encounters, I bumped into one of Madame Mestral's disciples. Turns out, Electra—that's her name—is friends with Caroline Foster. According to her, Mestral and Caroline have never met each other."

"I guess Madame Mestral wasn't on her way here after all."

"No, but that isn't the interesting part. Apparently, Caroline Foster didn't write *Magic & Mayhem: The Haunted Forest Murders.* She's letting a friend use her name. A friend who was a witness to Tommy Forrester's murder."

Ben gave me the look. "You're jumping to conclusions again. How do you know this play has anything to do with Tommy's death?"

Fair enough. I was making a leap with my assumption. "I'm going with instinct, not logic, on this one."

"Trusting your sixth sense for a change." Ben slipped his arm around my waist, "You know I'm a big believer in the power of a person's intuitive capabilities."

"Come on, lovebirds," Louie called out, "the Green group's being led inside."

We followed the others into a small, old chapel with carved wooden pews. The first piece we saw was an adaptation of "In the Court of the Dragon," a short story by Robert W. Chambers, about a man besieged by malevolent forces in the midst of a church service. It was made all the more chilling because the audience served as the protagonist's fellow congregants. Approximately thirty minutes in length, after it was over we were brought back to the holding area.

"Is that it?" Lupe asked. "They didn't even mention my Tommy."

"We still have two more plays to see," Louie said.

"Why did they bring us back here?" Lupe did not look happy. "My feet hurt."

"Danny told you we would be doing a lot of walking tonight. Why did you insist on wearing such ridiculous shoes?"

We all looked down at her stiletto-heeled, laced from toe-to-thigh, leopard-patterned boots.

"These are for walking, Luis. You can tell by all the little animal spots. People wear them in Africa—they're safari boots."

"Only if Lou Reed's your safari leader." Louie's remark went over Lupe's head.

"I think the plays have varying running times, so they use this as a place for the audience to wait until all the groups are done." I spotted a cement bench nearby. "You can sit here until they call us again. Let me go find out what we'll be seeing next."

Our group must have been the first to return because I noticed a number of people streaming in through a stone archway on the opposite side of the garden. I flagged down one of the ticket takers. "Excuse me, do you know which play my group will be seeing next?"

The young man dressed as a nineteenth-century undertaker looked at my ticket. "Green's scheduled to be in the mausoleum, which means 'You Know They Got a Hell of a Band' is next up."

"Thanks." Must be the one Jack's in. I was really getting anxious, and maybe more than a tad nervous, to see The Haunted Forest piece supposedly written by Caroline Foster. If Caroline's anonymous friend turned out to be the long lost Cissy Forrester, her play could unravel the real story of what happened up at the old Cobb Estate back on that fateful October day in 1966.

Making my way back to the others through the ever-thickening crowd, someone caught a hold of my arm. Assuming it was Ben, I turned to give him a playful slap. "Elvis?" I said to the man in the white jumpsuit.

"Your very own personal hunk of burnin' love, darlin'."

"Jack?"

"King Jack to you."

It was incredible how much he looked like the real Elvis, somewhere in-between his svelte and portly days.

"What are you doing out here? Ben said you're performing in one of the plays."

"I am. Ya don't think I go round lookin' like this, do ya? I came to grab somethin' to eat between shows." Jack held up a bag of popcorn. "This gig's a last minute thing, I rushed right over without eatin' dinner. Want some."

I shook my head. "Not hungry, thanks. Are you acting, singing, or both?"

"A bit of everything. The play's based on a story by Stephen King. It's kinda cool. A couple on a road trip get lost and wind up in a strange town called Rock and Roll Heaven. Elvis is the mayor. I ran lines with my buddy, Frank, when they were rehearsin' the play—so I already knew the part. It was a no brainer to call me when he got sick. Plus, I fit the costume."

"Your makeup job is pretty impressive. If you hadn't opened your mouth, I would have never recognized you."

"Yeah, Caroline—the makeup lady—is first class."

I needed to meet this woman and find out more about her secretive playwright friend. "Will you introduce me to her after tonight's performance?"

"I'd love to, babe. But I got the feelin' she's not plannin' on stickin' round till the end. She told us to be careful because we'd be responsible for any touch-ups between shows." Jack scarfed down the remainder of his popcorn. "Gotta vamoose—looks like they've gathered together the last of the tribes."

The garden was overflowing with people. And the ushers were directing the different color groups to their various departure points. I was going to ask Jack where the makeup room was located, but he disappeared into the crowd. The Green group was assembling in front of the outdoor columbarium near the bench Lupe was sitting on.

"Sorry I took so long," I apologized to my concerned theatre companions. "We're seeing the show Jack's in next."

"Is that the one about the alleged murders in The Haunted Forest?" a female voice with a cool, cutting edge asked.

I looked over my shoulder, standing behind me were Lilith, Lucious and Bonnie.

"Good evening, Roberta," Lucious said. "Thank you for the heads up on tonight's theatricals. It truly is amazing what surfaces when one enters a few choice words into a search engine."

My worst fear realized. Looks like my big mouth put them onto Cissy Forrester's trail. Of course, as I had come to realize, being on her scent and actually finding her were two divergent propositions. "I didn't notice any of you in the audience for the first play."

"Punctuality is a bourgeois pursuit," Lilith said dismissively. "Aren't you going to introduce us to your friends?"

A tricky request—since they think Louie's my boyfriend, and I neglected to tell Ben about my dinner with the infamous Solar Lodge's head honchos. "Sure…well… you all know Louie. This is his aunt…I mean…his niece, Lupe. And this here is my brother, Danny."

"And who is the gorgeous hunk of manhood standing next to you?" Lilith said in a deep-throated, seductive voice.

"Do tell," Lucious joined in on Lilith's lascivious sentiments.

"Ah…this is…Ben…"

"Cohen," Ben jumped in, "Ms. Law and I are colleagues." He gave me a conspiratorial wink.

I wasn't sure if Ben was picking up on my vibe or reading my mind, either way I was relieved.

"Are you a hypnotist, too?" Bonnie asked.

Lupe answered her, "No, he's a parapsychologist."

"I'm Lilith, by the way. And this is my husband, Lucious, and our dear friend, Bonnie." She took Ben's hand. "You must come to the next meeting of our group. My husband and I love to collaborate with promising candidates."

"And which group is that?" Ben asked.

I needed to change the subject—and fast. Ben warned me to steer clear of the Solar Lodge. I didn't want him finding out from anyone but me that I'd chosen to completely ignore his advice. "Lilith deals in artifacts and antiquities, she's especially interested in ancient Egypt."

As I hoped, Lupe picked up on my cue. "You must meet Samir."

"You're the lady who channels the entity Roberta told me about," Lilith said. "I would love to book a session with you."

"You have me confused with Madame Mestral," Lupe said. "She lives with Danny and me in Angelino Heights."

"I take it you and Danny are lovers?" Lucious surmised with his one-track mind.

Lupe appeared flattered by the absurd assumption. "No, we've never taken our relationship to the next level."

Danny looked confused, probably trying to figure out what level they were actually on.

"He's my lover," Louie reflexively answered.

"You're the lover of the brother and the sister?" Lucious perked up. "Is this a ménage à trois?"

Realizing he'd put his foot in it, Louie tried to cover as best he could. "No…it's more of an open relationship."

"We better rethink your application, Danny," Lilith said. "I may have underestimated you."

"No need," Danny drew back, "my schedule's quite tight. I signed up for a rather intense ukulele class."

Lilith turned her attention back to Lupe. "So how do I book a channeling session with your Madame Mestral?"

"She's been cutting back on her private sittings due to personal health reasons. We're holding a seance on Halloween, I think there are still some empty chairs."

"Book us in for a party of three," Lucious said.

"All people holding Green tickets, please follow me," an usher announced.

As the crowd pushed forward, I fell back. This might be my only chance to meet with Caroline Foster and I wasn't going to miss it.

Ben noticed me lagging behind. "Shake a leg, Roberta."

"I'll catch up with you later and explain everything," I said to Ben, as he blended in with the others. Now all I had to do was figure out where the makeup room was located. Luck was on my side, Electra was back behind the concession stand.

"You're going to miss the next play," Electra said.

"I need to speak with Caroline Foster before she leaves. Her playwright friend may be in danger."

Electra looked worried. "I'll take you to her, as long as you don't let on I told you anything about her not being the writer of the play."

"Deal."

We walked into the main building—up and down marble staircases—through one long hallway after the other, lined with niches containing cremated remains—until finally arriving at what appeared to be a storage room. The door was open a crack and the room was dimly lit.

"If she's still here, she'll be in there." Electra left me to my own devices.

I pushed open the creaky, wooden door.

A lone woman, in a floppy black hat, sat on a chair across from the makeup mirror.

"Caroline?" I said.

The woman swiveled round to face me. It was Angela Fowler.

CHAPTER THIRTY-FOUR

All Things Dark And Dreadful

I WAS SO FLABBERGASTED, "Angela?" was the only word I managed to get out of my mouth.

"Dr. Law what are you doing here?" Even though it was nighttime and she was sitting in a dimly lit room, her eyes were still hidden behind her trademark shades.

"It's Ms. Law. I'm a Certified Hypnotherapist, not an MD. Please, I'd prefer it if you call me Roberta. I'm looking for Caroline Foster."

"You just missed her."

"Are you working on this production, too?"

"I helped with some of the set and costume design. Totally off the books though—not even a program credit. It was as a favor to my old friend, Caroline. I owed her one—big time."

Why? Did she let you use her name on the play you wrote? Is Angela Fowler really Cissy Forrester? She was referred to me by a psychologist, suffered from crippling panic attacks, refused to take meds, and had a paranoid fear of being followed. Her family wasn't in the picture and she hinted at a dysfunctional, possibly abusive, childhood parental relationship in my office the other day. She also had some kind of connection to Madame Mestral, which put her in the driver's seat of Lupe's Corvette on more than one occasion. But what happened to her fear of death and all things Halloweenish? Here she was hanging out at a cemetery and working on a macabre theatrical production in her spare time.

I tried to tiptoe into the subject. "Doesn't it bother you to be here?"

"Not anymore. I thought Dr. Jenkins told you about my break-through. I'm cured."

Looking at her sitting there all alone in the same getup she had worn to my office—trench coat, floppy hat, sunglasses—the word "cured" somehow didn't fit the bill.

"You got my message, then. I think we should schedule at least one follow-up to insure your success is long-lasting."

Angela was quiet and appeared to be pondering my suggestion. Or maybe not. To tell the truth, it wasn't easy to ascertain what was going on behind her protective disguise.

"I trust her…she think it's for the best," Angela whispered.

"Are you speaking to me?"

She lowered her voice and continued to talk under her breath. Though I couldn't make out a word of what she was saying, it sounded like she was in a heated argument with herself.

"Angela, are you okay?"

"She's fine!…I'm fine…" Angela's breathing was erratic. Her trembling hand grabbed onto her chest as she slumped into the chair.

I pulled out my cell phone. "I'm calling 9-1-1."

Angela grew frantic when she saw what I was doing. "Don't! Please god, don't!"

Fearing I might kill her, I put down my phone and ran to her side. "What can I do for you?"

She reached for my arm. "Be my friend."

My eyes welled up. Her pathetic plea was so desperate and spoke of an unfathomable loneliness. I squeezed her hand and her breathing steadied.

A few seconds later she sat up, acting like nothing had happened. "I need to use the ladies' room, if you'll excuse me." Angela rose from the chair and walked through a door at the back of the room.

I waited patiently, concerned for her welfare and hopeful I would be able to elicit more background information on her shrouded past.

"You gotta get out of here or I'll lose my job." Electra had returned. "They're about to change shows again. Sometimes the cast comes down here to touch up their makeup."

"Can I wait until Angela gets back?"

"Angela? Who's she?"

"A friend of Caroline's. She helped with the sets and costumes."

"Never heard of her." Electra looked at her cell phone. "People are going to start showing up here any minute."

"Let me knock on the restroom door to make sure she's all right." I headed for the door Angela had gone through.

"There aren't any facilities in there. It's a back exit. But keep going that way," Electra joined me, "we're less likely to bump into anyone."

The door opened into a shabby stairwell—Angela wasn't anywhere in sight. She'd given me the slip, yet again. I followed Electra back to the holding area, where I rejoined my party.

"You missed Jack's moment in the sun," Louie said. "He made such a convincing King of Rock and Roll, I'm going to get in touch with my German looky-likey pals on Monday and see if they can offer him any bookings on the Deutschland Doppelgänger Circuit."

"Aren't doppelgängers supposed to be doubles of living people?" Ben said.

"Elvis isn't dead," Lupe advised. "He's using the name of his deceased twin sibling, Jesse."

"I suppose Samir told you this?" Louie said.

"No, I read it in a newspaper at the grocery store. Mark my words, one day we will sing together."

Louie rolled his eyes. "Get out the disappearing ink."

"Where were you during the show, Roberta?" Danny asked.

I noticed Lucious, Lilith, and Bonnie were standing within earshot of us. "It's a long, complicated story. I'll fill you in later."

An usher wandered through the crowd. "All patrons holding a Green ticket, please follow me."

"Finally!" Lupe perked up. "I'm going to meet my Tommy."

"She does realize he's dead, right?" I said to Louie out of the side of my mouth.

"Since she's still holding out on Elvis, I'm not so sure anymore."

The audience followed the usher from the holding area to an outdoor location containing bona fide cemetery plots—as in tombstones sticking out of the ground. It was dark—it was damp—it was downright spooky.

Louie carried Lupe the last part of the way because her heels kept sinking into the moist earth. "You're throwing out these suicidal boots when you get home."

"Don't be such a prima donna," Lupe chastised, "I'm light as a feather."

Folding chairs were set up on the lawn, amongst the trees and headstones. My gang was directed to the first row—Lucious, Lilith, and Bonnie were seated directly behind us. We weren't right on top of anyone's grave, but close enough.

"I do love a good piece of fiction," Lucious said.

Turning to face him, I couldn't help myself, "My sources tell me this piece is based on true events."

"Please, spare me the naiveté," Lilith sniped. "They say things like that to up the ante on the free publicity."

"No, Roberta's right," Lupe weighed in. "I've confirmed it with Samir. My Tommy's murder will be solved tonight."

"Your Tommy?" Bonnie and Lucious said simultaneously.

Oops! Didn't get a chance to tell Lupe that Tommy was Bonnie's son, and Lucious was his best friend.

"Don't mind her," Louie said. "She's also planning a tour with Elvis."

"Tommy was the victim of a tragic accident," Lucious said adamantly. "It's very upsetting for his mother to sit here and listen to all this nonsense about murder."

"Yes," Bonnie confirmed, "my son's case was thoroughly investigated by the police and ruled an accident."

"If anyone says otherwise," Lilith threatened, "they can expect to be on the receiving end of a vicious lawsuit."

This trio was getting extremely agitated over a play they hadn't even seen yet. Before they had a chance to work themselves into a fit, the sound of eerie background music came from out of the trees, signaling the start of the show.

The scene opened on two men—one in his early twenties and one in his forties—dressed in black hooded robes, chanting. They were busy prepping an altar for some sort of sacrifice; other than this, there was no set to speak of.

I could hear snippets of animated whispering going on behind me, but not enough to decipher what was being said amongst the members of the Darvell party.

A third young man, wearing the same type of robe, entered the scene. He had the body of a girl slung over his shoulder.

"I see she didn't come willingly, Luther," the older man spoke.

"No, High Master, she put up a fight as usual. I got in to an altercation with her brother." Luther deposited the limp body onto the altar.

"We're going to have to do something about Timothy. His homecoming has proven to be a contentious one." The High Master draped a scarlet red cloth over the inert girl. "Too bad, I thought his development was coming along rather nicely until he got drafted overseas." He clenched Luther's shoulder. "At least you managed to return to me intact."

Luther/Lucious—Timothy/Tommy—the characters names were so thinly disguised, I was surprised not to hear any further mumbling from the Magus and his entourage.

"Are we performing the full ritual tonight, High Master?" the other young man asked.

"Not yet, Ray. But soon, very soon. We must be patient. She has just come into her full womanhood." The High Master turned to Luther. "Did her mother prep her as instructed?"

I took a quick look behind me.

"Yes," Luther answered.

Bonnie Lawson shifted uncomfortably in her seat.

"Good, your seed must not be fully implanted until the stroke of midnight on All Hallows' Eve at Devil's Gate Dam. We will succeed where Parsons and Hubbard failed—our Magical Moonchild will be conceived and born."

The whole thing was getting too *Rosemary's Baby* for my tastes. If this did turn out to be a roman à clef type play, its implications were far-reaching and close to home. At best—Lucious, the man seated behind me, was an accomplice to rape and murder. At worst—he was the rapist and murderer.

Another young man took the stage. Dressed in jeans and a leather biker's jacket, he appeared from behind a stone crypt. "Get away from my sister, Fred."

"Now, now, Timothy, I told you to call me Dad," the High Master said. "Ray, can you take care of this nuisance? I have some important work to finish."

The girl on the altar sat up. "Where am I?"

"Run, Chrissy! Run!" Timothy shouted.

Chrissy took off into the night.

"Luther, find her!" Fred, the High Master, commanded.

A scuffle ensued between the remaining men.

Fred held onto Timothy's arms while Ray pummeled him with a series of punches.

Breaking free of Fred's grasp, Timothy picked up a silver chalice from the altar and launched it at Ray's head.

Ray fell to the ground.

"Get up, you lazy good-for-nothing." Fred kicked Ray in the side, then lunged at Timothy.

Timothy, dodging out of the way, tripped and fell next to Ray.

Fred ran over to Ray and helped him to his feet. "Here," he handed Ray a large rock, "finish him off."

A staggering Ray lifted the rock above his head and, using his full force, hurled it down onto Timothy's head. He turned and reeled backwards before collapsing in a heap.

Luther ran back in, "She got away, I can't find her."

"Never mind about her," Fred said. "I need you to help me dispose of these bodies. Let's pack this stuff away in my car first."

The two men picked up the altar and exited.

A weeping Chrissy reemerged from behind the crypt and went to her brother's side.

The scene went dark and the actors came forward to take their bows.

I was so caught up in the last few minutes of the piece, I forgot all about Bonnie Lawson and the Darvells.

"My poor, sweet, Tommy." Lupe stopped applauding and wiped a tear from her eye.

People all around us were getting up to leave, when I heard the cackle of a walkie-talkie. "How bad is it?

A voice from behind me answered back, "I think the old lady's dead."

CHAPTER THIRTY-FIVE

A…My Name Is Angela

I FELT A TAP on my shoulder. "Do you know if anyone attended tonight's performance with this woman?"

I turned and saw Bonnie collapsed in her chair—unconscious and alone.

"Yes," I answered. "Her name's Bonnie Lawson. She came with a couple, Lucious and Lilith Darvell."

"So these people are friends of yours?" the usher asked.

"More like passing acquaintances," Louie said.

"Pay no attention to my uncle, she's my fiancé's mother," Lupe said. "Is she going to be okay?"

When did her imaginary boyfriend get promoted to fiancé?

The usher did a double take before continuing. "We need to contact her next of kin." He turned to Danny. "Are you the son?"

"No, he's my ex," Louie answered.

The usher looked over at Ben.

"I'm with her," Ben grabbed my arm.

Lupe pointed to where the action of the play had taken place. "Her son was killed over there."

If the usher seemed perplexed by Lupe's first delusional admission, this one really messed with his head. He pressed the button on his walkie-talkie. "Larry, it's Steve. Call 9-1-1 back. We might have a double homicide down here."

"She's talking about the play," I corrected him, "there isn't another body."

"Did you copy that, Larry?" Steve asked.

"Roger," Larry replied.

The EMTs arrived on the scene and checked Bonnie's vital signs.

"I've got a pulse," one of the EMTs said. "It's weak, but it's there. I think she may be in shock."

They strapped Bonnie onto a stretcher and slipped an oxygen mask over her face.

Steve spoke into his walkie-talkie, "The old lady's alive, Larry." He took me aside. "Do you want me to have them take a look at her?" he indicated toward Lupe, "She seems a bit confused."

"Thanks, we have it under control."

The EMTs rushed the stretcher into their truck.

"Do you know which hospital they're taking her to?" I asked Steve.

"Probably Huntington Memorial, it's less than five miles away. Can I get her friends' contact info from you? The House Manager is going to want to get in touch with them."

I gave him the Darvell's phone number, though after abandoning her that way, I doubted if they cared whether Bonnie lived or died.

My theatre companions and I made our way back to the parking lot.

"You see? Now do you doubters believe?" Lupe hobbled along in her designer safari boots. "Samir was right, Tommy was murdered."

"I'm convinced," Ben said. "After what I witnessed in my office today, there's not a doubt in my mind. Madame Mestral is legitimately channeling a disembodied spirit."

"You know I always trusted her abilities," Danny said.

Louie threw his hands in the air. "Fine, I give in. But what's this business about Tommy being your fiancé? You're lucky they didn't cart you off, too. The poor guy did have a fiancé and it certainly wasn't you."

Louie's chastising triggered a bell. "That's right!" I thought. According to Tommy's obituary, he was engaged. But to whom? And what became of her? Did she know anything about what happened to Tommy and Cissy? I decided it would be a good idea to contact Holy Family Church tomorrow and see what I could find out.

"We haven't heard a peep from you, Roberta?" Danny prodded.

"Okay, I'll admit it, Mestral's Egyptian pal hasn't steered us wrong once. Bonnie Lawson's severe reaction to the play, coupled with the Darvell's disappearing act, seems like more than mere coincidence. What they saw tonight shook them up in a big way."

"Big enough to land Bonnie in the hospital," Louie agreed.

"Yes, but was Bonnie's shock brought on because her secret was exposed?" Ben hypothesized, "Or was it because a secret had been revealed to her for the first time?"

"Good point," I said. "That might explain Lucious and Lilith's strange behavior."

"I think those two are operating from a whole new level of strange," Louie added.

"All will be revealed at Madame Mestral's Halloween seance," Lupe prophesied.

"You're not still planning on letting them attend?" a nervous Danny asked.

"Why not?" Lupe said.

"Because Lucious is a murderer." Louie sounded as apprehensive as my brother.

"Accomplice to murder," Ben corrected him. "If the play is to be believed, Tommy was killed by the Ray character."

Louie unlocked his SUV. "You're not making me feel any safer, Ben."

A defiant Lupe weighed in, "For the sake of my Tommy, we will proceed as planned."

"I have an idea," Ben said. "Maybe you could ask Officer Sanchez to sit in on the proceedings."

Louie brightened up. "Can't go wrong with a man in uniform."

"If he agrees to go," I said, "he'll have to be undercover. No need to scare them off before we get started."

"Invite him." Lupe got into the SUV. "Now let's get going, I need to get my beauty rest."

"Before you leave," I recalled my last conversation with Dr. Jenkins, "would it be all right if I asked one other person?"

"No need to worry," Lupe said. "I've already included Benjamin in my head count."

"It's for someone else—a fellow colleague. He's very interested in what I've told him about Madame Mestral and would love to observe her abilities first hand." I wasn't completely devoid of suspicion where The Madame was concerned. The pill collection I stumbled upon in her bedroom still nagged at me. Carl's assessment would go a long way toward allaying any lingering doubts about the state of her mental health.

"All right," Lupe said. "He's the last one—the guest list is closed. Madame Mestral doesn't want this turning into a concert event. Call me in the morning and I'll add his name."

* * *

First thing Saturday morning, which translates into eleven in my world—No, Ben didn't sleep over! But he left at three a.m., so we're making progress—I called Lupe and got Carl Jenkins' name added to Mestral's seance guest list.

Second thing I did—while nursing a cup of coffee and a toasted sesame bagel smothered in smoked salmon schmear—was get in contact with Holy Family Church in South Pasadena.

"Hi, I was wondering if I could get some information about a parishioner whose funeral service was held at your church."

"Sure, do you have the date?" the woman on the other end of the line asked.

"He passed away on the sixteenth of October. Give me a second, I have the exact date somewhere." I sifted through the scant bits of information I had collected. "Here it is. The obituary lists the date of the service as Friday, October twenty-first."

"I think you have the wrong church. No funeral masses were said here yesterday.

"Oh, excuse me, I didn't give you the year. It was 1966."

"That was way back, before we switched to computerized records. I'll have to put in a request to have those files pulled from our off-site storage facilities."

"How long will it take?"

"Two weeks or longer. The company we use is located out of state."

Not what I wanted to hear. All I needed to know were a few details about the service like was Tommy's fiancé there? If so, what's her name? And did Cissy throw herself on top of her brother's casket as it was being lowered into the ground?

"I don't suppose you have the same pastor?"

"No, I'm afraid not."

This one's a long shot. "You don't happen to keep lists of attendees in those files?"

"We don't nowadays. Of course, I'm not sure what went on before I was born."

"Thanks for your hel—"

"Wait!" I heard the woman snap her fingers. "One of the old church secretaries is here today helping out with the Fall Festival. She may be able to answer some of your questions. I'll send someone to get her."

"That would be wonderful, thank you."

"Hold on while I flag down an altar girl," the woman said. "Valerie, would you be a love? Run over to the Fifty Plus Club bake table and ask Angela Fowler to come see me in the office."

CHAPTER THIRTY-SIX

What A Difference A Death Makes

I COULDN'T BELIEVE my ears. "Did you say the former secretary's name is Angela Fowler?"

"Yes, she's a longtime parishioner," the current admin assistant said. "But she hasn't worked here in years."

Granted, Angela Fowler wasn't the most unusual name in the world. Though running into each of them at places with a connection to Tommy Forrester's death seemed out of the ordinary. I heard the voice of a child in the background.

"Thank you, Valerie," the woman said. "I'll let the caller know."

"Has she already left?" I asked.

"No, she's still here. There isn't anyone available to man the bake table for her right now. Things should calm down after lunch. If you give me your number, I'll ask her to give you a call."

If it was *my* Angela Fowler, I didn't want to risk her taking flight before I got a chance to speak with her. "Is your Fall Festival open to the public?"

"Absolutely, we've been hosting this fair for over forty years. Admission is free, prices vary on the food and games."

I wasn't planning on playing any games, Angela's ongoing hide-and-seek shenanigans were wearing me thin. "Will you do me a favor? Please don't mention this call to anyone. I think I may know Angela and I want to surprise her."

"No problem. Would you like directions?"

"Think I'm good, I've been in your neighborhood before."

*   *   *

The Fall Festival was in full swing when I arrived—alive with noise, laughter, and movement. There was a Ferris wheel, a pirate ship, a dunk tank, a double splash slide and bounce houses—this was definitely a kid-centric event.

Following my nose and my stomach, I headed for the food stalls located next to the game booths. While buying a kosher hot dog, I spotted baked goods for sale at one of the craft tables across from the Wheel of Fortune. An attractive woman in her late sixties, sort of a Gloria Steinem type, was placing red velvet cupcakes on a display stand.

"Pardon me," I said to Ms. Cupcake, "I'm looking for Angela Fowler. Do you know when she'll be back?"

"She is back," the woman said, "I'm Angela Fowler."

These were not the words I was hoping to hear. So much for assuming she would turn out to be *my* Angela Fowler. "I was speaking to a woman in the church office earlier, she said you worked here as a secretary back in the Sixties and might be able to help me with some information."

"I'll try, though I only worked part-time while I was a student."

"You wouldn't happen to recall anything about a funeral held here in 1966? It was for a young man named Tommy Forrester."

"I haven't heard his name in years," the woman said wistfully, "but I remember it like it was yesterday. We attended South Pas High together. I had a gargantuan schoolgirl crush on him."

This was a very fortunate turn of events. "I'm trying to find out what became of his sister. I've heard varying stories of what happened to her after her brother died."

"Poor Cissy, she was completely lost after Tommy was gone."

"Did you make any of those killer brownies of yours this year, Angela?" a man in his early thirties, pushing a stroller, asked.

"I did, Bob," Angela replied. "Sold the last one a half hour ago. Can I interest you in a cupcake?"

"Did you bake them?"

"Sure did."

"In that case, I'll have two."

Angela completed the sale and returned to our conversation. "Where were we?"

"Cissy Forrester," I reminded her. "Did you hear any talk about her behaving strangely at Tommy's funeral?"

"Nothing comes to mind, I attended Tommy's service. All of Tommy's old pals showed up, except for the ones who were serving overseas in the war. It was so tragic the way Tommy managed to survive Vietnam, only to die so soon after his return home."

"So nothing about Cissy's behavior stood out to you on that day?"

She shook her head. "Lots of weeping like the rest of us." Angela's eyes lit up. "Actually, there was one thing which seemed peculiar to me. A good friend of Tommy's, Roy Hastings, wasn't present at the funeral. I found out later he enlisted right after Tommy died and shipped out before the funeral. I didn't see why he couldn't wait until after Tommy was buried, but I guess grief affects each person differently."

Was Roy Hastings the real name of the character that delivered the fatal blow to Tommy in last night's play? The guy named Ray. This didn't make much sense to me because I was left with the distinct impression Ray had died too. "Do you know what happened to Roy?"

"Last I heard he went missing in action." Angela cast her eyes downward. "There was a lot of heartbreak during that era."

Looks like Tommy's killer was hit with some bad karma. Since Bonnie's second husband, Edward Lawson, is deceased as well, the only remaining participant in Tommy's murder and Cissy's sexual abuse is Lucious Darvell.

I had watched enough *Law and Order: SVU* to know the statute of limitations had run out on Cissy's case, though I wasn't so sure about Tommy's. Lucious did willingly help cover up a murder, I knew this made him some sort of accessory to a felony. Whether or not he could be charged after all these years was beyond my armchair detective purview. Though without Cissy Forrester to testify against him, it seemed improbable he would ever be brought to justice.

"May I ask why you're inquiring about Tommy's funeral?" Angela asked.

I didn't want this woman to think I was whacko, so I wasn't about to get into the whole Madame Mestral, Samir, and Lupe deal. "A friend of mine who knows…I mean…knew Tommy told me Cissy disappeared when she was still a child. Then, recently, I was introduced to their mother, Bonnie Lawson. She told me Cissy had a severe emotional breakdown at the funeral, and threw herself on top of Tommy's casket as it was being lowered into the ground."

"That did happen," Angela said, "only it wasn't Cissy who had a meltdown. Poor Mrs. Lawson must have been having a senior moment. She has Cissy confused with Tommy's fiancé."

Was it a momentary brain lapse or did Bonnie deliberately mislead me? She was getting up there in age. But it was also possible she was trying to hide her own involvement in her daughter's sexual assault. Last night's performance revealed she was the one in charge of prepping Cissy for the ritual in The Haunted Forest. Maybe if I track down the fiancé I can get a better idea of what was going on in Tommy and Cissy's home. "Any chance you know the whereabouts of Tommy's bride-to-be?"

"Like I said before, it was a heart-rending period. Linnie was committed to Camarillo State Mental Hospital. She took her life there on the first anniversary of Tommy's death."

"So where is Cissy now?"

"Your friend was right, she disappeared a few weeks after Tommy died. Cissy was last seen near Devil's Gate Dam. The police eventually figured she was one of Mack Ray Edwards' victims. He abducted, molested and murdered a number of children in the area during the Fifties and Sixties. Edwards was finally caught and sentenced to death in 1970. I remember reading in the paper he hung himself in his San Quentin cell not too long afterward."

"Well, thanks for clearing things up for me, Angela. Sorry I dredged up all those unpleasant memories." I surveyed the bake table. "Pack up a half dozen of those cupcakes for me." It was the least I could do.

"No need to apologize, they're all in a better place now." Angela placed the cupcakes in a box. "I think after I finish up here today, I'll head over to Mountain View Cemetery and place some flowers on Tommy and Caroline's graves. They're buried next to each other. Hope I don't have any problems getting in, Father Doyle tells me there's a play being performed right near their burial site. Not sure how I feel about that."

"Who is Caroline?" I asked.

"Tommy's fiancé, Caroline Foster. Linnie was her nickname."

CHAPTER THIRTY-SEVEN

Get Me To The Temple On Time

A NGELA FOWLER'S—as in church cupcake lady's, not disappearing new client's—disclosure of the previous day had created quite the conundrum for me. Tommy Forrester knew an Angela Fowler and a Caroline Foster—the former, an old high school classmate—the latter, his fiancé. It seemed to be more than happenstance I should become professionally acquainted with a different Angela Fowler, who was friends with another Caroline Foster, and they should both be involved with a play about Tommy Forrester's murder.

I put in a call to Angela when I got back home on Saturday afternoon, and left a message about setting up the follow-up appointment we discussed. If we could manage to get through an entire hypnosis session before she took to her heels, maybe I could decipher her true identity. It was now late Sunday morning and she still hadn't responded.

While getting ready for Ben's cousin Aviva's wedding that afternoon I thought I heard a faint knock on my front door. This was confirmed by Lex's sudden dash into the foyer, followed by a series of his deepest, "Halt! Who goes there?" barks.

Half-dressed in bra and panties, hair a mess, I peeked through the peephole. It was Angela Fowler—my Angela Fowler—wearing her indispensable black floppy hat and sunglasses. "Hang on a sec!" I ran to my bedroom and threw on a robe before opening the door.

"Guess I caught you at a bad time," Angela said, turning to go.

"No...no...don't go!" I wasn't going to let her slip away again.

"Sorry to bother you at home," Angela gingerly entered, "I knocked on your office door first, but no one answered."

"I don't usually see clients on Sunday—except in emergency cases. Are you all right? Did you get the message I left?"

Head hung down, she spoke quietly. "I guess I'm okay. In your voicemail, you mentioned something about my disappearing on Friday night."

"Yes, where did you go? You said you needed to use the ladies' room, then slipped out the back way."

Angela trembled and swayed.

Afraid she was going to pass out, I took her by the arm. "Come in." We walked into the living room and over to the paisley easy chair. "Have a seat."

"Could I have some water?"

"Sure," I hustled into the kitchen, quickly filled a glass, and returned before she had a chance to escape. "Here you are."

Angela took the water from me. "I don't remember disappearing on Friday night." She stared into the glass. "In fact...the last thing I remember is sitting in the makeup room talking with you...I mean...it's the last thing I remember until picking up your message half an hour ago."

"Has this ever happened to you before?"

She nodded her head. "Lots...I'm scared."

"Have you told Dr. Jenkins about this?"

"No, I'm not supposed to."

"Is someone threatening you, Angela?"

"Yes," she hesitated, "I think so."

"Who?"

"Some of Caroline's friends."

The plot thickens. Since my first encounter with Caroline Foster was at the Solar Lodge meetup in the back room of It's All About The Bean, I decided to test out a few names. "Is it any of these people? Lucious Darvell? Lilith Darvell? Bonnie Lawson?"

"Those names all sound familiar."

"What about Madame Mestral?"

She nodded.

Bingo! Like I suspected, Mestral *is* mixed up in this scheme.

Okay, I've assembled a cast of characters. Now I need to figure out the plot. First, what's their motivation? Defraud Lupe of her money? Louie says she's managed to stash away a few bucks over the years. Get the deed to her property? That one strikes me as the most plausible. A prime Victorian in top-notch shape can fetch a bundle in the LA real estate market. Mestral has already moved her kooky church onto the premises. Maybe the Abundant Beings Church of Divine Energy and the Solar Lodge are acting as tax-shelter front organizations for this supernatural flimflam operation. It's all smoke and mirrors—including the supposed "ripped from the headlines" play I saw at the cemetery on Friday night. I seriously doubt Angela Fowler and Caroline Foster are the only ones using assumed identities.

Whoa! Back up there, Roberta. Remember, you met the real Angela Fowler yesterday. How can you be sure today's surprise encounter isn't part of the plan? It would certainly explain a lot about this client's unpredictable behavior. On the other hand, she might be sincerely trying to come clean with me—hence the threats.

"Angela, I think it would be in your best interests if you allow me to hypnotize you."

She sipped her water.

"If you want to get to the bottom of these blackouts, this is the best method I know of using for finding out what's going on."

More silent sips.

Her hesitation was most likely fear-based. Fear I was going to reveal her as a fake—or fear she would at last discover the true source of her affliction. "So what's it going to be?"

She put the glass down on the coffee table. "I'll do it."

Victory!

"Only I can't do it right now."

Defeat.

Angela stood up. "Do you have any openings on the twenty-eighth?" Her demeanor had shifted. She displayed a cool confidence.

"I can get you in earlier than Friday if you like," I said, trying to mask my eagerness.

"No need, Friday will be fine." She walked toward the front door.

"Can you come by at nine?" I wanted her in first thing, even if it meant bumping another client.

"Will you do me a favor and text the particulars to me?"

"No problem."

Lex, who had been napping in the foyer during all this, got up to see his friend out.

Angela looked down at Lex. "I hope your dog won't be present, I'm not overly fond of animals."

Since when? She insisted on him being in the room with her during her last appointment. "He only sits in on sessions when invited by the client."

"Good." She opened the door and left.

Lex slumped back down on the floor.

"Don't let it get to you, fella. Unlike me, some gals can be kind of fickle."

* * *

Ben and I had arranged to meet at Temple Emanuel in Beverly Hills. Since he had spent Saturday night at his mother's in Malibu and I lived in the San Fernando Valley, it made more sense to do it this way. Thanks to my unexpected visit from Angela Fowler, I made it there just under the wire.

The wedding, held near sundown, was filled with tears, laughter, breaking glass, and a passel of friends and family. Aviva and her groom, Nev, looked radiant standing together underneath the chuppah. I was impressed with the ceremony's relative speed—twenty minutes versus the hour long Roman Catholic ones I'd attended.

"That was short and sweet," I said to Ben, as we made our way out to the cocktail reception in the courtyard.

"My people like to waste no time getting to the most important part," Ben said, taking a canapé from a passing tray.

"Which is?"

"Food!" Ben popped the appetizer into his mouth.

Despite having a mouth full of wild mushroom phyllo triangle, he looked particularly dashing in his custom-made dark gray suit with maroon shirt and silver tie. My three-quarter sleeve, burgundy, lace midi dress was the perfect match for his stylish wedding attire—as well as the red, yellow and orange tones of the autumn-themed decor.

Ben snatched another canapé. "Better eat something, Roberta. Jewish weddings use up a lot of energy."

He wasn't kidding. I was on the floor—dancing the hora in one of the party rooms—faster than you can say, "shake that tokhes shiksa."

"I'm heading back to our table," I said to Ben about a half hour into the workout. "This goy gal's got to take a break."

"I warned you," Ben shouted over the music. "Dinner should be served soon. Come get me when the first course arrives."

We were seated at a table near the front of the room, close to the stage and the raucous klezmer band. Ben's mom, Barbara Goldberg, was alone at the table fussing with her smartphone.

"I'm still getting used to this new phone of mine. It has one of those huge display screens." Barbara passed her cell to me. "So why can't I find the camera?"

"Are you sure it has one?"

"Don't they all? These eyes of mine haven't held up as well as the rest of me." Barbara looked stunning, as usual. A statuesque woman in her mid-to-late sixties, her thick, shoulder-length, silver hair complemented the form-fitting sapphire dress she wore.

"Found it!" I handed her back the phone. "It was hidden in a folder for some reason."

"New assistant setting up phone is the reason," she said sternly. "I'll have a word with him on Monday."

Barbara is not the type of lady you want to mess with; I did not envy the fellow. "Can I pick your brain for a moment?"

"I'm all yours."

"Ben mentioned you worked as a clerk on the 'Boy in the Box' case."

Barbara nodded her head. "Not a trial I'm likely to forget."

The band launched into another rousing rendition of *Hava Nagila*.

"Recently, I stumbled upon a group in South Pasadena claiming to be the Solar Lodge."

Barbara's somber face matched the tone of her voice. "I'm all ears." She looked up at the Klezmer Kats. "We need to go somewhere we can talk. Come." I followed Barbara to the powder room. "Tell me everything you know."

I started at the top, recounting my experiences at the Abundant Beings Church of Divine Energy, Pardo's Potions, the meetup at It's All About The Bean, the Darvell's dinner party, and the play at Mountain View Cemetery.

Barbara brought me up to speed with what she knew. "Bonnie Lawson, her husband, Edward, and Lucious Darvell were all members of the original Solar Lodge. Thirteen people from the group were arrested in the summer of '69 when their compound in Vidal was raided. The others, including two of your dinner party companions, fled California and warrants were issued for their capture. All charges were eventually dropped against them due to entrapment issues."

"Did anyone serve time?" I asked.

"Four people received felony convictions and spent six months in jail. Another four got three months for misdemeanor violations. The Lawsons and Lucious Darvell got off scot-free. Though I've always maintained my suspicions about them, since they'd all been persons of interest in the disappearance of Cissy Forrester a few years earlier. But that case was eventually attributed to Mack Ray Edwards."

I thought back on my conversation with Angela Fowler—the former church secretary. "Yesterday I met someone who knew Cissy, she mentioned him to me."

"I've never heard of your Madame Mestral, though. Of course, that doesn't mean anything. From what you've told me, she's probably operating under an assumed identity."

The door to the ladies' room opened. A platinum blonde—chest spilling out of a skintight, gold lamé mini-dress—waltzed in on us.

"Trixie," Barbara said drily, "still shopping at Frederick's of Hollywood, I see."

"Frederick's is a sexy lingerie store," Trixie replied icily, "not that you would ever need any."

"Pardon me," Barbara snapped back, "I thought you were wearing a corset."

Trixie turned her attention to me. "Hello, Bobby. Are you Barbara's date for the evening?"

"It's Roberta. And no, I came with Ben."

"How is my dear ex doing? Still in the ghostbusting biz?"

"He's a paranormal researcher and he's doing quite well."

"Aviva mentioned you would be here this evening," Barbara said.

Trixie looked in the mirror, reapplying her ruby red lipstick. "Yes, I'm accompanying Ben's Uncle Mort."

"So this is more of a shopping excursion for you then," Barbara said.

Trixie looked perplexed.

Barbara continued, "A chance to survey the current crop of Cohen men."

Trixie had quite the reputation in the Cohen family. Her first husband was Ben's father; he left Barbara to make Trixie his trophy wife. A few years later, she walked out on Ben's father and eloped with Ben. It did seem unusual the way she was always feeding from the Cohen trough. A sex therapist by trade, I wondered if she had ever bothered to take a good hard look at her own sexual predilections.

"It's been a dubious pleasure, as usual, Trixie." Barbara walked over to the door. "Coming, Roberta? We can finish discussing what to do about the Lucious Darvell problem later."

"Has dear, sweet Lucious done something to upset you ladies?" Trixie asked, fluffing her hair.

The words "dear" and "sweet" did not readily come to mind when thinking of Lucious Darvell. Could she possibly be referring to the same man? Or was there another imposter in our midst?

CHAPTER THIRTY-EIGHT

If You Knew Trixie

"**H**OW DO YOU KNOW Lucious Darvell?" I asked Trixie.

"He and Mort have a mutual friend." She waived an ostentatiously large diamond ring at Barbara and me. "Don Pardo, the best jeweler in Beverly Hills, introduced us."

"You and Mort are engaged?" Barbara asked in a tone of jaded amazement.

"Not quite yet," Trixie played with the ring on her finger, "I'm using it as a placeholder. When he does pop the question, I promise you'll be the first person I tell."

Barbara smiled. "What an unwelcome honor."

I shifted the conversation back to the topic that interested me most. "You better be careful, Lucious is the leader of a kinky sex cult."

"Honestly, Bobby," Trixie laughed. "I don't get why Ben is attracted by your bush-league charms. We're living in the twenty-first century, you need to broaden your sexual palette."

Why I felt I needed to issue a warning to a gold digging sex therapist escapes me—Trixie was no babe in the woods—or the sack.

"Mort and I consider ourselves erotic explorers pushing past the bounds of conventional coupling."

"TMI." Barbara pushed the powder room door open. "Let's get back to the table, Roberta—before we lose our appetites."

No sooner had we made our exit than Barbara and I ran right into Mort, who was hovering around outside. Though in his early seventies, on a good day Mort could easily pass for eighty-five. The years had not been kind. "Did you gals happen to see Trixie?"

Barbara nodded and pointed back at the restroom door.

"Is anybody else in there?" Mort seemed antsy.

"Not that I noticed," I said.

"Good." Mort popped a purple pill in his mouth and peeked inside. "Daddy's home and he has a big surprise for baby Trixie." He winked at us, then ducked inside the ladies' room.

Barbara looked at me and sighed. "Once an asshole, always an asshole."

Ben was seated at the table when we returned. "Where have you two been? They're about to bless the challah."

"We ran into your ex-stepmother-slash-ex-wife," Barbara said. "She's snagged herself another Cohen man."

"Yeah, I know," Ben said. "Dad mentioned it to me the other day."

"How is your father?" Barbra said dryly. "Busy chasing schoolgirls?"

"You can ask him yourself," Ben said. "He and Aunt Sylvia are headed this way."

"Darling, you look fabulous!" Aunt Sylvia gave Barbara a warm embrace. Sylvia Tenenbaum—mother of the bride—is a petite, sporty- looking woman in her late fifties. She is also the younger sister of Ben's dad.

"Don't undersell her, sis. She's a knockout this evening." David Cohen is a tall, tanned, dashing man in his late sixties. Think George Hamilton meets Pierce Brosnan meets George Clooney.

"To what do we owe this unaccustomed visit?" Barbara asked David.

"I think it's best if I allow Sylvia to explain."

"You know how Aviva insisted on hiring Echo, that ditzy friend of hers, as the Wedding Planner? It's really all my fault, I should have stood my ground and hired Becky Weiss like I wanted to…"

"Cut to the chase, Sylvia." Barbara was losing her patience.

"You were probably wondering what's up with these three empty seats." Each table had place settings for six. "Well, that yutzi made duplicate place cards for three of our guests and left three other people without seating assignments."

"Dad, are you one of the ones without a table?" Ben asked.

David Cohen nodded his head.

"How fitting, first you're gone—and now you're forgotten," Barbara said sarcastically. "Don't stand there like a schlemiel, David. Pull up a seat."

"Thanks so much, doll." Sylvia gave Barbara a peck on the cheek. "I knew you'd understand. The other couple are here somewhere, they should be joining you momentarily." She turned around and made a beeline for the head table.

Part of me suspected Sylvia was using this as a ploy to disguise her true intent of playing matchmaker for the ex spouses. Though they'd never admit it, I could tell more than a few burning embers remained.

"So who's the mystery couple?" Barbara asked.

David shook his head. "Sylvia didn't say."

"It looks to me like everyone is already seated." Then I noticed a disheveled-looking couple hurrying into the reception hall, causing me to revise my earlier assessment of Sylvia's intentions. "I think that's them over there." I pointed out the giddy pair.

"Oh, no," Ben sighed.

"Of all people," David groused.

"Lord help us," Barbara moaned, "not Mort and Trixie."

"Hello, lovebirds—current and former." Trixie plopped herself down beside David. "It feels like old home week."

"More like old homewrecker," I overheard Barbara mumble under her breath.

"What was that?" Trixie was looking into her compact mirror—fluffing her mussed up hair.

"Just talking to myself," Barbara said.

A panting, sweaty Mort occupied the seat next to mine.

"Is everything okay?" David asked his older brother. "You look like you just came from a workout at the gym."

"I'm fine." Mort wiped the back of his neck with a hanky.

Trixie giggled suggestively.

Barbara and I knew she was sniggering about her recent powder room assignation with Mort. And judging by the looks of recognition on their faces, so did Ben and his father.

One of the caterers rolled a cart—containing a large challah—out onto the dance floor.

"Shit, I almost forgot!" Mort stood up. "Sylvia asked me to make the hamotzi."

Not understanding what Mort was talking about I looked at Ben.

"It's a traditional blessing over the bread," Ben said. "An honored guest is usually asked to do it."

"And sometimes they'll ask someone because they look as old as dirt," Barbara added.

A hush fell over the room as Mort recited the simple prayer. "Baruch ata Adonoy, Eloheinu melech ha-olam, ha-motzi lechem min ha-aretz." He cut the loaf of challah into pieces. Then he took the first slice, dipped it in salt, and took a bite.

"That was beautiful, Mort," I said when he returned to the table. "What does it mean?"

Mort held up his knife and fork. "Let's eat!"

"Blessed are you God, King of the Universe, Who brings forth bread from the earth," Ben whispered in my ear. "Uncle Mort's a bit of an a-hole."

"So I've heard."

When you consider the fact Trixie had—at one time or another—been lovers with every man seated at our table, the rest of the evening turned out much better than expected. In between trips to the restroom, Mort and Trixie kept pretty much to themselves. While Barbara and David looked like they were on the road to rekindling their relationship.

Over the course of dinner and dancing, out of earshot of Trixie and Mort, I filled Ben in on my evening at the Darvells, my continuing suspicion of Madame Mestral, and the possibility I may have discovered Cissy Forrester.

Patient as always, Ben listened intently and gave me some valuable feedback. Though he was still solidly in The Madame's camp. "I got some pretty impressive EMF readings off her the other day."

"Let's say, for the sake of argument, I accept your assessment of her psychic abilities. It doesn't necessarily make her an honest player. She may be using her gift to take advantage of vulnerable people."

"That is a possibility," Ben agreed. "For your own safety, I think you need to get the police involved."

"How? It's not like I have any solid evidence to present them."

"Why not give Officer Sanchez a heads up? He's used to the kind of unusual situations you get yourself entangled in."

He was right. It didn't matter if Mestral was a fraud or not, in either scenario something illegal had happened or was about to happen.

* * *

Ben and I said our goodbyes at one in the morning. Other than some hand holding and a few stolen kisses here and there, we were the perfect Duggar-style, dating role models. Frankly, I was okay with the way things worked out. All that rigorous dancing had me wiped. I was looking forward to an undisturbed sleep date with my memory foam mattress.

Lex greeted me at the door, tail wagging, anticipating his long overdue evening snack.

"This is a bribe, boy." I reached into the cookie jar and pulled out two, rather than his customary one, bone-shaped biscuits. "I'm pooped. And while we're on the topic, instead of your usual walk around the block tonight, I'm going to let you take your evening constitutional in the yard."

Lex grabbed the treats from my hand.

Taking this move as a tacit agreement on his part, I opened the back door. While waiting for Lex to return, I remembered my promise to text Angela her appointment info. After locating her file in my office, I pulled out the form containing the spotty personal data she had provided at our first session. Her date of birth jumped out at me—October 16, 1966—the same day Tommy Forrester had died. My heart skipped a beat at this odd coincidence. Why had I not noticed this earlier? Probably because prior to this I had no reason to think she was Tommy's sister. Then a disheartening realization sunk in—Cissy Forrester was twelve years old when her brother died. Angela couldn't possibly be Tommy's sister.

* * *

The four days leading up to Angela Fowler's appointment were routine and uneventful. I tried to reach Lucious or Lilith, but was unsuccessful. Their maid told me they were called out of town unexpectedly. Did this spur of the moment trip have anything to do with what happened at the play last Friday? I inquired about Bonnie Lawson. She told me she was in ICU at Huntington Memorial Hospital and things didn't look promising.

Friday was a dull, gloomy day. The smell of rain teased the air, though it rarely delivered on its suggestive gesture. Never knowing quite what to expect from Angela, I cleared my morning schedule in anticipation of a challenging session with my skittish new client.

Nine o'clock rolled around—then nine-fifteen. By nine-twenty I put in a call to check on her whereabouts. "The number you have reached is not accepting calls at this time," said a canned voice message. Is she blocking my calls or did she forget to pay her bill?

I went outside to see if she was parked on the street or hiding behind the cedar hedge, afraid to come to my door. No luck. As I headed back into the office, Lupe's yellow Corvette turned onto my street and pulled up in front of the house. The woman who got out of the vehicle wasn't Lupe—or Mestral—or Angela. It was

Caroline Foster. Or perhaps I should say, the woman who was using Tommy Forrester's deceased fiancé's name.

"Where's Angela?" I asked.

"She asked me to come in her place." Caroline walked up to me, right hand extended. "I don't believe we've met, Ms. Law."

I shook her hand, wondering if I should be afraid of this woman. "No we haven't, Ms. Foster. That is your name, right? Caroline Foster?"

"Yes."

I didn't have a clue what this person was up to, but I knew I needed to find out. "Why don't you come in and tell me what this is all about?"

Caroline followed me inside.

"Have a seat." I motioned toward the black leather recliner.

"I know this is a rather unorthodox situation," Caroline began.

"That all depends on what you expect to accomplish here today." I sat down behind my desk.

"I've come to be hypnotized for Angela."

"You're absolutely right. This is an extraordinary state of affairs. How can my hypnotizing you help Angela?"

"The idea of not being in control terrifies her."

"Hypnosis is not about turning over control of yourself to someone else. It's a natural state of consciousness we access all the time. All I'm doing as a hypnotherapist is facilitating a client's journey to realize a set of predetermined goals. If Angela would stick around here long enough to find this out, I'm sure I could allay any apprehensions she's harboring."

"Believe me, I understand your position." Caroline appeared sympathetic, though I was still trying to figure out her angle. "Unfortunately, Angela's not the easiest person in the world to reason with about certain things. She trusts me. If I go through the process and give it a two thumbs up she'll cooperate with you. Otherwise, I highly doubt she'll ever go through with it."

She had me over a barrel. First of all, I wanted to prove to Carl Jenkins I had helped effect any real change in Angela's behavior. Though she claimed her work with me to be a total success, it wouldn't take him long to realize she was playing him. Secondly, I had to find out if she was in cahoots with Mestral—or the Darvells—or both, and uncover their endgame.

"All right, I'll do it—with one caveat—you have to come clean with me first."

Caroline looked mystified. "I don't catch your drift. People say I'm an open book."

"Is Lupe Lopez one of those people?"

"I don't know a Lupe Lopez."

"Really? Then why are you driving around in her car?"

"Angela loaned me the car. It belongs to a very close friend of hers named Madame Mestral. She lets her use it whenever she needs to. I'm sure she informed her I would be driving it today."

"Maybe she did, the problem is it isn't hers to loan in the first place. Mestral borrows the Corvette from a woman named Lupe Lopez, and she has no idea her vehicle has been turned into a Zipcar."

"I'm so sorry." Caroline sounded genuinely contrite. "Believe me, I wasn't aware of the situation and I doubt Angela knows anything about it either. She's not the sort of person to take advantage of others."

She was calm. She was rational. And I believed her. "How do you know Madame Mestral?"

"I've never met her. Like I said, she's a friend of Angela's. They've known each other for a while, but I'm afraid I don't know where or how they were introduced."

"Which one of you wrote the play, *Magic & Mayhem: The Haunted Forest Murders*?"

Caroline hesitated before answering. "I did."

"That's not what I heard. Are you sure you're not letting a friend use your name as a smokescreen?"

She appeared to be pondering her next response. "Anything I say to you in here today will be considered confidential?"

"It will, if you decide to become a client—with certain exceptions proscribed by California law."

"I do plan on having you hypnotize me."

"Then fill out this paperwork," I handed her a clipboard, "and we'll make it official."

She hastily filled in the forms and gave them back to me.

I scanned the documents, everything seemed to be in order. In the section, "What Would You Like To Accomplish Through Hypnosis?" she had written, "Help a friend."

"Am I a client of yours now?" she asked.

I nodded my head. "So who wrote the play?"

"Her name is Cissy Forrester."

CHAPTER THIRTY-NINE

Who Aren't You

C ISSY FORRESTER *did* write the play about her brother Tommy's murder. Finally, some confirmation I'm not barking up the wrong tree. "Caroline, how are you and Angela connected to Cissy?"

"Angela and I met each other through Cissy, though Angela has known her longer."

Now for the million-dollar question. "Are you and Angela using pseudonyms?"

"I don't know what you mean. Cissy's the one using my name as a nom de plume."

I wasn't quite certain of the best way to broach this topic, so I figured I'd plow on through and see how she reacted. "When Cissy was a child there was another Angela Fowler and Caroline Foster in her life. Both of them knew her brother, Tommy—one was an old high school chum and the other his fiancé."

Caroline looked perplexed, but her tone was matter-of-fact. "I don't know what to say except they're not what you'd call unusual names. Cissy is a bit of an odd duck, she may have sought us out because of it."

"What do you mean?"

"She's a hermit, doesn't get out much and for the most part keeps to herself. I'm much closer to Angela."

"Where did you meet her?"

"Angela?"

"No, Cissy."

"It seems like I've known her forever," Caroline rubbed her forehead, "I can't seem to recall when or where we met though." Her face appeared flushed. "May I please have a glass of water?"

Having become leery of dematerializing clients, I had stocked a few bottles behind my desk. "Here you go," I handed one to her, "there's a clean glass on the table beside you."

She poured the contents into the tumbler and drank it down in a couple of gulps. Hopefully, she wouldn't need to use the restroom before our session ended. "So when are you going to hypnotize me?"

"Soon. One more background question, how do you know the Darvells?"

"Who are they?"

"The people who run the Solar Lodge. You handed a play flyer to my brother the night we attended one of their meetings at It's All About The Bean."

"I thought you looked familiar," Caroline said. "Cissy asked me to go. Something to do with her friend, Madame Mestral, and a guy named Samir. I'd report back to her about what I had seen there. Personally, I find the organization to be on the freaky side. When I mentioned I felt uncomfortable attending those meetings, she asked me to go once more and make sure I got a flyer into your brother's hands. She described what he looked liked and I did as she asked. I figured he must be a producer. People will go to crazy extremes to land a deal in this town. An actress friend of mine joined AA and NA to make some offline connections."

Caroline seemed on the up and up. Based on what she told me, it appeared she and Angela were innocent pawns in Mestral's con game. Now I had to determine if Cissy Forrester really was *the* Cissy Forrester. And, if she turned out to be legit, was The Madame taking advantage of her or was she a willing co-conspirator? But I would have to place my speculations on hold for the moment, I had a new client to put into trance.

I picked up the personal data form she completed. "It says on here you've never been hypnotized."

Caroline shook her head, "Not to my knowledge anyway."

"Hypnosis is a natural state we all slip in and out of, a good example of this is what is known as 'highway hypnosis.' You're driving along the road listening to the radio or thinking about your schedule for the day, and next thing you know you've missed your exit. Your subconscious mind operated the car for you, while your conscious mind was concentrating on something entirely different. A similar thing takes place when you get wrapped up in a movie or a novel. The passage of time gets distorted, hours slip by in what feels like minutes. Maybe someone walks in the room and taps you on the shoulder—startled—you jump! This happens because your attention has been completely focused on a book or the TV. Your body's still in the room, but your mind is in an illusory location."

"I thought hypnosis was more akin to being asleep," Caroline said.

"That's a popular misconception fueled by pop culture and standard hypnotist lingo. When a hypnotherapist says 'deep sleep' to someone, what's really being invoked is a state of intense relaxation."

"So what you're saying is you're not going to subject me to any Svengali-like 'look deep…deeper…into my eyes' business."

I laughed, "In a nutshell—pretty much. So is there anything you want to work on? I know you wrote down you're only doing this to help Angela overcome her fear of going into trance. I don't see any reason why we can't accomplish that along with a personal goal."

"Let me mull it over for a minute." Caroline sat there still and quiet. "You know I don't remember much about my childhood, everything's sort of foggy. My clearest recollections start around the age of fourteen. I'd like to go back and see what I've forgotten."

Fishing around in someone's mind to retrieve memories is not a very reliable pursuit. The subconscious makes no distinction between fantasy and reality. I didn't want to inadvertently trigger a case of false memory syndrome. "Are you hoping to find confirmation of some event in particular?"

Caroline shrugged, "I don't know…maybe see if I was a Brownie…find out what my favorite activities were…my best subjects in school."

Her request seemed innocuous enough for me to proceed. What harm could come from revisiting some schoolgirl pursuits? I walked over to Caroline and adjusted her chair into a full recline. "I'll start by leading you through a progressive muscle relaxation."

"Sounds good to me. I'm all about relaxing."

I walked over to the windows behind my desk. Lex was curled up on the patio, near the purple bougainvillea, basking in the morning sun. After closing the shutters, I walked over to the bookshelf and turned on the CD player. The soothing mix of ocean waves lapping the shore, combined with tranquil, alpha state inducing music, was a useful tool for facilitating a smooth transition into the hypnotic state. "Are you comfortable?" I asked Caroline.

"No complaints," she said.

"All right, let's begin by taking a series of long, deep breaths." I adjusted the volume on the music and returned to my seat. "Allow yourself to tune in to your own natural rhythm with each cleansing inhale…and each relaxing exhale. You may notice your eyelids feeling heavier and heavier with each successive breath…when you find you can no longer keep them open…let them close naturally."

Caroline's eyelids fluttered shut, her breathing continued to deepen.

"Now I want you to bring your attention to your feet…as you become aware of the weight of your shoes, you will notice a relaxing sensation moving through your lower extremities up into the rest of you body…this might feel cool to you…or possibly warm…it may even tingle…however it seems to you…this soothing energy will gradually spread throughout your entire body."

Her feet gave a slight twitch, indicating she was fully cooperating with my subtle commands. I could tell by the quick responses, she was a highly suggestible subject.

After another ten minutes of this unwinding process, I performed an eye challenge test—a technique used for gauging hypnotic depth. "You are so relaxed now you may not have noticed your eyes are stuck shut… you may try to open them…but the more you try…the tighter they become. No need to worry about any of this…just take another breath and go even deeper as I count backwards from ten…nine…eight…seven…going deeper and deeper…six…five…allowing yourself to go as deep as you need to…four…three…two…the physical world recedes as you go deep down inside yourself…one…zero…deep sleep!" I snapped my fingers.

Caroline appeared to be resting comfortably. Her breathing slow and steady.

"I would like to take you for a ride in a special elevator. If you are agreeable to this, please raise the middle finger of your right hand." It was important to run something like this by the client, in case they were claustrophobic.

She raised her finger in the air, signaling I could proceed.

Each floor the elevator stops on represents a different age in a client's life. So I would know which floor we'd be starting our journey from, I checked the birthdate written on her client info sheet—October 16, 1968. There was that date again, though this time it was two years after Tommy Forrester's death and Angela Fowler's birth. My intuition told me something out of the ordinary was going on here. Perhaps she had not been upfront with me after all.

"When were you born, Caroline?"

She did not move. She did not speak.

I rephrased the question as a direct command and spoke in a louder voice. "Tell me your birthdate."

Caroline was still non-responsive.

In my studies, I learned of subjects who could rapidly reach profound Theta trance levels, and slip into a form of hypno-paralysis beyond the reach of sound. Some only ignored certain words or phrases, others had been known to blot out entire people. I'd also heard of cases where people with a history of psychosis could experience a hypnosis-triggered break with reality, and use the hypnotic state as a convenient escape route. If Caroline had listed any past or present mental health issues on her form, I would have insisted on a medical referral before proceeding.

I walked over to the recliner and touched Caroline's hand—she was ice cold. Her measured breathing maintained its pace. I took the soft, gold and blue throw—decorated with images of sun, moon, and stars—from the back of the recliner and draped it over her body. Taking her hand again, I squeezed it gently as I spoke, "Where are you, Caroline?"

Her voice was barely audible. "In an elevator."

Phew! A case of selective hearing. Feeling somewhat encouraged by her speech, I decided it was safe to proceed. "Which floor are you on?"

"The fourteenth."

The age her childhood memories begin. "Let's go down a few floors."

"I can't," there was panic in her voice, "it's stuck!"

Stroking her hand, I reassured her. "Everything's all right, you are not alone. Though you can't see me, I am with you—guiding you—making sure you are safe."

The tension left her body.

"I'm activating a switch which overrides the system, the elevator should start to move at any moment."

"It's moving now," she said.

"We'll take this slowly. At each floor the elevator stops on, you'll encounter yourself at the corresponding age. So on the thirtieth floor, you'll be thirty…on the twentieth floor, you'll be twenty… and so forth. We'll make our first stop at the twelfth floor. Let me know when the doors open."

"They're opening," she said.

"What do you see?"

"Angela is standing there."

Funny, she should be seeing herself standing there. "Step out onto the twelfth floor and look for your younger self."

"Angela won't let me, she's blocking the way."

At this point I wasn't sure if she was encountering her real life friend, Angela, or a metaphoric representation created by her psyche to shield her from a long-buried childhood trauma. Since it wasn't my intention to engage in a psychotherapeutic fishing expedition, I thought it best to move on. "Let's close the doors and go down two more floors."

"Angela wants to get on the elevator with me." She sounded anxious.

This sounded like a good idea. A person's subconscious mind was wired for self-preservation, taking imaginary Angela along for the ride would provide an extra measure of insurance. "Invite her inside and we'll be on our way."

"She's standing next to me." Caroline's voice had steadied.

"Next stop, tenth floor." I waited two beats. "The doors are opening. What do you see?"

"It's Cissy. She's crying."

Was this real Cissy or representational Cissy? "Would you like to get off the elevator and comfort her?"

"My feet won't move."

Another block. "Does Angela want to go to her aid?"

"She's stuck, too."

"Why don't you ask Cissy to join you?"

"She's afraid." The voice had changed, it sounded familiar, but it definitely wasn't Caroline speaking.

"Are you all right, Caroline?"

"I think so," her voice answered from afar.

"She's fine," the other voice said.

"Who are you?" I asked.

"Angela Fowler. We had an appointment set up for today. Sorry I'm late."

CHAPTER FORTY

Revelation 10

NGELA FOWLER'S VOICE coming out of Caroline Foster's mouth was not something I'd bargained for, this put a whole new spin on what I was up against. Though I'm not a trained psychologist, it looked like I may have inadvertently uncovered a DID (Dissociative Identity Disorder)—what used to be referred to as multiple personality disorder. I needed to immediately inform Dr. Carl Jenkins of this latest development, though my first challenge was to safely bring Caroline/Angela out of trance and back into conscious reality in one piece—whatever that meant.

"Angela, may I please speak with Caroline again?"

"I sent her away, this is supposed to be my appointment." Her voice was more strident and self-assured than usual.

"True, though you did ask her to go into hypnosis for you."

"She did and now I'm here to continue."

We were at a standstill. I wanted to bring her out of hypnosis and quickly wrap up the session so I could confer with Dr. Jenkins. I was leery of doing this while Angela was dressed as Caroline, since I wasn't sure if this type of incongruity could trigger a severe abreaction.

"Is Caroline on the tenth floor?"

"No, Cissy won't let us get off the elevator."

In my shock, I'd forgotten all about Cissy blocking the entrance to the tenth floor. When Angela wouldn't let Caroline get off at the twelfth floor, she joined her in the elevator—shortly after, Caroline vanished. Would the same thing happen if Cissy got on-board—would Angela morph into Cissy Forrester?

"Invite Cissy onto the elevator."

"Cissy wants us to leave." Angela was agitated. "She's not ready to come forward yet."

"Should we move on to the eighth floor?"

"No," she said adamantly. "I don't want to disappear like Caroline."

At last I had found Cissy Forrester, trapped inside her own subconscious, hiding behind the guise of two protective fragments of her personality—Angela Fowler and Caroline Foster. It was only fitting she would adopt the names of two of the young women in her brother's life. From what I was able to piece together, up until the moment of his death, Tommy had filled the role of protector in her life. With him gone, she needed to seek sanctuary elsewhere.

"Angela, the elevator doors are closing and we are heading back up to the twelfth floor where Caroline picked you up." I decided to employ some reverse logic. "I want to thank you for your invaluable contribution to today's session."

"Is that it? Are we through?" She picked up on my subtle suggestion.

"For now. Twelfth floor! Doors are opening."

"Should I get off here?"

"If you wouldn't mind." I waited in silence for her to exit. "Next stop, fourteenth floor!" If things were going as planned, an empty, imaginary elevator was on its way to pick up Caroline Foster and bring her back to my office. "Fourteenth floor! Doors are opening." I patiently waited before asking my next question. "Caroline, are you on the elevator?"

"Yes," her voice was weak.

"Are you alone?"

"I'm never alone," she replied.

Ain't that the truth. I rephrased my query. "Do you see anyone else on-board the car with you?"

"No one."

"Doors closing! I'm putting the elevator in express mode. The next stop will be the present day. You will rest comfortably until we arrive at your floor."

I took this opportunity to closely scrutinize Caroline's appearance. She didn't look at all like Angela Fowler. She was a redhead, not a blonde. It didn't look like she was wearing a wig, though Angela's blonde bob could have been a fake. Angela always hid her hair under a floppy black hat and her eyes behind oversized sunglasses. I'd never met her as Cissy Forrester, so I had no idea what she looked like when presenting herself under her true persona. As Caroline, she'd done an incredible special effects makeup job turning Jack into Elvis. Compared to that, I'm sure creating these different looks for herself was bush league.

Moving back behind my desk, I finished bringing her out of trance. "Doors opening, please exit the car." I gave her a moment before continuing, "Are you off the elevator, Caroline?"

"Yes, I am."

"Good…I want you to visualize yourself floating on a cloud of peace…in a sea of tranquility…not a care or worry in the world. As I count from one to five…you will bring this pleasant feeling of lightness back with you…leaving behind any memory of what you experienced here today…you will awake refreshed and energized at the count of one…two…three…four…five…eyes open…wide awake!"

Caroline's eyes popped open and she snapped out of trance right on cue.

I was relieved the session was over. "How do you feel?"

"A little groggy," she yawned. "Is that normal?"

It was the only normal thing about her hypnotic journey. "Yes, some clients feel that way when first coming out of trance. It should wear off momentarily. Do you have any questions or observations you'd like to share with me?"

A quizzical look came over her face. "I can't seem to remember anything. Are you sure I was hypnotized?"

"Hypnoamnesia is common in deeper states." And when I put in a post-hypnotic suggestion directing you to forget. I wasn't sure how she would react to finding out she was a splintered fragment of Cissy Forrester's personality. It seemed prudent to maintain the status quo until I notified her psychotherapist.

"What am I going to tell Angela when she asks me what it was like?"

"Be honest." I wasn't sure if my post-hypnotic suggestion would be binding on her alter egos. "How do you feel right now?"

She stretched out her arms. "Never felt better, it's like I had some kind of mental massage."

"Tell Angela that, it should soothe her qualms about completing a session with me."

After I felt reasonably assured the hypnosis had not left any negative aftereffects, I sent Caroline on her way and reached out to Dr. Jenkins.

His secretary answered, "Dr. Jenkins' office. How may I assist you?"

"It's Roberta Law. Is he in?"

"Yes, but he's asked not to be disturbed. Can I take a message?"

"I'm calling about one of his patients. It's an emergency."

"Hold, please."

I was barely sixteen bars into hearing ABBA sing—appropriately enough—"SOS" when Carl picked up the phone. "What's the matter, Roberta? Has Angela gone missing again?"

"In a way. Something happened while I had a friend of hers in hypnosis today. Not that I'm an expert, but I'm pretty sure she has a split personality."

"I'm confused, what does her friend's hypnosis session have to do with Angela?"

"I was doing an age regression when somewhere between the ages of twelve and ten, Caroline—that's the friend's name—turned into Angela."

"So you think this Caroline person is one of Angela's alters?"

"Yes and no," I took in a deep breath, "I think both Caroline Foster and Angela Fowler are alters for someone else—a woman named Cissy Forrester."

There was complete silence on the other end of the line.

"Carl, are you still there?"

"Yes...yes," Carl sounded distracted, "I need a moment to take this all in and process it."

"Caroline Foster showed up for Angela's appointment this morning. She was twenty minutes late, and told me Angela had asked her to come in her place because she was afraid to be put under. She wanted Caroline to tell her what hypnosis felt like and assure her it was safe before experiencing it herself."

"I thought you already hypnotized her. What about that big breakthrough she had?"

"We did have a second appointment together and managed to make it through the initial interview, but she snuck out of my office while I was moving my dog, Lex, to another room."

"I thought you were using the therapy dog in conjunction with her sessions." Carl did not sound pleased.

"Lex was instrumental in getting her to actually come into my office and talk with me. I felt he would be a distraction during trance work." The more I tried to explain myself, the worse I felt about the whole situation. "Believe me, Carl, it was never my intention to mislead you. Things got out of hand. I scheduled today's appointment to try and get to the bottom of what was going on."

"Looks like the bottom you found is only the tip of the iceberg." Carl's voice was still stern, but more relaxed.

"As soon as I stumbled upon the splinter personalities, I brought her out of hypnosis."

"Where is she now?"

"I gave her a post-hypnotic suggestion to prevent her from remembering what happened here today and sent her home."

"Thanks for the heads up, Roberta. I didn't mean to be terse, you caught me off guard. It's a little startling to find out a patient is not who you thought they were—frankly, I'm embarrassed I didn't catch this myself."

"I appreciate your understanding, Carl."

"What you've told me about Angela—I mean, Cissy—puts her entire case into a new light. Did she mention anything about her brother?"

"She hinted at a turbulent childhood and told me she was estranged from her family, but she never mentioned any siblings specifically.

"His name was Tommy. He died in a tragic hiking accident."

CHAPTER FORTY-ONE

Torn Between Two Alters

T HIS WAS SUCH foreign territory to me. "Is it common for alters to have the same siblings as the original personality, Carl?"

"It's rare, but not unheard of, why do you ask?"

"Cissy Forrester's brother is named Tommy, too, and he supposedly died in a hiking mishap like Angela's. As a matter of fact, the date of his death—October 16, 1966—coincides with Angela Fowler's birthday. And Caroline Foster, the other alter, was born two years later on October 16, 1968."

"Interesting. What else did you uncover about Cissy Forrester?"

"Here's my theory, for what it's worth. Cissy was the victim of ritual sexual abuse at the hands of her stepfather, Edward Lawson. Her mother, Bonnie, was either complicit or chose to ignore the whole thing. I think the molestation started when she was ten years old, after her brother was drafted and sent to Vietnam. Upon his return, Tommy Forrester suspects something sinister is happening to his sister. On the day of his death, he tracks his stepfather to the Cobb Estate aka The Haunted Forest, a popular hiking area. He catches him, along with his best friend and another fellow, preparing to rape his sister as part of some crazy devil worshipping ceremony. In the process of rescuing his sister, Tommy gets murdered and Cissy witnesses the death of her beloved brother. The trauma of that moment causes her personality to split and Angela Fowler is born."

"You had quite the productive session, Roberta."

I was proud to have made such a favorable impression.

But Carl wasn't through. "There's one problem with your theory. Not one alleged case of satanic ritual abuse has ever been substantiated. A high percentage of patients diagnosed with DID make claims of this nature. Many of us in the field have come to the conclusion these memories are nothing more than another symptom of their underlying mental condition. I don't think it would be wise of us to reignite another moral panic like we experienced in the Eighties, do you?"

Carl was referring to the rash of false accusations lobbed at people in infamous cases like the McMartin preschool trial. I certainly didn't want to be the instigator of the next media-fueled cause célèbre. And I wasn't about to tell him how an ancient Egyptian entity named Samir guided my haphazard investigation of the Tommy Forrester case.

"Maybe I've let my imagination get the best of me."

"Your brother mentioned you have a theatrical background."

"Yes, I was an actor prior to becoming a hypnotherapist."

"Why don't we chalk up this overenthusiasm to your inherent thespian nature?" There was a note of condescension in his voice. "I'll take over from here, starting with the resumption of my duties as Cissy's exclusive therapist."

I felt like a fool. "Whatever you think is best, Carl."

"I have to go now, my next patient is waiting."

"Goodbye, Carl. Are we still on for the thirty-first?"

"The thirty-first? Oh...yes...it almost slipped my mind—the Halloween seance. I'll be there to evaluate the inscrutable Madame Mestral, as promised. One more thing before I go—you did a great job, kid. If it wasn't for your hypnotic skills, I might never have discovered Angela's secret."

I was relieved to hear Carl's parting remark and know he didn't consider me to be a total nincompoop.

* * *

Halloween fell on a cold, dreary Monday. The weather suited my mood and seemed like a fitting backdrop for an evening spent contacting the spirits of the dearly departed. The weekend leading up to the big event had been low key. I decided to forgo the Hell's Papas gig at the CIA and spend some quiet time at home. When I wasn't curled up with Lex in front of the fireplace—catching up on my reading—I was munching popcorn in front of the flat screen, binge watching my way through my Netflix queue. So I was looking forward to getting back out into the world, even if it was *the otherworld*.

After breakfast I checked in with Lupe to confirm everything was going ahead as planned. "Hi, it's me. Are we still on for tonight?"

"Roberta, I'm so glad you called. I'm worried about Madame Mestral. She's been under the weather all weekend."

"Has she been having one of her spells?" I didn't have much sympathy for the so-called medium. The way she had latched onto Cissy Forrester—a person with a severe mental illness—using and manipulating the woman for her own personal gain was a despicable act.

"I'm not sure, she's barricaded herself in her room. I've been bringing her meals up on a tray. She picks at her food, I swear she hasn't eaten more than a few bites. I think this seance has put too much pressure on her, maybe we should call it off."

The Madame wasn't going to worm her way out of this one so easily. No more hiding behind her conveniently timed health scares. I'd alerted Officer Sanchez to my suspicions, and he got in touch with a couple of his buddies assigned to the Bunco Unit over at the LAPD's Rampart Division. I offered to wear a wire, but the other officers suggested a cheap recorder app for my iPhone would suffice. They said I could drop by the station after the seance and they would listen to the playback to determine if anything illegal was going on.

"You know how it is with performers, Lupe. It's not unusual to get pre-show jitters."

"Madame Mestral is not a performer!" I'd touched a nerve. "She is the most gifted sensitive of our era."

More like the most gifted con artist. "I'm sorry, Lupe. I didn't mean to diminish her psychic abilities." Not. "She's a very resilient lady, I'm sure she'll be fine. Call me if you need anything, I'll see you later."

Since, at Madame Mestral's insistence, the seance had been scheduled to begin between eleven-thirty and midnight, I still had plenty of opportunity to hand out some treats—along with a few scares—to the neighborhood kids. My house had developed a bit of reputation as the local go-to place for a first-class All Hallows' Eve experience, and I didn't want to disappoint. Keeping with tradition, I had not scheduled any clients and Louie was coming over to help me get the place in proper horrific shape. Now that my work with Angela/Cissy was behind me it was safe to get my spook back on.

Louie showed up with lunch at noon. "I picked up some burritos from Sharkey's. Did you finish assembling your Trick-or-Treat bags?"

"Check." I pointed to several large, stainless steel bowls lined up on a table in my foyer.

Louie followed me into the dining room. "What's left to do?"

"Let's see," I pulled up the list on my iPad, "the outdoor lights are hung, the flying bats are rigged, the tombstones are planted on my front lawn. I could use some help setting up the fog machine, the corpse in the coffin, and the outdoor speaker for the haunted house sound effects. Are you sure you don't want to stick around for the antics?"

"Would if I could, but this shindig at my aunt's is already cutting into my evening at the WeHo Halloween Carnaval. Soon as I leave her, I'm slipping into a dazzling, red-sequined, evening gown with a big ole slit up the side, and a flashy auburn hairpiece worthy of Wigstock."

"Going as Ginger from *Gilligan's Island*?"

Louie snapped his fingers and did a head roll, "You betcha, girlfriend."

"What? No shoes?"

"I have those castoff ruby slippers of Lupe's stretching away on a rack, as we speak."

"Is Danny going with you this year? I know how he hates to wear costumes."

"I managed to talk him into it. He's going as The Professor."

"Dungarees and a shirt—so he's going dressed as himself."

"Pretty much, but it'll work as a costume as long as he stays by Ginger's side."

"So there's a method to your madness."

We put the finishing touches on my House of Horrors, and Louie had me in hair and makeup by four o'clock. "Are you sure you want to go with the same Bride of Frankenstein look?"

"It's a neighborhood tradition. I don't want to disappoint the little ones venturing out on their first Trick-or-Treating expedition."

"Aww," Louie said, cosmetic brush in hand, "I had no idea you were such a sentimental sort of ghoul. Who's manning the smoke machine for you this year?"

"Ben's coming by right after work."

"In costume?"

"No, he said he wouldn't have enough time to get dressed up."

"Party poop." Louie positioned the black-and-white striped fright wig on top of my head.

"Make sure you get a snug fit," I adjusted the cap underneath, "the darn thing fell off last year and Lex ran into the backyard with it."

"Are you dressing him up as Igor again?"

"No way, that was a one-off. I think stealing my wig was his way of taking revenge on me for making him wear a costume."

Louie teased the Bride's hair into an even more exaggerated beehive. "Well, you know what they say, 'hell hath no fury'…"

"Like a pissed off beagle." We both laughed.

"Let me add a couple more scars," Louie took an eyeliner pencil to my face, "and then I think we're done."

'Whatever you say—my skin is your canvas."

"Voilà!" Louie handed me a mirror. "Perfection."

I surveyed his work. "You are a master."

"Now I've got to beam myself out of here and do my own transformation."

After Louie left, I slipped into my simple—yet tasteful—white muslin shroud and proceeded into the kitchen to get my hand-carved jack-o'-lantern. I went outside and placed the pumpkin on my front window ledge. It was already dusk, so I lit the candle inside. In the distance I heard the nervous laughter of children making the rounds from house to house. They would be arriving on my doorstep at any minute, and my smoke machine needed to be up and running. Wondering what was keeping Ben, I turned to go back inside. As I crossed the threshold, a rustling sound came from behind the sour orange hedge beside my door. Thinking a possum had decided to claim squatter's rights in the eight-foot high bush—and wishing to avoid a close encounter of the marsupial kind—I quickly stepped inside my foyer.

A hand grabbed hold of my right shoulder.

Frozen, I opened my mouth to scream. All that came out was a weak rasp.

The stranger pulled me back.

I reeled around to confront my assailant and found myself face-to-face with Frankenstein's monster.

The bolt-necked creature growled, "Woman," as he pulled me into his chest.

Sniffing trouble, Lex bounded to my rescue. The fiend slipped him a couple of skull-shaped dog biscuits, which he readily accepted—tail a wagging. Obviously, trouble wasn't the only scent he was tracking.

"Those treats better not be from China," I said.

"You know I know better than that. Where's his Igor outfit? I wore this getup because I thought we'd make a stellar Halloween trio."

Ben, Lex, and I walked into the living room together. "He heard you weren't getting dressed up, so he decided to follow suit. You know how headstrong beagles can be, especially when it comes to wardrobe decisions. Why'd you change your mind?"

"I didn't. Thought I'd surprise you for a change."

"It worked. You almost gave me a heart attack, sneaking up on me that way. I didn't even see your car out there."

"I parked it on the next street."

"You're an enterprising monster when you want to be. Can I get you a drink?" I reached for the bottle of Vampire Pinot Noir sitting on my coffee table.

Ben nodded his head, "A little hair of the bat would go down just fine."

I picked up a cut-crystal goblet and was about to pour when the doorbell rang.

"Rats! I'm not ready yet. Will you run into the dining room, and hit the switches for the fog machine and the sound effects, while I get the door?"

Ben stood up. "My bride's wish is my command."

The bell rang again, accompanied by the pounding of insistent little fists.

"Coming!" I grabbed a handful of goodie bags and slowly opened the door. "Welcome to my castle."

"Trick-or-treat!" the small group of kiddies shouted. There was a shimmering fairy princess, a bobby-soxer in a pink poodle skirt, and a tiny Count Dracula.

They were accompanied by an older kid, about twelve or so, wearing an oversized, red, crushed velvet suit with zebra print cuffs and lapels. He had a giant, purple fedora on his head and a huge, gold dollar sign hung from a long chain around his neck.

"And who are you supposed to be?" I asked the boy in red, as I dropped my offerings into their plastic pumpkins and sacks.

"I'm a pimp."

Interesting choice.

"This is for you." Huggy Bear shoved an envelope into my hand.

"Oh, is this for UNICEF?" I said in a surprised tone.

He laughed. "Is that what you call your dog?"

I turned to look behind, not realizing Lex had followed me to the door.

"Dumb name," the kid said before I had a chance to answer him.

"No, he goes by Lex." I looked down at the crumpled envelope. "I don't understand? What is this about?"

"Some lady in an old yellow car gave me five bucks to give it to you." He and his pals scattered across my lawn, over to the neighbor's house.

Ben took the envelope from me. "It's got your name on it."

"Go ahead, look inside."

He tore open the letter and read the contents. "Do not leave home tonight. Your life is in grave danger."

CHAPTER FORTY-TWO

Let's Call The Whole Seance Off

I ALERTED OFFICER SANCHEZ about the threat I received from Mestral. He told me the note could just as easily be interpreted as a warning, and there was no way of proving who sent it, but he would pass the info along to his buddies over at Rampart Division. The Madame's feeble attempt at scaring me off had made me more determined than ever to expose her.

The last Halloween straggler, a teenager—why is there always a lone teenager?—showed up around ten p.m. With the treats portion of the night out of the way, I put in a quick call to Lupe before heading over to her place.

"Hello," Lupe answered.

"Hi," I said.

"I've been expecting your call, Roberta."

"You have?"

"Yes, Madame Mestral had a premonition earlier this evening. She told me you would be calling to cancel."

"Actually, I want to know if it's okay if Ben and I come by early. We've given out the last of the Halloween candy and figured we could help you finish setting up for tonight."

"You're welcome anytime, though there's not much left to do." Lupe paused before continuing. "I'm still worried about Madame Mestral, it's not like her to be so off the mark with her predictions. These spells of hers are becoming more frequent and intense. She really has been having a rough go of it the past couple of days."

Wait till she sees how rough it gets when she lands in the slammer. I tried to put Lupe's mind at rest. "After tonight's seance, she can look forward to a nice long rest."

* * *

Still in costume, Ben and I arrived at Lupe's about a half hour prior to the main event. Seconds after we parked, an Access Paratransit van pulled up in front of Ben's Tesla. A blind man with a German shepherd stepped out of the vehicle. Bald-headed and tall—well over six feet—a dark overcoat covered his portly torso. His eyes were hidden behind a pair of wraparound shades.

"That must be Dr. Jenkins," I said to Ben.

"You've never met in person?"

"No. I keep forgetting he's blind. It's a good thing we got here early, he may need some assistance maneuvering the steps leading up to Lupe's." Ben and I got out of the car. "Dr. Jenkins?"

"Yes," he turned toward the sound of my voice, "is that you Roberta?"

I took a few brisk steps toward him. The German Shepherd snarled and lurched forward.

Dr. Jenkins snapped the lead. "Stop!" The dog immediately sat by his master's side, panting. "Please forgive, Hank. He's a very special type of service dog. Besides guiding me around everywhere, he's also trained to serve as a bodyguard. For some reason he sensed danger."

"Gee, I don't know what I did to spook him. I usually get along famously with animals. Maybe I was moving too quickly?"

"Could be. He's not fond of sudden movements."

"Do you think he'll be okay during the seance? Madame Mestral and her entities are not the most predictable or sedate characters."

"I'm sure he'll be fine, he's very obedient." Dr. Jenkins patted Hank's head. "Are you alone? I sense another presence nearby."

"Permit me to introduce, Dr. Ben Cohen."

Ben took Carl's hand, "Pleased to meet you, Dr. Jenkins."

"Please, call me Carl, Dr. Cohen."

"Only if you return the favor and call me Ben."

"What's your specialty, Ben?"

"I'm a parapsychologist."

"I see you're quite determined to get to the bottom of this Madame Mestral woman, Roberta."

"She can be quite tenacious when her suspicions are aroused," Ben said.

"So I've noticed," Carl said. "Have you heard anything from our errant client lately?"

I knew he was referring to Cindy Forrester since she was the only client we shared in common, although his choice of adjective struck me as strange. "Nothing since her appointment this past Friday. Why?"

"I haven't been able to get a hold of her. She's not returning my calls."

A chill ran through my bones, I couldn't tell if it was caused by the brisk wind that had kicked up or something else. "Brrr, let's go inside and get a cup of Lupe's Mexican hot chocolate."

Fourteen, steep, cement steps led up from the street to the front door of the Victorian house. Since there was no handrail, I offered Carl my arm. Hank walked alongside us. Ben followed from behind. When we reached the top, I turned the small, brass handle in the center of the door. A bell sounded on the other side.

Lupe answered. "Aren't you all a bit old to be trick-or-treating? I only give out candy to children." She slammed the door on us.

"We must be at the wrong house," Carl said.

"No, it's the right place. I don't think she recognized us; Ben and I are wearing costumes. We came right over from scaring kids in my neighborhood. He's Frankenstein's monster and I'm his bride."

Carl chuckled, "She must think I'm dressed as old De Lacey, the blind man who takes the creature in."

Ben and I laughed along with him, glad to know he had a sense of humor about the incident.

"Let me give this another try." I rang the bell a second time.

Lupe peered out from behind the sheer, white cotton curtains covering the oval-shaped glass in the door.

"It's Roberta and Ben," I shouted.

Lupe pointed at Carl.

"This is my guest, Dr. Jenkins."

"Why is everyone wearing a costume?" Lupe asked, reopening the door. "I'm not throwing a Halloween party here tonight. This seance is serious business."

"Ben and I dressed up to hand out candy at my place, then we came straight over here."

We followed Lupe into the living room. "Were you passing out candy also, Dr. Jenkins?"

My back stiffened, unsure of how Carl would react to Lupe's unseemly remark.

"Unfortunately, this isn't a costume," Carl said in an even tone.

Realizing her gaffe, Lupe switched topics. "Does your seeing eye dog get along with cats?"

"Hank doesn't pay much mind to cats."

"My gato, Hector, feels pretty much the same way about perros."

"Good," Carl nodded, "then we shouldn't have any problems. Cats and dogs are best kept at a respectable distance."

"Not always," Lupe disagreed. "I read about a blind dog who has a Seeing Eye cat for a friend."

"Will wonders never cease," Carl noted with condescension.

Lupe continued, apparently not picking up on Carl's slight, "Please make yourselves comfortable, each participant has an assigned seat."

The white chairs used on Sunday had been cleared from the room. A large, round, teak table surrounded by nine, straight-backed, wooden chairs had been set up in front of the blazing fireplace. According to the place cards, Ben and I were seated next to each other. Carl was between Madame Mestral and Lilith Darvell.

I escorted Carl to his chair. "Who came up with the seating chart?"

"Samir decided on the number and location of seats. He says nine is a most propitious number for such events, representing both magic and heaven. It's a sacred number in Egypt "

"Ah, yes, 'nine is divine,' " Carl said. "The freemasons consider it the eternal number of human immortality. Yet, when you flip it over it becomes a six—the number of the beast."

I sat down next to Ben. "Whatever you do, Carl, don't mention that to my brother when he arrives. Danny still battles religious delusions."

"Isn't all religion a form of delusion?" Carl said.

Ben joined in, "I take it you're not a fan of Jungian psychology, Carl."

"While sympathetic to religion and the power of its symbolism, Jung was more of an agnostic. In my life experience, I have found the avoidance of all things spiritual to be the most prudent path."

"Madame Mestral will turn you into a true believer," Lupe stated with unwavering certainty. "She'll be downstairs shortly. Would anyone like a drink in the meantime?"

"I'd love a cup of your special hot chocolate, if you have any," I said.

"There's a fresh batch of champurrado brewing in the kitchen right now. Can I interest anyone else in a cup?"

"Count me in," Ben said.

"Nothing for me," Carl said. "Would it be possible to get a bowl of water for Hank?"

"Of course," Lupe replied.

I stood up. "Let me give you a hand."

The front bell rang.

"I'm fine, Roberta. Could you see who that is for me?"

I walked into the foyer and opened the door.

Lilith Darvell stood alone on the porch. "Is this Lupe Lopez's residence?"

"Yes. Where's Lucious?"

"Do I know you?"

"It's Roberta Law. I'm wearing my annual Halloween attire."

Lilith scanned my body. "It's a good look for you." She pushed past me. "Is Lucious here?"

"No, I thought you were coming together."

"Change of plans. He had some pressing business to attend to, told me to meet him here."

"It's still early, Madame Mestral hasn't even joined us yet."
Lilith followed me into the living room. "You've already met Ben.
This is Dr. Carl Jenkins, you'll be sitting next to him. Carl, this
is Lilith Darvell."

Lilith slid onto the chair. "I hope that thing doesn't have fleas."

Hank growled.

Carl jerked the dog's collar. "Hush!"

I'd never seen such a decidedly unfriendly service dog, though I
might have to give his behavior a pass where Lilith was concerned.

Lilith cautiously eyed Hank. "Would you mind removing him to
the other side of you? It would put such a damper on the evening if
he bit me and I had to call Animal Control to come put him down."

Carl repositioned the dog, though he didn't look too
happy about it.

Lupe returned with the refreshments. "Welcome to my home,
Mrs. Darvell. Is your husband not joining us?"

Lilith was looking down at her cell phone. "I'm sending him
another text. Hopefully, he'll answer this one. It's not like him to
be incommunicado."

Louie called out from the foyer, "Ginger and The Professor
have arrived! Where is everybody?"

"In here!" I answered.

Danny and Louie joined the rest of us in the living room.

"Ay, caramba!" Lupe clasped her chest. "You had the surgery!"

"Calm down, already." Louie pulled the falsies out from under
his evening gown. "I keep telling you I'm gay, not transgender."

Lilith looked over at me. "I thought you two were a couple."

"So did I," Lupe agreed.

Ben put his arm around me. "She's all mine."

Danny followed suit with Louie. "And I've called dibs on him."
My brother turned his attention to Dr. Jenkins. "Carl, it's been
ages, how are you doing?"

"Right now—slightly confused—but I'm sure it will pass. Any
idea when we're going to start this seance? I have an early day
tomorrow."

A gong sounded upstairs.

"It's time," Lupe said.

Madame Mestral sauntered into the room wearing a diapha-
nous, purple kaftan. Her long, dark hair was hidden underneath a
Queen Nefertiti style headdress. And her feet were clad in silver,
Aladdin toe sandals. "My guides have informed me," she dramat-
ically swirled around, "they are ready to lead us into the ether."

CHAPTER FORTY-THREE

With A Little Help From Her Entities

T HE MADAME DID NOT seem the least bit under the weather. And judging by the way she glided in, I'd be willing to bet she had dipped into her pharmaceutical stash in preparation for the big event. She took no notice of the costumes some of us were wearing, and appeared to be in a partial trance state.

"You'll be sitting here," Lupe pulled out Mestral's chair for her, "between Dr. Jenkins and Mr. Darvell, as Samir requested."

"Who is this Samir I keep hearing about?" Carl asked, as Mestral settled in beside him.

"An ancient Egyptian entity Madame Mestral channels," Lupe answered.

"Really?" Carl smirked. "Will we have the pleasure of meeting him before the night is through?"

"We better," Lilith said. "He's the reason I showed up here tonight. Maybe he can help me get a line on some hard to find antiquities I've been trying to track down."

Mestral braced her hands, palms down, on the table. A vibration, which appeared to be emanating from the very core of her being, gradually overtook her body. "Yeow!" she screeched. "What a magnificent gathering Madame Mestral has assembled before me tonight," Samir's voice blasted out like a shockwave.

I reached under my shroud to activate the recording app on my iPhone.

"Surrender all your electronic gadgets to Lupe," Samir barked.

Damn it! She's a shrewd operator.

Lupe went around the table collecting phones.

"I need to hold onto mine," Lilith said. "My husband hasn't arrived yet. He may need to reach me."

"He will not join in our circle," Samir pronounced. "Not in a physical sense."

Lilith's unflappable air evaporated. "What's that supposed to mean?"

"All will be revealed," Samir snapped. "Patience is a virtue, even in the most amoral."

I was expecting Lilith to come back with one of her snide retorts, but she handed her phone over without a word and shrunk into her seat.

"Will we be able to continue without nine people present?" Lupe asked.

"A king will arrive to save the day," Samir assured her.

I'm dying to see how she pulls that one off.

The front doorbell sounded.

"He has arrived," Samir said.

Lupe walked toward the dining room. "Luis, be a dear and answer the door while I put these phones away."

Even with all the makeup he had slathered on his face, Louie looked as white as a sheet. "M-m-m-me?"

"I'll go," I said, anxious to expose Mestral at her game. Taking a deep breath, I flung the door open—Jack? "What are you doing here?"

He stepped over the threshold. "Elvis is in the buildin'. Sorry, 'bout bein' late. I rushed over soon as the show came down."

"Who told you to come here?"

"A little Goth chick named Electra. She asked me to show up as a favor for a friend." So she *is* in on this. "It's the least I could do after bangin' her at intermission."

"Right this way, Jack. Come join the party."

"Hey, how'd ya know my name?"

"It's Roberta."

"Whoa, Red." Jack looked worried. "Ya know I was just kiddin' 'bout gettin' my rocks off backstage with that baby vamp."

Sure. "You can take the seat on my right." I turned to the others. "For those of you who don't already know him, may I present the one and only, Jack Hensler.

Lupe burst out laughing, "Samir, you have such a playful sense of humor."

Carl had a bemused expression on his face. "I think I'm missing something."

"Jack's wearing an Elvis costume," I said.

"He *is* the King of Rock and Roll, after all." Louie still looked rattled.

Mestral clapped her hands. "Let us begin!" Samir bellowed.

Lupe dimmed the lights and placed a brass candelabrum in the center of the table. She lit each of the five white tapers before sitting down between Lilith and Louie.

"Our circle is complete," Mestral said in her lisping Spanish accent—Samir had taken a powder. The Madame nodded at Lupe.

"Please join hands," Lupe requested, "and close your eyes."

Everyone did as instructed—everyone except me. In addition to keeping watch on Mestral, I wanted to observe Lilith. Her husband, Lucious, had to be in cahoots with The Madame. His no-show was obviously a prearranged deal. The reasoning behind their grand scheme still escaped me, but I was sure we were all in for one hell of a show.

Madame Mestral's bowed head bobbed up and down, there was a labored quality to her breathing that I had not noticed prior. My fellow participants were quiet and still. A low, steady snore emanated from Dr. Jenkins vicinity, I suspected the culprit to be Hank. All that growling and snarling had taken its toll. I was about to nod off myself when a sudden chill wind whipped through the room. The candle flames danced wildly, though I could not detect the source of the breeze.

"Please forgive me," a weak voice spoke through Mestral, "I didn't know what was going on."

"Bonnie is that you?" Lilith asked.

"Yes," the distant sounding voice answered.

Lilith continued, "Are you dead?"

"I think so."

Lilith's quasi-verification of who was speaking was not enough to make a believer of me. With no way of confirming if Bonnie Lawson had passed away, I had to grin and bear it until Mestral's spectral performance drew to a close and I could put in a call to the hospital.

"Bonnie, where is Lucious? Is he okay?" Given the emphatic nature of Lilith's inquiry, I wondered if perhaps she didn't know where her husband had gotten to after all.

A male voice spoke, "Mrs. Lawson can't answer any more questions until she is properly debriefed. Come along with Dr. Greystoke now, madam."

In addition to his medical duties, it looked like the Victorian physician served as a sort of between worlds PR agent.

"Who killed my Tommy?" Lupe blurted.

"The young lady says the killer is close by," Sheila O'Hara spoke through Mestral. "But she's not prepared to speak the name yet, mum."

The Madame was pulling out all the stops, eliciting the aid of her full cast of characters and throwing in some new ones for good measure.

"And *who* might this young lady be?" I asked.

"She says her name is Cissy Forrester," Sheila replied.

Now I had her dead to rights—pun intended. "Cissy Forrester is alive!"

"What's she doin' hangin' out with a bunch of dead dudes?" Jack asked.

Louie jumped in, "Why didn't you tell me you found Tommy's sister?"

"That girl committed suicide years ago," Lilith added.

"Dr. Jenkins can back me up," I said, defending my position.

"Carl?" Danny said. "Is this true?"

"As of Friday, it seemed to be so. Though I can't vouch for her whereabouts at the moment."

In the midst of all the chatter, while the others still had their eyes closed, Madame Mestral got up from her seat and wandered away from the table. I tried to see where she was going, but the room was too dark.

"Do you hear that?" Lupe asked.

"It sounds like a child crying," Ben said.

Lupe opened her eyes. "Where is Madame Mestral?"

Carl and Lilith remained seated at the table, while the rest of us traced the plaintive sobs to the window on the other side of the room. Mestral's curly-toed slippers protruded from underneath the purple velvet drapes.

"Madame Mestral," Lupe called, "is everything okay?"

The weeping continued, reminding me of the night I found her in the fetal position on the floor of her closet.

Lupe was at a loss. "What should we do?"

"I think it would be best if we ended this seance," Danny advised. "She's been very stressed lately, the pressure is too much for her to take."

Ben concurred, "She does seem to be channeling a lot of entities at a very rapid pace. This constant displacement of her personality may be taking its toll."

I put my hand on the curtains and pulled them slightly open.

"Step away! Can't you see she's afraid?" Samir chastised. "Cissy will appear when she is ready to do so and not a second sooner. She won't let the murderer escape again."

"Okey-dokey," I said, moving back to my seat.

"This is ridiculous," Carl protested. "I will not be a party to this woman's breakdown." He got up so abruptly, he spooked Hank.

The guide dog stood there looking dazed, unsure of who or what was the enemy threatening his master.

"Not so fast, my friend," a man spoke from behind the drapery.

Lilith ran toward the voice. "Lucious, why are you hiding?"

"He's not back there," Carl insisted. "It's some kind of trick."

Lilith froze in her tracks. "How would you know? You've never even met my husband."

"On the contrary, my dear," Lucious spoke. "We knew each other during our youth."

Carl yanked Hank's collar and turned toward the foyer.

Lucious continued, "Our paths had not crossed for many years. Until today—when he killed me. Right, old pal?"

CHAPTER FORTY-FOUR

Leaving On An Astral Plane

UPON HEARING CARL had killed her husband, Lilith collapsed in a heap on the floor. Danny went to her aid. Lilith's visceral reaction convinced me she wasn't involved in any shakedown operation.

"Carl—I mean, Roy, contacted me early this morning to arrange a meeting concerning Cissy Forrester," the voice of Lucious continued from behind the curtains. "He said the missing girl had resurfaced and he needed my assistance getting her out of the way. I already had my suspicions about Cissy's reappearance. However, Roy's resurrection came as quite the surprise. Everyone thought he had died in Vietnam. Turns out all he lost over there was his eyesight."

"This is insane," Carl shouted. "You people don't actually believe this hocus-pocus drivel?"

"You did tell me you lost your eyesight in Vietnam," Danny said.

"I saw you kill my Tommy in the cemetery the other night," Lupe said.

"And Lucious *is* unaccounted for," Louie added.

Carl Jenkins must be Tommy's friend, Roy Hastings, the guy the real Angela Fowler told me about at Holy Family Church's Fall Festival. And Roy Hastings must be 'Ray,' the character from Cissy Forrester's play who delivers the fatal blow to her brother. This explains his sudden enlistment in the army right after Tommy's death, he wanted to get as far away from the scene of the crime as possible—some place no one was going to come looking for him.

Carl pulled Hank close to his side as he pushed past Ben and me. "You're all certifiable."

Madame Mestral appeared from behind the drapes, her voice was low and timid, "Roy Hastings, you murdered my brother. You know it and I know it, and soon the whole world will know it"

Carl paused at the entrance to the foyer. "Cissy?"

Mestral moved toward Carl, "I'm not running anymore," her speech grew stronger with each word.

Hank snarled as she approached.

"Tommy has waited a very long time for justice," she said, closing in on her brother's assailant.

A growling Hank strained against his collar.

"Not one step closer, Cissy," Carl threatened.

Mestral continued walking. "You don't scare me anymore."

Carl dropped Hank's lead. "Attack!"

The dog leaped for Mestral's throat. Before any of us had a chance to react, Hank let out a pained yelp in mid-air and fell to the ground at The Madame's feet.

"Carl Jenkins aka Roy Hastings, you're under arrest for the murder of Thomas Forrester and the attempted murder of Madame Mestral," said Officer Sanchez, Taser gun still in hand. "Can Elvis, Ginger, and Frankenstein help me move this dog to a secure location until Animal Control arrives." He cuffed Carl and looked over at Danny. "How's Mrs. Darvell doing, Professor?"

"She'll be fine." Danny escorted Lilith to her seat.

"Where did you come from?" I said to Sanchez.

"He's been sitting in my kitchen eating churros and drinking champurrado," Lupe answered, while the men moved the unconscious Hank into the pantry. "Madame Mestral asked me to phone him, she had a strong premonition something terrible was going to happen here tonight. I wanted to cancel, but she insisted we continue as planned."

I couldn't ignore the evidence any longer—The Madame was a bona fide medium. Sadly, this realization couldn't save Cissy Forrester. Her use of Madame Mestral as a channel was proof positive of her demise. My greatest remorse was in knowing I had been the one to alert her murderer to her existence.

Mestral had not budged from the spot she was standing in.

"I'm afraid I've misjudged you," I said.

The Madame did not acknowledge me, so I repeated myself. Still no response. "Danny, you better take a look at her, too."

Danny went over to Mestral. "She's appears to be in a state of catatonia."

"The strain was too much for her," Lupe said. "I knew I should have gone ahead and called the whole thing off."

"I'll call an ambulance," Danny said.

A tremor went through Mestral's body. "No doctors," she lisped emphatically.

"Where is my husband?" Lilith was oblivious to The Madame's current state.

"His body or his soul?" Mestral asked flatly.

"Both," an anguished Lilith replied.

"His corporeal self will be found in the Arroyo Seco river basin near Devil's Gate Dam—his vital force is with the devil himself."

A distraught Lilith rushed over to Mestral, grabbed her by the shoulders and shook her violently. "No, it can't be so," she railed.

The Madame reacted like a limp rag doll.

Sanchez and the others came back into the room. "Perhaps you should wait elsewhere, Mrs. Darvell," he interceded. "Let me radio for a car to escort you home."

"I'll take her," Jack offered. I wasn't sure if he was being gallant or attempting to fill his Tantric dance card.

Not long after they left, Animal Control arrived to collect Hank and Officer Sanchez took Carl/Roy in for booking.

Through it all Madame Mestral remained stoic. We were worried about her condition. Danny had managed to get her to sit down, but she would not acquiesce to medical intervention.

It was late and Ben was ready to go, but I knew I couldn't leave without finding out what happened to Cissy. "Madame Mestral, there's something I need to ask you. Where is Cissy Forrester?"

Mestral took a long deep breath, then slowly exhaled. "I fear she's hiding somewhere in the dark recesses of my mind."

"Yes, I understand. What I meant is what did Dr. Jenkins do with her body? We should alert the police to the existence of another victim."

The Madame closed her eyes and slumped over in the chair, body vibrating to the point of convulsion.

"Please, Roberta," Lupe intervened, "no more of this tonight. She needs to rest."

"Do not worry, my sweet songbird," Samir's voice roared, as Mestral's head jerked up with a sudden force. "She will soon be at perpetual rest, as will I."

"It's those spells of hers, isn't it?" Danny said.

"Yes and no," Samir said.

"Has her excessive EMF exposure put her health in jeopardy?" Ben asked.

"On the contrary," Samir let out a belly laugh, "it has been her saving grace."

"I don't get it." Louie looked as confused as I felt. "What's the matter with her?"

"Nothing's the matter with her, the problem exists with another."

"Is The Madame ill or not?" I asked, barely concealing my impatience with the ancient Egyptian's game of verbal cat and mouse.

"Madame Mestral does not exist, at least not in your current limited understanding of consciousness. Let me summon someone to explain this in a more concrete fashion." Samir's voice dropped to a whisper, "No need to hide anymore, it's safe to come forward."

Mestral's body contorted. The next words were not Samir's, but Cissy's, "You wish to speak with me?"

"Do you know who I am?"

"Roberta Law, Angela and Caroline's therapist." Even in the afterlife her fragile psyche was split.

"What did Dr. Jenkins do with your body?"

"You mean Roy?"

"Yes, Roy Hastings."

"He raped me," her voice held a slight tremor, "along with my stepfather and Lucious."

She was still fixated on the moment her ego shattered. I needed to nudge her consciousness to more recent events. "Do you remember Roy hurting you in the past few days?"

"I know he wanted to, but he couldn't find me. After he heard about Caroline and Angela hiding me, they introduced me to Madame Mestral. The girls knew she would keep me safe."

After all my suspicions about Mestral, it looked like she was going to emerge the heroine of this saga. Though in the end, she couldn't protect Cissy from her fate. "But, he did locate you."

She shook her head, "No, he didn't. I found him—here—tonight—with all of you. And he'll never be able to hurt anyone again." Her head tilted to one side and her overall demeanor shifted. Samir spoke, "At this juncture it is best if the rest of us fade away. You can carry on from here, Cissy. My human friends will assist you in the process." Mestral's face went blank.

The Madame was on the verge of keeling over when Ben stepped in and caught hold of her collapsing body. "Call 9-1-1."

Lupe reached for the phone. "Forgive me, Madame Mestral. I must call for a doctor."

Danny checked The Madame's pulse. "It's another one of her fainting episodes."

"I'll get a wet cloth for her forehead." Louie ran into the kitchen.

A dazed Mestral reached for the Egyptian hat atop her head and pulled it off, revealing a shock of white hair instead of her usual dark tresses. "Where am I?"

"You're at my house, Madame Mestral," Lupe said.

"Madame Mestral and the others are gone." She cautiously rose to her feet, studying the room and the people in it, as if trying to get her bearings. The stupefied look on her face gradually faded. "My name is Cissy—Cissy Forrester. And I'm here to stay."

* * *

Discovering Madame Mestral was one of Cissy Forrester's alters posed more questions than it answered. While munching churros from the Day of the Dead care package Lupe had packed for us, Ben and I discussed the implications on the drive back to my place in the early morning hours.

"Does this mean Samir, Dr. Greystoke, and Sheila O'Hara are also alters?" I asked.

"Good question." Ben took a bite from the churro I was holding.

"Danny still believes she was legitimately channeling them as Madame Mestral. Which makes me wonder something else…"

"Can an alter be psychic, if the original personality is not?"

"Bingo!"

"Well, some of the things Madame Mestral's entities divulged could not possibly have been known by Cissy."

"Yeah, Bonnie Lawson's appearance and that whole Lucious business was pretty out there. Officer Sanchez said the hospital confirmed the time of Bonnie's death. It occurred while the seance was in progress. He's got a search team going out to look for Lucious' body as soon as the sun comes up."

Ben glanced at the dashboard clock. "Which should be any minute now."

"Tired?"

"Depends, what do you have in mind?"

I closed my eyes and conjured up one of my wildest sexual fantasies. "Turn on your extrasensory spyware."

A naughty smile appeared on Ben's face. "Interesting use of neck bolts."

The car came to a stop in front of my house. I waited for the usual sedate goodnight kiss.

"Have you ever wondered about those white lightning streaks in your hair?" Ben opened his door. "Let's climb into bed and I'll show you what put them there."